Praise for Lorelei James' *Cowgirl Up And Ride*

Rating: 5 Angels and a Recommended Read! "... From the first pages the chemistry sizzles and we're taken on a no holds barred ride into some super hot sexual shenanigans...with *Cowgirl Up And Ride*; we're offered an open door into the hearts and minds of a very big family...From beginning to end I couldn't put it down, I didn't want to leave AJ, Cord or any of the amazing people in this book."

~ *Rachel C., Fallen Angel Reviews*

Rating: 5 Blue Ribbons "Perfectly matched, Cord and AJ take center stage and had me believing that anything was possible when powerful emotions are coupled with witty and fun dialogue. COWGIRL UP AND RIDE is a sexually charged and incredibly emotional story that is a fabulous addition to an already well-written and received series. Ms. James manages to outdo herself with each book..."

~ *Jenn L., Romance Junkies*

Rating: 5 Hearts "The love scenes between Cord and AJ burn the pages...a lot of depth to all of the characters and they really draw you in. If you love strong and sexy cowboys, this is the book for you."

~ *Jacquelyn R. Ward, The Romance Studio*

Rating: Grade A- "The sex scenes between Cord and AJ are hot, hot, hot. This one is fraught with emotion as well as fun and filled with family...It's a whole new level of writing...and this author proves that with each word she puts on paper."

~ *Sandy M., The Good, The Bad, The Unread*

Rating: 4.5 Nymphs **"...**the characters of AJ and Cord are well rounded and intense...blistering hot when it comes to their physical relationship. The story is filled with many great recurring and new secondary characters, many of which add great depth to the book and series."

~ *Mystical Nymph, Literary Nymphs*

Rating: 4 Cups "...keep the fire extinguisher nearby because *Cowgirl Up and Ride* is a scorching read...Lorelei James crafts impressible characters...Her excellent cast makes this story flow well, creating a great read."

~ *Cherokee, Coffee Time Romance*

Look for these titles by

Lorelei James

Now Available:

Rough Riders Series:
Long Hard Ride
Tied Up, Tied Down
Rode Hard, Put Up Wet
Rough, Raw and Ready

Wild West Boys Series:
Mistress Christmas

Dirty Deeds
Babe in the Woods
Running With the Devil
Wicked Garden

Print Anthology:
The Beginnings Anthology

Cowgirl Up And Ride

Lorelei James

A Samhain Publishing, Ltd. publication.

Samhain Publishing, Ltd.
577 Mulberry Street, Suite 1520
Macon, GA 31201
www.samhainpublishing.com

Cowgirl Up And Ride

Print ISBN: 978-1-60504-087-5
Digital ISBN: 1-59998-895-X

Editing by Angela James
Cover by Scott Carpenter

First Samhain Publishing, Ltd. electronic publication: March 2008
First Samhain Publishing, Ltd. print publication: February 2009

Dedication

To the rough, gruff men—and the women who love them.

Chapter One

Amy Jo Foster had loved Cord McKay her entire life.

It didn't matter he was thirteen years her senior. Or he'd once dated her older sister. Or his little sister was her best friend. She fell for him hard the day she'd fallen off her horse.

That hot, dusty afternoon teased the edges of her memory. She'd been clip-clopping along on the gravel road connecting the Foster and McKay ranches when a rattler spooked her pony and bucked her off. She'd twisted her ankle on the unexpected dismount, unable to scramble away from either the angry snake or the truck barreling toward her.

Her life flashed before her eyes.

But the tires on a big Ford dually locked up and the truck skidded to a stop. A young man jumped out, swooped in and picked her up. His work-roughed hands tenderly brushed rocks from her knees and wiped the tears from her dirty face. He carried her to the passenger side of his truck, burned rubber over the snake and drove her home, keeping hold of her hand as she sobbed.

Amy Jo had a devil of a time climbing out of his rig, not because of the injury to her ankle, but mostly because she hadn't *wanted* to get out. She remembered sitting in that truck cab, surrounded by the scent of horses, of chewing tobacco, of hay, dust and the underlying tangy aroma of his cologne, and she'd wanted to stay right there with him forever.

With his dark good looks, bold smile and gentle ways, Cord had become her ideal, her dream, her savior, her prince charming in battered cowboy boots and a sweat-stained white Stetson.

No man had ever held a candle to him.

She'd been a whopping five years old at the time.

So, Amy Jo secretly worshipped Cord McKay throughout the years. Even after he moved to Seattle. Even after he returned to Wyoming married to a floozy from the West Coast. Even after the woman birthed a son. Even after the idiot abandoned Cord and their baby Ky.

She'd especially loved Cord then because she'd ached to pick up the pieces of his broken life. To make him whole. To crack the bitter shell he'd erected around his heart. To show him real, everlasting love was worth waiting for. In her core, her heart, her very soul, Amy Jo knew she was meant to be that one special woman.

Problem was she hadn't been a woman at the time either; she'd been a shy eighteen-year-old girl.

Too young.

The other problem was Cord hadn't seen her beyond the clumsy blonde pig-tailed friend of his little sister. Or as a family acquaintance with a neighboring ranch. Or recently as his son's babysitter.

That'd been the worst kind of torture. Being in Cord's house. Hearing Ky rambling from sunup to sundown about his father. Seeing Cord's unmade bed—one side rumpled, one side pristine. His lone coffee cup in the sink. Catching a whiff of his shaving cream as she lingered in front of the same bathroom mirror he used every day.

Seemed Amy Jo spent her life waiting for her chronological age to catch up with the age of her soul. Waiting for other people to believe she was old enough to know her own mind, even when she'd made it up at the tender age of five.

Now that she was twenty-two, she could stake her claim.

Standing in front of her bedroom mirror, she adjusted her cleavage in the skin-tight shirt the color of ripe apricots. She applied a coat of shiny pink lip-gloss. Finger combed her hair and inhaled a deep breath.

In all the hours she'd fantasized about Cord McKay, he'd never really noticed her.

Come hell or high water, Amy Jo would change that tonight.

Chapter Two

Cord McKay scowled at his beer. He scowled at everyone in the whole damn bar. Why had he come here?

Right. No reason to be home, sitting alone, wondering what the hell to do with himself. Couldn't do chores at night or else he'd be doing that. He'd rattled around the empty house for the last two days at loose ends.

Earlier, when he'd slipped on a Matchbox car and nearly fell on his ass, he'd automatically yelled, "Ky, come down here right now and pick this up..." The silence hit him like a load of hay bales. His son wasn't there. Ky wouldn't be around for another forty-two days.

Not that Cord was counting or anything.

The band struck up a cover of George Strait's "All My Exes Live In Texas" and boots thumped as dancers crowded the tiny wooden dance floor.

Cord upended his beer and tugged his Stetson down his forehead a notch. His ex didn't live in West Texas, rather on the West Coast. The twangy tune served as a reminder of the disturbing events of the last month.

Ky's mother, Marla, had called out of the blue, demanding to see their son.

The son she'd abandoned.

Naturally, Cord flat-out refused. Then Marla turned nasty and threatened to drag Cord to court, throwing around words like "joint custody" and "parental rights". Words that sent shudders down his spine and ice into his soul.

Kyler McKay was his son. *His*. Marla had handed over Ky's care to him the day he'd been born. She'd lasted six months after Ky's birth before she'd hightailed it back to Seattle for a temporary separation. A tearful Marla returned to Wyoming a year later with her tail tucked between her legs, full of apologies, proclaiming she'd changed, wanting another chance to make things—their marriage and motherhood—work.

She'd only lasted three weeks that time.

Cord had filed for divorce. Marla hadn't contested it, as she hadn't contested his demand of full, sole, permanent custody of Ky.

No doubt he struggled as a single parent, but luckily his family lived nearby and they helped him out. Consequently, Ky was a happy, bright, well-adjusted, four-year-old boy surrounded by uncles, aunts and grandparents. Ky didn't need a mother and they sure as shootin' didn't need her. Cord had told Marla as much over the phone.

But Marla wouldn't back down about the visitation rights. Cord took the matter to his attorney. The lawyer's advice was to let the boy stay with his mother for the seven-week period she'd requested. It surprised Cord when his own mother sided with the lawyer, claiming it would be good for both Ky and Cord.

Seven days ago he and Ky had hopped a plane and flew to Seattle. Cord insisted on being there as a safety net before he passed Ky over to Marla, a mother Ky didn't remember at all.

Leaving his son in the care of a virtual stranger hundreds of miles from home was the hardest thing Cord had ever done. A million bad scenarios raced through his mind. He'd almost turned around and flew right back to Seattle after he'd landed in Cheyenne. Let his brothers and cousins run the massive McKay ranch for a few weeks. God knew, Cord had pulled their weight more than a time or two. They owed him.

Cord's mother talked him into coming home, giving Ky time to adjust before making a rash decision. Ky seemed fine whenever Cord talked to him on the phone, which had calmed his fears somewhat.

Somewhat. Damn, he missed his kid something fierce.

So, here he was killing time in the local honky-tonk, wondering how he'd get through the next month and a half without going insane. Wondering if the next time he stumbled over one of Ky's toys whether he'd break down and bawl like a lost calf.

The chair next to Cord's squeaked as a big body flopped beside him. He tilted his hat up and saw his cousin Kade's shit-eating grin.

"Fancy seein' you here, Cord."

"Don't get used to it."

"Don't worry, I know you ain't here trollin' for a piece of ass." Kade's dark eyebrows rose in challenge. "Are you?"

"Fuck off."

Kade's baritone laugh boomed. "You talk to Ky today?"

"Twice."

"Cool. How's the little guy doin'?"

"Good. Misses his horse more than me."

"Sounds like a typical McKay response. How're *you* doin'?"

"I'm here, ain't I?"

"Must mean you're bored already, huh?" Kade's gaze swept the bar. "Who you here with?"

"Colt is supposed to show up."

"He'll show up late, if at all." Kade snorted. "Last I knew he was hookin' up with some stripper from Lusk. I swear he's nailin' three-quarters of the women in the tri-county area."

"Jealous?"

"Hell yes, I'm jealous. He gets more pussy in a week than I get in a year."

The haggard waitress dropped off a fresh beer and took Kade's order. Cord asked, "Is Kane here?"

"Nope. He's got a hot date. Everyone is gettin' laid but us, cuz." He shot Cord a devious look. "Unless you're lyin' to yourself, me, and your mama on why you're really here?"

"Not hardly. I don't have time for the bullshit that goes along with the privilege of gettin' my rocks off once or twice."

"Man, that's harsh. You tellin' me you wouldn't make time if someone came along?"

Cord's beer stopped halfway to his mouth. His attention

wandered to a woman swinging her hips on the dance floor.

Oh yeah. He'd make time for her in a fucking heartbeat.

Holy hell. Her legs went on forever. His gaze started at the heels of her high-heeled silver boots, gradually traveling up along the sexy line of those shapely legs, ending at her luscious ass barely hidden beneath an extremely short denim skirt. When her dance partner twirled her, Cord caught a glimpse of bright red bikini panties.

Lust whomped him in the gut.

He'd been so busy checking out her ass he hadn't seen her face. Her backside faced him—not that he was complaining—and a cheap straw cowboy hat covered her head. Her strong, tanned arms slid around the wide shoulders of the lucky cowboy as she sashayed closer to grind her pelvis against his. The cowboy whooped, clamping his hands on her ass in a dirty dancing move that'd make Patrick Swayze jealous.

It caused a burst of envy in Cord too. Nonchalantly he asked, "Kade, who's the chick on the dance floor?"

"Which one?"

"The one with the never endin' legs puttin' on the show in the miniskirt."

Kade squinted. "You mean AJ?"

AJ? Not a familiar name. "Yeah."

"She's quite the dancer, huh?"

"Sure is."

AJ performed a shimmy-shake with her hips, while snaking her arms above her head. The movement caused her tight lace shirt to slide up, exposing the smooth curve of her lower back.

Cord withheld a groan. Nothing was sexier than that dimpled section of a woman's back above her ass. Nothing.

With the exception of those unbelievably hot legs.

Every wicked undulation of her hips resulted in the fringe on her skirt swishing across the back of her firm thighs. He'd never been jealous of a skirt before now, but he sure as hell was right then.

"She seein' the guy she's dancin' with?"

"Mikey? Nah. Not for lack of tryin' on his part. AJ doesn't

lack for partners."

"I'll bet."

"She's sweet as the day is long. How your sister hasn't corrupted her is beyond me. She ain't as wild as Keely, but ain't for want of volunteers to take her for a walk on the wild side."

Walk? Hell, Cord would take her for a ride on the wild side. Binding her mile-long legs around his waist as he drove into her hard and fast. Feeling those slender thighs draped over his shoulders as she rode his face.

Jesus. Been an ice age since he'd had a woman, especially a buckle bunny cowboy-toy like her—built for speed with curves that'd lead a man straight into temptation.

Cord nursed his beer, his eyes never straying from her twisting form. Still, something about her seemed...familiar.

AJ threw back her head and laughed. Her straw hat tumbled to the floor.

Come on, baby doll, bend over and pick it up.

She twirled his direction and Cord finally saw her face.

If his lips weren't pressed against the beer bottle, his jaw would've smacked his knees.

The blonde sexpot with the killer legs and fantastic ass was none other than little Amy Jo Foster. His astonished gaze zeroed in on the cleavage spilling out of her V-necked blouse.

Nothing little about her now.

Talk about degenerate behavior. He'd been ogling his much-younger sister's best friend. His son's former *babysitter.*

Christ on a crutch.

Good thing she'd never waltzed into his house dressed like that—a sex kitten on the prowl. He'd've been arrested for his lewd thoughts alone. Dammit, why couldn't he stop wondering whether her nipples were pale pink like her lips or cherry red like her undies?

Amy Jo's large silvery-gray eyes met his for a moment. The *come-hither* smolder she aimed at him nearly knocked him off his damn barstool.

Where'd she learn that "fuck me now, Big Daddy" stare? She was too damn young.

She's old enough.

And he was old enough to know better.

Wasn't he?

Apparently not.

Amy Jo shrieked as Mikey lifted her up, gifting Cord with another glimpse of those sexy panties.

Cord bristled at seeing Amy Jo manhandled. Oh, he'd teach that pup with the roving paws a thing or two about manners.

Right. You'd love a chance to teach her a thing or two about how a real *man would handle her.*

Before Cord's butt left the chair to rescue her, Amy Jo broke Mikey's hold and stooped over to retrieve her hat. This time when their eyes met, she licked her lips and smiled seductively. Wantonly. Like she was picturing him buck-ass nekkid in just his damn hat.

Another wave of lust heated his balls. Then he knew the kiss she'd given him at Carter and Macie's wedding reception last year hadn't been a result of too much champagne.

His brain flashed back to the wedding dance at the Bar 9. The early autumn night held a bite of chill as the evening's festivities were winding down. Dozens of couples boot-scooted on an improvised dance floor beneath a white tent. He'd drifted off, preferring to drink a Fat Tire beer alone. Amusing himself by watching Ky and a couple of boys chasing giggling girls around in the preschool version of two-stepping.

A swish of fabric caught his attention. He turned when Amy Jo sidled up, wearing an ankle length dress the color of sunshine, which fit the fresh, clean, sunshiny scent flowing from her.

He managed a smile. "Amy Jo."

"I thought that was you, hiding over here all by your lonesome."

"Story of my life."

Silence stretched as thorny as the rose bushes lining the walkway.

Cord shifted his stance. Lately, being around Amy Jo made him feel like a tongue-tied fool. He couldn't tell her how pretty she looked without sounding like a total letch. He couldn't mention how goddamn good she smelled without coming across like a deranged bloodhound, or worse—some kind of hopeful horndog.

When in doubt... "Nice night," he offered lamely.

"That it is." She shivered discreetly. "If a bit chilly."

Should he act gentlemanly and offer her his suit coat? Nah. She'd probably think he was an old coot.

Which he was.

Dammit. Say something. Anything.

"You havin' fun?"

"Absolutely. Weddings are always fun, aren't they?"

Cord bit back a smart retort and swigged his beer.

"Why aren't you out there cutting a rug like the rest of your McKay brothers and cousins?"

With his beer bottle, Cord gestured to Ky and the kids. "Someone's gotta keep an eye on them so they don't dunk each other in the stock tank."

"Are you always the responsible one?"

"Yep. I reckon it goes with the territory of bein' the oldest."

"Isn't just the providence of the oldest child to be forced into responsibility." She sighed. "Don't you ever want to..."

He gave her a strange look. "What?"

A smile bloomed on her face before it faded. "Never mind. Ky did a great job as ring bearer today."

"That he did, besides refusin' to let go of Callie Morgan's hand."

"Can't say as I blame him. A cute girl who can rope and ride as well as he can?" Amy Jo's trill of laughter was as sweet and fleeting as the evening breeze. "Poor boy is smitten."

"Seems to be an epidemic in the McKay family of late." He glanced over to see his brother Colby and his wife Channing slow dancing, as well as the newlywed couple Carter and Macie entwined together, lost to everything but each other. A feeling close to jealousy tightened his stomach.

Not jealousy. Just indigestion.

Get a grip, McKay. This happily-ever-after wedding bullshit is addling your brain.

During his silent bout of self-pity, Amy Jo glided in front of him. Right in front of him. Lord. She was nearly as tall as he was in those ridiculously sexy yellow high heels.

"Why aren't *you* smitten, Cord McKay?"

Cord had nothing to say to that. He studied her, half-wary, half-curious about her intentions.

"You could be smitten with me." Keeping their gazes locked, she slowly angled forward and kissed him. Just a feather-light press of her soft mouth to his. As his lips were getting with the program, she withdrew slightly, letting their heated breath mingle for a second before she sank her teeth into his bottom lip. She gave a playful tug, followed by a thorough flick of her wet tongue to soothe the sting. "Because I'm definitely smitten with you." She sauntered toward the tent in a cloud of chiffon and pure temptation.

Cord remembered licking his lip, realizing she tasted as warm and sweet as autumn sunshine. He'd been too stunned to chase after her, chalking up the teasing kiss and challenging words to booze and the party atmosphere.

He hadn't thought about it again until now. As a matter of fact, he hadn't seen Amy Jo since she'd moved to Denver last year to attend massage therapy school with his sister. His mother kept him updated on Keely's exploits, which usually included tidbits on Amy Jo and her family.

His mother relayed the turn of bad luck in regard to Amy Jo's mother, Florence. Evidently she'd fallen from her horse and broken her leg. Amy Jo's older sister, Jenn, called Amy Jo home temporarily to help out with Florence's recovery.

Just how temporary was the situation?

The McKays' association with the Fosters spanned several decades. After Floyd Foster died four years back, Cord and his dad made a generous offer to buy the Foster ranch outright. But as Florence's only grandchildren lived nearby, she wasn't ready to sell the family homestead. And the McKays could afford to wait until she was.

Maybe the time had come.

A flash of metallic fringe brought his awareness back to Amy Jo exiting the dance floor. Cord sat up, straightening his hat, fully expecting she'd stroll to his table to flirt with him. Or at least beg him to dance with her. Or make good on the sultry promises she'd offered him with her smoky eyes. He'd be polite, but he'd gently discourage her attentions.

But Amy Jo flounced to the bar.

Chapter Three

What the hell?

Cord's eyes narrowed as the bartender rang a cowbell and lined up a full shot glass. Amy Jo slapped a five on the bartop. A group of young cowboys egged her on. She clasped her hands behind her back, bent forward, slid her lips down the shot glass and tipped her head, gulping the cloudy white liquid without using her hands.

Her throng of admirers whooped and hollered. Crumpled bills piled up on the bar napkin next to a bottle of Budweiser.

Amy Jo returned the glass to the bar the same way she'd taken it. She made a show of smoothing the bills and secreting them in her bra. Her sleek platinum hair tumbled over her left shoulder as she turned to smile at a guy creeping up behind her.

A small drop of milky liquid clung to the corner of her mouth. Sweet Jesus, it looked like a drop of...

Her smoking hot gaze hooked Cord's. She brought her finger to that spot, wiped the droplet and sucked her fingertip between her full pink lips.

His cock went hard as a fencepost.

Then Amy Jo whirled around and ignored him.

The little cock tease. When he got his hands on her...

"Cord? Man, you okay?"

Startled, Cord looked at Kade and was glad his cousin couldn't see the hard-on he was sporting under the table. "I'm fine. Why?"

"Looked pretty pissed off there for a sec."

"Just thinkin'."

"You thinkin' about another beer?"

"If you're buyin'."

By the time the round arrived, so had his brother Colt, with a tiny, curvy brunette on his arm with tits the size of watermelons, who appeared to be about fifteen.

Like you have any place to judge, pervert, lusting after your kid's babysitter.

"Sorry I'm late. Was a little distracted." He gave the woman a drunken leer, snagged an extra chair and they sat—with her straddled across his lap. "This is Jasmine. Jasmine, this is my older brother Cord, and my cousin, Kade McKay."

Jasmine studied them both carefully before a brazen smile stretched her glossed-up lips. "They cloning Chippendale cowboys in Wyoming now? All you big, gorgeous McKay guys look alike."

Cord and Kade scoffed at the Chippendales comment.

"Not clones, but Kade has an identical twin brother, Kane," Colt offered.

"Really?" Jasmine batted her fake eyelashes. "I've always wanted to be packed between hot-lookin' twins. Mmm. My kind of cowboy sandwich—with lots of beefcake."

Kade choked on his beer.

Cord frowned.

Jasmine cranked her head around to smile at Colt. "Do your other brothers look like you and your cousin?"

"Colby does. Cam and Carter take after our ma."

"Pity. You ain't pulling my leg? Kade looks like he could be your brother."

"We look alike because our fathers are twins who married sisters, so we're double cousins," Colt explained.

"*Double*. Mmm. Another one of my fav-o-rite words." Jasmine slunk across the table like a stripper in heat as she sought Kade's attention. "So you up for a little double trouble, cowboy?"

Kade shot Colt a hopeful look. "For real?"

"Yep. Jasmine has lots of energy and some...interestin'

ideas. She's told me she's up for anything tonight."

"Anything?"

"Yeah. Any kind of rodeo you're up for," Jasmine cooed. "I'm itchin' to ride. Or be rode. Or whatever."

Kade grinned. "I'm in."

Jasmine squealed, "Yee-haw! Let's hit the road before he changes his mind, partner."

"Cool beans. We'll meet you at the Boars Nest, Kade." Colt winked at Cord as they stood. He clamped Jasmine to his side since the woman was practically dry humping his leg. "Sorry, bro. See you tomorrow."

Kade downed his beer and threw a ten on the table. "Hate to bail, but you know how it goes."

"Actually, I don't. You get offered threesomes often?"

"Hell no. Why do you think I said yes so damn fast?" He clapped Cord on the back and disappeared out the side entrance.

Cord slouched in his seat. The bad idea to drown his sorrows was getting worse by the minute. Talk about being out of date and out of place. Things'd changed since he'd been on the dating scene.

No they haven't. You're just blocking out some of the raunchier moments from your misspent youth.

Maybe that was true. But he still felt damn old at thirty-five. And he noticed Jasmine didn't ask *him* to join in their fun and games—not that he would've if she *had* asked.

Who was he kidding? He'd've done it in a New York minute.

He sighed, primed to leave, when Amy Jo darted onto the dance floor with some fresh-faced buck who had three extra pairs of hands.

Rather than go home to watch lousy TV alone, he settled in and watched her. She'd two-step a couple of numbers with one guy, flit to the bar for a fresh drink, and drag a new dance partner to the floor.

Cord hid in the darkened corner for over an hour, tracking every enticing sway of her slim hips, every smooth glide of those long legs, every exaggerated shoulder roll, every sexy chest shimmy, every toss of that sleek platinum hair. Not once did

Amy Jo acknowledge him, even though she was as hyper-aware of him as he was of her.

Her sexy little ass shake turned him on more than if she'd have been buck-ass naked grinding her crotch on a brass stripper's pole.

When she was alone at the bar Cord moseyed up behind her. "Evenin' Amy Jo."

She tossed him a quick grin and granted him a not so quick once over. "Surprised to see you in here, Cord. And it's AJ now, not Amy Jo."

"My mistake. Why the name change?"

"New attitude, new name." She resumed drinking her beer.

Cord scooted close enough to catch a whiff of her sunshiny scent. He noticed sweat beading on the curve of her neck below her ear and had the strangest desire to place his mouth there and gently suck the salty droplets clean away.

A beat passed and she didn't acknowledge him.

"I didn't know you liked to dance."

"There's a lot you don't know about me."

I'd like to learn. Every. Damn. Thing.

"Who are you here with?"

Amy Jo—AJ—faced him fully. "Who are *you* here with?"

"No one."

"That why you came looking for me? Can't find anyone better to hang out with?"

"No. Didn't know you thought so highly of me."

She shrugged.

The classic brush off—a pointed reminder on why he avoided the bar scene. He flashed her a fake smile. "Anyway. I came by to say hello. I'm headin' home and I wondered if you needed a lift."

AJ arched a slim brow. "You offering to give me a ride, cowboy?"

Cord curbed his response, *you can ride me any time, any place, as long as you want, cowgirl*, and cleared the lust from his throat. "Yeah."

The band announced the next tune, Willie Nelson's "Always

On My Mind" and AJ shook her head at yet another eager, happy-handed cowboy approaching her for a dance. "Thanks for the offer, but no."

"You sure? You've been drinkin' pretty heavily the last couple of hours. Probably shouldn't be drivin'."

"How would you know how much I've been drinking?"

"Because I've been watchin' you. Closely. Every step and every sip, darlin'. I couldn't take my eyes off you and you damn well know it." Her confidence slipped; he moved in. "You *like* that I've been watchin' you, sweet Amy Jo."

"AJ," she corrected softly.

"You like that I've been watchin' you, sweet *AJ*."

"So while you were watching, did you see anything you liked, McKay?"

"Oh yeah." His gaze landed on her lush mouth.

"Right. Give me a break."

Cord managed to drag his eyes back to hers. "You callin' me a liar?"

"No. I'm calling your bluff."

"Meaning?"

"Meaning, I know you'll look your fill, burn my clothes away with your sexy eyes, but you're too damn polite to do anything more than gawk at me."

Cord nearly choked, "*Polite*?"

"Polite. Responsible. Chicken. Whatever." She stared at his lips and ran her pink tongue over her teeth. "Tell me, Cord, don't you ever just wanna say to hell with what's expected of you and do what makes you feel good?"

"Every damn day."

She reached up, letting her fingers fiddle with a button near his shirt collar. "Then tell me why you don't?"

"I'll tell you anything you wanna know, baby doll, as long as you answer a question for me first."

"Okay."

"Look at me."

When AJ's lust-filled eyes met his, it took every ounce of restraint not to smash his mouth to hers, hike up that sassy excuse of a skirt, spread those silky thighs wide, and nail her against the closest paneled wall.

Focus.

"Can I buy you a drink? Like the shot you did earlier?"

"You wanna see me do a blowjob?"

Cord froze.

She laughed. "See why I won forty bucks?"

"Just for sayin' that raunchy word out loud?"

"No. For doing it."

He lifted both brows. "Doin' what?"

"Giving them a group blowjob. See, the object is the same with the drink as it is with the act, shoving the glass in your mouth as far as it'll go, keeping a tight grip with your lips. Then you tilt your head and suck hard and deep, bracing yourself for the warmth spilling down your throat as you try to swallow it all."

He growled, "What game are you playin' with me, little girl?"

AJ stood on the tips of her boots. "I haven't been a little girl for a long time, Cord McKay."

"Believe me, I noticed."

"About damn time."

If he leaned in a fraction of an inch, he could lay a hungry kiss on those ripe lips, not innocent like the flirty smooch she'd teased him with last year. Would this bolder AJ take the initiative?

She didn't. Instead, she lifted a shaking hand to his cheek. Her fingertips delicately traced the outline of his neatly trimmed goatee, lingering on the short hair above his upper lip. A chaste, yet erotic caress to make his cock stand up and take notice if it wasn't already rock-hard.

"No games. If you want to play with me, all you have to do is ask. I'll be here tomorrow night, waiting for your answer."

AJ spun on her bootheel and vanished into the sea of bodies on the dance floor, leaving Cord McKay absolutely pole-axed.

Chapter Four

When Kade walked into the Boars Nest, the old ranch house he shared with his brother Kane and his cousin Colt, the first thing he noticed was Jasmine on her knees giving Colt a blowjob.

Colt's hands gripped Jasmine's head as he hammered his hips into her face. "More. Take it all. Wider. Oh yeah, baby, here it comes. Suck it down."

This wasn't a new scene. Normally the wilder stuff happened behind the bedroom doors. Threesomes were old hat for his brother Kane, and Colt, hell, even sometimes their cousin Dag, hence Kade's eagerness to participate.

Colt's neck arched and he groaned. Jasmine made happy humming noises. Then Colt's semi-erect cock slid out of her mouth. "Christ, Jazz, you suck like a fuckin' dream. Baby, that was amazin'." He finally noticed Kade. "Hey, cuz."

"Hey."

"Thank God somebody is here to fuck me." Jasmine stood and eyed Kade with a grin. She snatched a condom from the coffee table and flipped him the square package. "Slap on a love glove, cowboy, and mount up."

Already? Kade started stripping. "Where we doin' this?"

"Right here for round one. We'll see how you hold up. If you got enough *try* to make it to round two and on to the finals." She bent over the back of the couch and waggled her ass at him. "Come an' get it."

"Have at her, buddy. I need a drink."

Kade ripped open the plastic package and rolled the latex down his cock as he walked to the sofa.

Jasmine smacked her lips when she saw his dick. "A bull's got nothin' on you."

"I ain't heard any complaints." Kade smoothed his hands up her back and rolled his hips over her ass. "Need lube, Jazz?"

"No. I don't need sweet words or soft kisses either. I need you to fuck me hard. Blowing Colt or watchin' someone else blow him makes me horny as shit."

Kade canted her hips, spread her pussy open with his fingers and slammed deep. "You weren't kiddin'. You are wet."

"Damn straight. More."

"Comin' right up." Kade pulled all the way out and thrust back in. She was so short he could hold on to her shoulders as he fucked her.

Jasmine's hand disappeared between her legs and he saw her frantically rubbing her clit.

Without missing a stroke, Kade said, "You want me to do that?"

"No. I'm better at it. You do what you're good at which is...God! Do I love a big cock. I'll bet you can go all night, cancha, cowboy?"

"Maybe not tonight."

She choked out a smoker's rasping laugh.

Sweat poured down Kade's body. He closed his eyes. It'd been a couple of months since he'd had sex; he knew he wouldn't last long. Damn. Should he hold off? How much longer before she came? And why didn't he care, like he did with his other lovers?

Because this is pure animalistic fucking. You're following her lead.

Colt wandered back in, still stark naked, sipping from a bottle of vodka. He flopped on the dilapidated easy chair. "Jazz, baby, I'm here watchin' another man rammin' his cock into your greedy pussy."

She moaned. Her hand moved faster between her legs.

"I oughta come over there and shove my dick in your mouth again. That'd get you off. Especially if I came on your face while he's comin' in your cunt."

Kade hissed, "Jesus, Colt, do you fuckin' mind?"

"She loves it when I give her a play-by-play of what I'm gonna do to her next. She loves it even better when I watch another man or two fuckin' her." Colt tipped his bottle to Kade. "But a little pain will make her come like you wouldn't believe."

Jasmine whimpered.

"What? No way."

"Trust me, she wants it. Bad. Smack her ass."

Kade kept plunging deep. He gritted out, "Is that what you want?"

"Yes, goddamn it. Smack it. Make it burn."

He'd stepped into the world of the surreal. He'd never done anything like this. Kade released her shoulders, spread his right hand across the globe of her ass and swatted her.

"Yes!"

"Do it again," Colt said. "Lower. Harder. By her pussy."

Kade loaded up and whacked her again.

"Almost there, Colt, please. That is so good."

Colt? This chick was aware Colt wasn't the one fucking her, wasn't she?

Two hard smacks and she started to come. When her spasming pussy muscles clamped down on his cock, he blew like a geyser.

After his head quit spinning, he staggered back. Whoa. Getting off besides by his own hand was always good, but that was...weird. Disjointed. Fast.

Colt went to Jasmine. Kade disposed of the condom and grabbed a beer from the kitchen.

When he returned to the living room, Jasmine was reclined on the coffee table, her legs spread wide. Colt was on his knees with his face buried in her pussy.

From where he stood, he saw Colt's head moving and Jasmine's absolute rapture. Colt twisted and plucked Jasmine's big nipples with one hand and had three fingers plunging in and out of her ass. The scene shouldn't have turned Kade on, but it did. His cock stirred. By the time Colt made her come,

Kade was completely hard again.

Jasmine sat up with a shameless smile. “Ready for round two?”

“Whatcha got in mind?”

Colt grabbed a handful of condoms and tossed him one. “She wants both of us at the same time, you fuckin’ her tits, me in her ass. Lube is right here. Let’s take this in the bedroom.”

In Colt’s room, Jasmine stretched out on the bed, letting her legs dangle to the floor. Kade straddled her waist and she played with her nipples as he lubed the valley of her cleavage.

Looking at her face, Kade realized he hadn’t kissed her. He didn’t want to kiss her.

Colt said, “Ready, Jazz baby?”

“I was born ready.” She arched when Colt impaled her. “Oh that’s good. Better than your fingers. Better than that dildo you used last night.”

“Honey, that wasn’t a dildo, that was your buddy Leroy.”

“That explains his limp dick then.”

They both laughed and Kade was clueless as to why that was so damn funny.

Kade held her tits together and eased his cock into the channel he’d created. Oh man. The lube made it slippery. She was a much tighter fit here than her cunt. As he glided in and out, his balls brushed her belly. He said, “Pinch your nipples harder.”

Jasmine liked being told what to do. She tried to lick the cockhead with his every upstroke. When she began to moan, he glanced over his shoulder and saw Colt playing with her clit as his cock tunneled in and out of her ass.

Colt grinned drunkenly at Kade. “Ain’t this great? Ain’t Jazz the best ever?”

“Yeah, she’s somethin’ all right.”

Colt thrust so hard the next four times, Jasmine’s body slid up the bed.

“Wait. This isn’t working for me, fellas.”

Kade and Colt both stopped moving.

She slapped Kade’s ass. “Scoot up. Let’s see how much of

that big dick I can get in my mouth. Then I can play with your balls. God, I love fat, furry balls like these."

He positioned his knees beside her head. He put his hands flat on the mattress and slowly fed his cock into her eager mouth. Jesus. It was fucking hot to watch the length disappear until her nose was buried in his pubic hair and his heavy balls dangled by her chin.

When he eased back, she said, "I can't suck, but I can do this." She rolled his sac between her fingers like she was throwing dice.

"Damn. That's good."

She giggled.

He'd gotten into a steady rhythm, a fast plunge past the soft palate to the back of her throat, followed by the teasing scrape of her teeth as he withdrew. Sweat dripped down his chest and landed on her forehead. It was right there. Right *there*. He said, "Suck it now. Suck it hard."

Jasmine hollowed her cheeks and wormed two fingers in his ass as he started to come.

"Motherfuckin' hell, woman, what are you doin'!"

She giggled again and pumped her fingers deep as his cock emptied into her mouth.

The bedroom door burst open.

Kane said, "Well, well, what do we have here? A fuckin' party? Can I join in?"

Colt laughed. "Always room for one more, eh Jazz?"

She moaned around Kade's cock and it sent a tingle straight to his balls. He tried to pull out but she bit down, evidently wanting his cock right where it was.

"Don't pay no mind to me, I'll just be getting acquainted with this pretty pussy. Oh look. It's all wet. Has it been cryin' for someone to pay attention to it?"

Kade glanced over his shoulder as his twin dropped to his knees beside the bed and started slurping Jasmine's clit.

She arched her neck and Kade eased his throbbing dick out of her mouth past those deadly teeth. "God, yes, suck hard. Fuck my pussy with your fingers too," she said to Kane.

Kane bit and sucked her clit, ramming what looked like his

whole hand in her cunt.

Jasmine screamed; Kane kept sucking and Colt said, “Jesus. I can feel her comin’. Her ass is tightenin’ around my cock like a fuckin’ vise. Can’t hold off.” He groaned and threw his head back.

Kade scooted off the bed and watched the scene unfold.

Colt dismounted like he’d hopped off a buckin’ horse and clapped Kane on the back. “Time for double trouble. I’ll be back.” He stumbled from the room with his bottle.

Then Kade noticed not only was Kane naked, he already wore a condom.

Jasmine sat up. “You guys really are identical.” Her gaze lingered on Kane’s cock. “In every way.”

“Do you know how unbelievably fuckin’ hot it is how much you love givin’ and takin’ pleasure? Very few women are so uninhibited. You’re the ultimate fantasy woman.”

Jesus, Kane. Lay it on a little thick why don’t you? He didn’t need to bother. Jasmine was a sure thing.

Why did that bother him? Isn’t that what he was supposed to want? Wasn’t that why he was here?

But he missed the burning glances. The flirtatious banter. The accidental touches. That slow build up of lust until you hit the combustion point. That was his ultimate fantasy these days.

“Far as fantasies go, I have one of being fucked at the same time by identical twins. Looking over my shoulder and seeing the face of the man taking my ass is the same face as the man that’s in front of me fucking my pussy.”

Kane grinned. “It’s your lucky day. The McKay twins are here to make your dream come true.” He leaned forward and gave her a sloppy, noisy kiss.

Whoa. Kade had no desire to kiss Jasmine. Ever.

“We’ll make you a Jazz sandwich,” Kane teased.

She giggled.

“Hey, bro, you mind takin’ the rear? I wanna suck these titties while I’m hittin’ the fuckin’ *Jazz*-pot here.”

Jasmine giggled again.

His brother tossed him a condom.

Kade lay back on the bed, resting on his elbows. Jasmine threw a leg over Kade's hip, aligning her hole with Kade's cock. Kade pulled her ass cheeks wide and pushed the broad head past that puckered pink opening and into the channel.

She made a happy-sounding moan and leaned back, putting her hands on the mattress by Kade's ribs and bouncing on his dick like it was a pogo stick.

Kane aimed and drove into her pussy. He set the rhythm, he'd thrust forward then Kade would bump his hips back. Kane lifted Jasmine's tits and slurped her nipples.

Jasmine was into it; Kane was into it. Kade just wanted the whole fucking thing to end. What'd started out as a sexy romp had become tiresome. Emotionless. A into B—then B switches places and C goes into B. It was mechanical sex. No anticipation. No lingering touches or unexpected caresses or slow, sweet kisses. No...connection.

Christ. He must be a fucking wussy-loser if he'd rather be rolling in the sheets playing kissy-face with some nameless woman than participating in a threesome with an uninhibited stripper.

The action increased. Kane pumped his hips, Jasmine started to come, Kane shouted and came.

Kade wondered if they'd notice that he hadn't come. In fact, his dick was semi-soft.

Jasmine laughed, lifted off Kade's pole and rolled onto Kane, keeping his cock inside her, biting his neck like a pesky little dog.

Definitely time to go.

He met his cousin at the door. A bleary-eyed Colt swayed into the doorframe and swigged the last of the vodka, before tossing the bottle to the floor. "You leavin' already? We're just gettin' started."

"She wore me out. See you guys in the mornin'." Kade showered and locked himself in his room. When he heard Jasmine screaming and the headboard banging into the wall again, he inserted his ear buds and cranked up his iPod.

ω

The next morning Kade rolled out of bed at five-thirty. He started the coffee and shoveled down a bowl of Lucky Charms. The house was disgusting. Dirty dishes piled on the counters. Empty beer bottles and cans everywhere. The garbage overflowed in the corner. He was half-afraid he'd see spent condoms and empty wrappers in the living room.

His brother stumbled in and headed straight for the coffee. "Man. I'm gonna be draggin' ass today. What're we doin'?"

"Dad said fixin' fence and the baler."

Kane groaned.

"Whose turn is it to clean up the house?"

"I dunno. Colt's probably. That's why it's a fuckin' mess."

"I'm sick of it. He can clean the place up tonight after chores or I'm changin' the locks and he can sleep in the fuckin' barn like the animal he is."

"Right, like that'll happen. Think he said somethin' about Jasmine bringin' some friends over tonight."

"Great. Then I won't be stickin' around."

"Why not?"

"Don't mention it to Dad today, but I told Uncle Darren I'd check out the problems he's havin' with that old Chevy of Grandpop's. Uncle Harland ain't any help because he's tryin' to keep an eagle eye on Dag. I'm surprised Dag wadn't here last night to join in the debauchery."

His brother scowled. "He and Colt got into it last week. Knock-down, drag-out fistfight at Ziggy's. Both drunk as shit. They ain't talkin'. For now. Won't last. Hell, they neither one of 'em probably remember. Don't know which one of 'em is in worse shape. They both drink too goddamn much."

"Ain't the pot callin' the kettle black, is it, bro?"

Kane shook his head. "I know when to stop."

Kade studied his brother. They might look exactly alike, but contrary to what Jasmine said, it wasn't like looking in a mirror. He and Kane were polar opposites in many respects.

"So how was your date with...what was her name? You were home early."

"Skylar? Nice woman." Kane stared into his coffee cup. "Too nice if you know what I mean. Probably be a dozen dinner dates before I'd get invited into her bed. I decided she wasn't worth it."

"We're getting cynical. If it ain't easy, we don't want it. And if it's too easy, it ain't worth nothin' either."

"Speak for yourself. I like havin' pussy flashed in my face all the goddamn time. And when did you designate yourself the moral compass for the whole damn house?"

"When I realized we're all headed the wrong damn direction, Kane."

Kane blinked with confusion. "You seem to be the only one who feels that way."

They finished the pot of coffee in silence.

Colt's bedroom door was still closed as they headed out. "Think we oughta wake up Sleeping Beauty?" Kane asked.

"Nah. He deserves to get his ass chewed by Uncle Carson if he shows up late."

"Or by Colby."

Kade grinned. "Or worse yet, by Cord."

"Ooh, that's just plain fuckin' mean, bro."

"Not as mean as me callin' Aunt Carolyn and tellin' her what an animal her son's become. If she sees this place she'll blow a gasket."

"Yeah, but then she'll tell Ma."

"Almost be worth it not to live in a pigsty."

"True."

"So which one of us is gonna talk to him about all this crap?"

Kane clapped his hat on his head. "I'll do it, but you'll owe me."

"Deal. What do you want?"

"Don't know. Let me think on it and get back to you."

Kade scowled. "I hate it when you say that."

He laughed. "Why do you think I do it?"

Chapter Five

"You wanna dance?"

AJ smiled at the hunky cowboy. "Thanks, but no. I'm sitting this one out."

A hopeful gleam lit his eyes. "Maybe later then?"

"Maybe." If things didn't go her way.

She crossed her legs and tugged her white mini-skirt. Pulled her lacy shirt down. Damn thing kept riding up and exposing her lower back. Her boot tapped on the metal rung of the barstool in time to the music. She tried not to look anxious, but Lord, she'd been waiting for this night her whole life.

Take a deep breath. He'll show.

What if he didn't? What if Cord McKay spent the day over-analyzing her offer like he over-analyzed everything else? She imagined him tooling around in his truck, doing chores, a look of concentration on his handsome face as he convinced himself he was too old for her. He had a kid to raise, a ranch to run and no time to be messing with his little sister's best friend.

But then AJ remembered how hot Cord's eyes burned every time he'd looked at her last night. He wanted her, but he didn't *want* to want her.

Too bad. If he did show up, she'd pull out all the stops and make herself impossible to resist.

She scanned the bar. Decent crowd tonight, lots of folks she knew. Then again, she'd lived in Sundance, Wyoming since birth; there were few people she didn't know. She waved at Bebe shooting pool at one of the back tables. Smiled at her buddy Liza and her fiancé Noah cozied up in a corner booth. When AJ spun back around, her pulse leapt. Her sexy fantasy man was chatting up the bouncers as he paid the cover charge.

Cord glanced up. Their eyes met. He moseyed along, checking things out.

She drained her beer, hoping he'd come to check her out.

Cord stopped in front of her. "I'm here."

"I see that." Her heart thumped wildly as his big frame practically cast her in shadow.

"Buy you another?"

"Sure."

"Don't go nowhere."

"I'll be right here."

He ambled away, gifting her with a glimpse of his tight buns and muscular legs encased in dark blue Wranglers. A denim shirt stretched across his wide shoulders. Oh man. Just looking at him made her melt. What would it be like to touch him? Feel that rough skin all over hers?

Barely a minute passed before Cord was back. Maybe he was anxious too. He handed her a bottle and offered a toast. "To a new attitude."

"I'll drink to that."

He rested his elbow on the table and studied her face as if he'd never seen her before. "You look different."

AJ resisted the urge to smooth her hair or wet her lips. "Bad different? Or good different?"

Cord's forceful gaze traveled from her mouth to her breasts and back to her eyes. "Oh, definitely good. Very very good."

Her belly quivered.

"So, AJ...you weren't pullin' my leg last night?"

She shook her head.

"You up for some fun and games?"

Her mouth was so dry she just nodded.

"Flattered as I am... Why me? You gotta know any one of the young guys in here would kill to have a shot at you."

AJ broke eye contact and scraped at the label on her beer bottle. Shoot. How was she supposed to answer that without giving herself away?

Cord's rough hand curled over her wrist and he idly stroked her knuckles. Her stomach jumped again. She glanced up, overwhelmed by the lust in his eyes.

"Jesus. You have the sexiest mouth I've ever seen. I can't think beyond tastin' that mole by the corner of your lips. Runnin' my tongue over it. Kissin' every inch of it on the way back to kissin' every inch of your mouth."

Warning. Don't let him sweet-talk you until you get a chance to speak your piece. She blurted, "Do you wanna dance?"

"Not to this."

"Why not?"

"Because the first time I put my hands on you, I want you close. Real close. Close as we can get with our clothes on without getting kicked out for lewd behavior."

The silence between them grew. AJ felt her confidence slipping. This was not the way she'd envisioned her night of seduction.

Then take charge.

She finished the beer and hopped off the barstool. "I want your hands on me now, Cord." She hooked her finger in his belt loop and towed him on the dance floor to the corner farthest away from the stage.

He placed his hot palm on the small of her back, urging her lower body against his, threading the fingers of his left hand through the fingers on her right.

AJ slowly dragged her palm up Cord's arm just to feel his muscles before she rested her hand on his shoulder. "Isn't this better? We can make the music fit our mood, not the other way around."

"Seems you're in a reckless mood." Cord stared at her, no hint of a smile. "Why're you flirtin' with me like this?"

"Besides that you are one hot, sexy cowboy?"

"Bullshit. Are you playin' some kind of game with me? Seein' if you can get the old man hot and bothered and then flit away to laugh about it with your girlfriends?"

"No. Geez, Cord. You have such a high opinion of me."

"Nothin' personal."

"Just women in general?"

"Yep."

AJ let her fingers trace the ridge of his collarbone. "I wouldn't tease you. But I will admit I have an ulterior motive in flirting with you so shamelessly."

His eyes hardened. "Why?"

"Because I want something from you."

"What?"

"For you to teach me everything you know about sex."

Pause. "Come again?"

"Oh, I'd like to come again and again." She smiled triumphantly at his stunned expression.

"You'd better be explainin' that."

"What I know about sex is what I've seen in the barnyard."

"That's it?"

"Well, that and some porn."

He gave her another skeptical look. "Is there a reason you're sharin' this information with me?"

"Yeah, but it's sort of embarrassing. You are looking at the only twenty-two-year-old virgin in all of Crook County."

Cord quit moving, causing AJ to stumble into him. The man was rock solid. Heck, everything about him was firm and broad and hard. Very hard. Mostly his eyes right now.

"This is some kinda joke, right?"

"No." She predicted he'd be suspicious, but mad? Yikes. She tried to snatch her hand from his to escape, like hightail it straight for the South Dakota border and not look back.

"Oh, no you don't, baby doll. You *don't* get to tell me somethin' that fogs my damn brain over and then dart away like a scared rabbit. We are gonna discuss this, in detail, right now, since you brought it up, Amy Jo."

She lifted her chin defiantly. "It's AJ."

"Fine, AJ."

"Could we keep dancing? You sorta stopped."

He spun them so his back was to the room. His deep blue eyes locked on hers. "Lemme get this straight. You ain't never been naked with a man. Now that you've decided you're ready to spread your gorgeous legs, you've picked...*me* to be the lucky one?"

"Yes."

A muscle in his jaw snapped. He opened his mouth. Closed it. Finally he said, "Christ almighty, do you know what that does to me? Hell. You don't, because you've never—"

"You can just say *no*, Cord."

His lips curled oh-so-slowly, in a decidedly predatory grin. "Here's the deal: I don't wanna say no."

AJ froze.

"Keep dancin', you sorta stopped," he teased.

Neither spoke for a few beats as they swayed together.

Cord placed his mouth to her ear. "But before I say yes, I'm curious about a couple of things."

His hot breath sent shivers down her neck, tightening her nipples against his chest. "Like what?"

"Like why you're still untouched. Because if this is a religious issue and if you're lookin' for a preacher and a weddin' ring, I ain't your man."

"I'm not."

"Good." He sighed in her hair. "Then why are you innocent? You are sexy as shit. Don't pretend there ain't been men sniffin' around."

AJ angled her head to feel Cord's smoothly shaven jaw rub over her cheek. Mmm. He smelled good. Warm skin beneath a hint of spicy aftershave. By the way his body tensed she figured he liked it when she rubbed him like a contented cat, so she kept right on doing it.

"AJ? You gonna answer that?"

"Okay. When did *you* notice I was sexy as shit, Cord McKay?"

He laughed softly. "Got me there."

"Exactly. I haven't been with a guy before because"—*I was too busy working my ass off*—"I didn't date in school. When Keely and I moved to Denver there were lots of guys sniffing around, but I was embarrassed to admit I'd never done it."

"Nothin' to be ashamed of. I still don't get why me. Lots of young fellas around here—"

AJ stopped dancing and jerked back from him.

But his iron grip didn't waver. "What?"

"Say no, but do *not* try to convince me that Mikey is a better choice for my first lover than you. Don't treat me like a child who can't choose between a grape or a cherry lollipop. I've thought this through. If you don't want a piece of me, say so and walk away."

"I want a piece of you, baby doll, like you wouldn't fuckin' believe. Just had to make sure this wasn't somethin' you decided on the spur of the moment."

"It's not."

"Then c'mere. You're gonna hafta get used to havin' your body against mine." Cord pulled her even closer. "Get used to feelin' my hands on you. All over you. All the time."

Her hormones did the happy dance.

The band segued into a slow, mournful ballad and AJ's eyes drifted shut. She lost herself in the sensation of finally being where she'd always dreamed: in Cord McKay's arms.

"How much experience *do* you have?" Cord murmured.

"You ask a lot of questions."

"I expect an answer to every damn one." His lips brushed her temple. "Where all've you been kissed besides your pretty mouth?" Cord's free hand slipped up her waist to her ribcage. His thumb lightly stroked the bottom swell of her breast before sweeping higher, across her nipple, until it was a hot, tight point. "Here?"

Her breath hitched. "Ah. No."

He twirled them, dancing backward, smoothly inserting his leg between hers. "Here?" He pressed up so she was riding his thigh. "You ever had a man's mouth tastin' your sweet spot?"

AJ softly moaned at the exquisite pressure and heat of his hard muscles rubbing her tender flesh. The thought of his tongue licking there made her throb with want.

"Yes or no?" he growled.

Dizzy, she managed, "N-no."

"Has any man ever touched this pussy?"

"No."

"You've touched yourself? Made yourself come?"

"Yes."

Cord hissed. "You're drivin' me crazy, thinkin' of all the things I'm gonna do to you. How many different ways I can make you come."

"Show me." AJ tightened her thighs around his. "Show me it all."

"Remember you said that." He blew softly in her ear and she shivered like a newborn babe. "Soon as this song ends, I'm goin' outside. Meet me by my truck in ten minutes. This is between you and me. No one else needs to know what we're doin'. Understand?"

"Uh-huh."

The final drumbeat sounded and Cord eased away from her. AJ locked her knees to keep herself upright.

"Ten minutes. And you'd better not be wearin' them sassy panties."

Chapter Six

Cord hadn't known what'd happen tonight. Hadn't been entirely sure she'd even be here. He hadn't expected AJ to ask him to teach her about sex and he sure as hell hadn't expected her to be a virgin.

A virgin.

Sweet baby Jesus. Had he ever been with a virgin?

Not that he recalled.

So why was he considering bedding the virginal AJ? She knew nothing about taking and giving pleasure. In truth, who was he to talk? Cord hadn't been in a steady sexual relationship since his ex-wife left him. Sure, in the last couple of years he'd slaked his lust on rare occasions, but did that qualify him to teach her?

Hell yes. Actually, it offered the perfect chance to prove to AJ (and himself) that screaming-raw-hot sex owed nothing to love—just to lust and opportunity, both of which'd been sadly lacking in his life lately. With Ky gone for the next few weeks...and AJ home temporarily...it was a win/win situation for them both.

Plus, being the first man to stroke that baby soft skin everywhere, to fuck that tight pussy with his fingers, his tongue, his cock. Those possibilities stirred primitive instincts he'd never believed he owned.

Cord heard bootsteps to his left. He watched AJ's approach with open appreciation. Damn. Her ample breasts swayed provocatively. Every roll of her slender hips sent the miniscule white skirt brushing across the tops of her thighs. Would she move that sinuously under him? On top of him? On her knees before him?

"I thought you might've changed your mind," he said softly.

"Not at all. It's just..." Her gaze flicked from him, to the cab of his pickup, to the tailgate and back to him. "Where are we doing this?"

"Baby doll, I ain't gonna throw you up against my truck and fuck you senseless for your first time." He grinned. "But that don't mean it ain't a future possibility."

AJ stared at him with those beautiful big silvery eyes.

"C'mere. Can't touch you when you're standin' so far away."

Cord offered his hand and walked backward until they were hidden in the space where the cab of his truck ended and the truck bed of his diesel pickup started. He curled his hands around her face, bringing her lush mouth to his.

She started to twine her arms around his neck. Cord growled, "Keep those hands by your side 'til I say otherwise."

"Okay."

He brushed his lips back and forth over the curved warmth of hers, then kissed a path to the tempting mole. A couple of light tongue flicks and he returned to her succulent mouth.

AJ's breathing was erratic. She'd licked her lips, leaving them moist and slightly parted. Cord darted his tongue inside, groaning at the sweet taste of mint and AJ. He angled her head, nibbling, licking, coaxing her tongue to play with his. She let him do whatever he wanted, but she wasn't the eager participant he'd anticipated. "You gonna kiss me back, AJ?"

Her eyes were a stormy gray. "Not if you don't let me use my hands."

"Fine. You can use—"

Then her hands were gripping his hair and she smashed her mouth to his.

No gentle exploratory kiss; she thrust her tongue in and devoured him. Tasting, sucking, God, *biting*, taking him to a whole new level of need with her hunger. AJ held nothing back, she kept kissing him harder, urging his mouth open wider, feeding him long, deep, wet kisses, touching his face, tugging his hair when he attempted to move away, stoking the fire higher until he was afraid he'd combust in his Wranglers.

Cord ripped his mouth free. "To think I was crazy about your mouth before I knew you could use your mouth like this."

"Don't stop," she panted against his throat. "Please don't stop. I want you. Kiss me again. And again. And—"

He cupped her face and took her mouth in a brutal show of possession.

AJ met his demands with unrestrained passion.

He bit a path up her jawline to her ear, keeping his body against hers. "Need to touch you."

"Yes."

"Hands back by your sides. That ain't a request." Cord teased her with fleeting, soft kisses, his hands slid down her throat to the buttons on her blouse. He unhooked them one by one, dragging his callused fingertips from the smooth skin of her belly to her bra. He sprung the front clasp and peeled the lacy cups back. Her heavy breasts filled his waiting hands.

She shuddered. "Cord—"

"Let me." His rough thumbs strummed her nipples. "God, you're so pretty. All creamy and soft and sweet." He rubbed his goatee and openmouthed kisses across the upper swells of her breasts. Cord curled his tongue around a rigid tip.

AJ arched into him.

"Like that?" He lapped and licked and blew a stream of air across the wet buds, but never sucked them completely. He glanced up at her when she made a frustrated noise.

Her top teeth dug into her bottom lip in her effort not to cry out. Yet her curious gaze remained on him.

Cord bent his head and suckled her. Hard. Deep. Thoroughly.

"Oh. I really like that."

He switched sides, taking his time, losing himself in her taste and the feel of her in his mouth. She writhed when he pushed the soft mounds of flesh together to tongue both nipples at the same time. "I wanna suck these as you're ridin' me. I wanna feel these tips diggin' into my thighs as you put your mouth on me. Do you want that, AJ?"

"Yes." She bumped her hips to his; her body knew what it

needed even if she wasn't sure how to get it.

As Cord kissed his way up to her neck, his hand inched down to the hem of her skirt. A few teasing strokes and his fingers crept up the inside of her silky thigh.

AJ's whole body tensed.

"Open your legs for me, baby doll."

She closed her eyes, allowing her head to fall back against the truck as her knees widened.

His fingers brushed her naked, damp sex. "You did take off them sexy panties. Good sign that you obeyed me." He nibbled on her ear. "You are wet. Means you like what I'm doin' to you."

"Uh. Yeah."

"Look at me."

Her eyes fluttered open.

Cord swirled his middle finger around her opening, coating it with her juices before he pushed it inside, greedily watching her face to see her response to the intrusion.

She gasped.

"Does that hurt?"

"N-no."

He pumped his finger in and out a couple of times before he added a second finger. "You like that?"

"Yes...but..."

"But what? Tell me."

"I-I...don't know. It feels good, but I want...more. Even when I don't know what more is."

He thrust his fingers deeper and swept his thumb across her clit. "This kinda more?"

"Oh. That feels so good."

Cord latched on to her right nipple, suckling strongly, twisting his fingers inside her, increasing the friction on her clit. His cock was hard as a baseball bat, and he was tempted to grind it into her hip, but the only thing he cared about was making her come. Watching her come.

Her legs shook. She started to moan. He softly bit down on her nipple. And AJ lost it. Her clit throbbed beneath his thumb. She squeezed her legs together trying to shove his fingers deeper into her channel. Her fingernails pierced the back of his neck as she urged his head closer.

It was one of the hottest things he'd ever seen and he'd forgotten her hands were supposed to be by her sides. So fucking unbelievable he was the first man to touch her this way.

Cord waited until she'd caught her breath before he removed his hand from between her legs.

She peeked at him from beneath lowered lashes, smiling shyly. "Wow."

He pinned her arms by her side and kissed her for several long minutes. "Come home with me. There's lots more I can wow you with tonight."

"I can't."

"I thought you wanted—"

"I do want this, and I want you. I'm not playing hard to get, Cord. But the reason I'm home is to take care of my mom. Jenn and I trade off, depending on her schedule. She's been there all afternoon and she's leaving at eleven. Someone has to stay with Mom in case she needs something and tonight that's me."

Cord stared at her as she refastened her bra and buttoned her blouse. "Why didn't I know this?"

"I'd planned on talking to you earlier, but I forgot while we were dancing. And then we came out here and, Lord, I couldn't think straight when you started touching me. See?" She laughed and pointed at the crooked row of buttons. "So I understand if you've changed your mind and wanna back out."

"Hell no, I'm not backin' out. I have a ranch to run during the day anyway. Can you come to me at night?"

"Probably right after supper."

"Tomorrow?"

She nodded.

"And every night after that?"

"If that's what you want."

"Oh, I want all right. We need to talk about somethin' else anyway." He shoved his hand through his hair and paced. "I ain't about to ruin your reputation and mine because once we start this, I know I can't keep my hands off you."

"That's bad?"

"Jesus, yes that's bad. I can just hear the goddamn cradle robber jokes. So what happens between us stays between us and will be conducted in private. No exceptions. We ain't gonna go dancin' or out to dinner. And it's all gotta end when Ky comes home."

"I'll be headed back to school around then anyway."

"Good enough. As far as birth control?"

"I'm on the pill."

Cord stopped moving. "A virgin on the pill? Why?"

"About six months ago I was having some female issues and our school health clinician advised I get on the pill."

He smiled. "No condoms. I'm down with that."

"You are…clean?"

"Yes." Cord slapped his hands beside her shoulders, caging her in. "Somethin' else you oughta consider, AJ. I'm demanding in bed. Very demanding. Since we'll only be spendin' a few hours a day together, I'll expect all that time will be naked time. And you better be prepared to say yes to whatever I ask or tell you to do."

"Within reason."

He lifted a brow. "Got a few conditions?"

"Yes. I won't be cooking, cleaning, washing clothes, dishes or floors—even if you have some master/slave fantasy and command me to do it naked." Her silvery eyes narrowed. "And don't think I haven't heard the rumors about the wild McKay men and their appetite for kink, threesomes and whatever. No multiples. Just you and me. That's it."

"Deal. But that means you *will* give me control. If I'm teachin' you, we'll do it my way. Anything I want, any way I want, any time, any place." Cord layered his body to hers, rubbing his cock into the soft notch between her thighs. "Feel how hard I am? You did that to me, baby doll. I'm gonna have to go home and jack off in the shower, imaginin' it's your hand around my cock. So when you come to me tomorrow, you'll owe me one."

"I can't wait to pay up." AJ gave him a flirty kiss and vanished into the night.

Chapter Seven

"Sweetheart, what time did your sister say she'd be here?"

AJ glanced at the clock. Jenn was over an hour late. "You know she always runs behind."

And of all the days for Jenn to be late...AJ should've been at Cord's house thirty minutes ago. Just thinking about what he might have planned made her heart race.

She slapped a lid on the goulash and wiped down the counters. Done. She'd be in her Jeep the second Jenn and her kids arrived.

AJ carried the mug of tea to the living room, which had become a hospital room since her mother's accident. A big adjustable bed inhabited the space, seeming out of place in a room fraught with doilies, lace, and ruffles. AJ's stomach clenched to see her stalwart mother bedridden. She'd never thought of Florence Foster as old—even though she'd recently turned seventy-one.

Age was merely a number, but AJ couldn't deny her mom was getting on in years. Her mother looked at least a decade younger than her biological age, but AJ noticed Florence slowing down when she'd come home for visits in the last year.

Work-roughened hands reached for the mug. "Thank you. You're the best daughter ever."

"You're just saying that because I don't fight over the remote with you the way Jenn does."

"What does she see in those blasted reality shows?"

"Beats me." AJ smoothed the bedcovers and straightened the stack of *Western Horseman* magazines. "You need an extra pair of socks?"

"Stop fussing, child. Lord, you're as bad as me. Now I understand how smothered you must've felt all those years."

AJ looked up. "What years?"

"When you were growing up, but your daddy and I couldn't help it, sugar. We were just so thrilled to have you in our life, our surprise baby, my early menopause gift. And how did we repay you? By slavin' you during your teen years." Her mother's eyes teared up behind her glasses.

"Mama, you trying to make me cry?"

"No. Just feeling like an old fool. You finally get off the ranch to start your life and now you're back here again, stuck taking care of me."

She handed her a Kleenex. "My life didn't 'start' when I went to school in Denver. My life has always been right here. So stop feeling guilty or I'll gorge on all the brownies to comfort myself." AJ kissed her crinkled brow. "*Stuck*. As if. Glad I still have you to take care of."

"I know. I miss your daddy every day too."

Jenn's minivan zipped up the driveway.

"I imagine you'll be off now?"

"I promised Liza I'd swing by and look at a couple of wedding things." A white lie. Better than the truth of Cord McKay having his wicked way with her.

Her eight-year-old niece, Krista, shuffled in followed by her six-year-old nephew, Mason, and four-year-old Ariel. They plopped on the couch without a word—which was not normal.

"Guys? Why so glum?"

"Because I left Alan," Jenn said from the doorway.

AJ glanced up. Jenn's face resembled a puffer-fish. Her eyes were bloodshot from crying.

"Why don't you guys eat the ice cream bars I brought outside while I talk to Grandma and Aunt Amy Jo."

The kids escaped out the porch door.

"You left Alan?"

"It's not like he hasn't left us first." Jenn snagged a tissue and dabbed her eyes. "I'm tired of him being on the road all the time. Alan told me if a dispatch position opened up he'd take it. The money is better and he'd be home every night. Guess what? I found out he turned one down. Last year. He didn't even talk to me about it."

"I'm so sorry."

"Me too. So is it okay if the kids and I stay here for a while, Mama?"

"Absolutely, you know this is your home."

"Thanks." Jenn said to AJ, "Will you help me unload some of the stuff from the van?"

"Sure." AJ looked at her mother. "Will you be okay for a bit?"

"I'm fine. Send in my babies with some of that ice cream. We'll snuggle up and have some Disney therapy."

Once they were outside, Jenn collapsed against AJ and sobbed.

AJ wanted to cry along with her, but she'd have to be the strong one in the family. Again. She should be used to it by now.

Jenn pushed back and wiped her face. "Sorry."

"Nothing to be sorry about." AJ unloaded suitcases and boxes. "Where is everybody gonna sleep?"

"I thought I'd take Mama and Daddy's room since she's not sleeping in there. I'll put Krista and Ariel upstairs next to you, and Mason in the spare room, okay?"

"That's fine." They carried everything into the house.

"I need a drink." Jenn opened the liquor cabinet. "Wanna get drunk with me? I can give you all the reasons why you shouldn't ever get married."

AJ glanced at the clock. "Look, sis, I have something I need to do tonight. It'll take an hour, hour and a half tops."

"You're leaving? But..." Jenn's eyes filled with tears.

"I'll be back as soon as I can. I promise. Then we can stay up and talk as late as you want."

She nodded and knocked back a slug of Jim Beam.

AJ grabbed her purse and was out the door.

Took ten minutes to reach Cord McKay's place.

AJ parked in front of the big house and stayed in the car, telling herself she was admiring the stunning structure, but in truth, she was scared. How would Cord react when she told him she couldn't stick around tonight? After she'd bailed last night? She couldn't stand it if she'd waited all this time only to have him change his mind because their damn schedules didn't mesh.

After she knocked on the screen door, he yelled, "It's open."

She hesitated in the foyer. "Cord?"

He poked his head out, pointed to the receiver next to his ear and gave her the five-minute sign.

AJ wandered into the kitchen. She'd been in this gorgeous house many times, but never when Ky wasn't underfoot. The place was huge and she knew from listening to Keely that Cord's ex-wife had demanded he build her a brand new log house with all the amenities when she'd agreed to relocate to Wyoming. The house boasted a formal living room and dining room, a family room, a huge master bedroom and bathroom, five bedrooms, four bathrooms, a state of the art kitchen and an outdoor hot tub. But even the ostentatious house hadn't been enough to keep her around.

How could she walk away from the spectacular vista of gold and green fields against the backdrop of the pine-covered hills spread out beyond the sliding glass door? The view was more amazing than the house, in AJ's opinion.

Bootsteps on the wooden floors stopped behind her. "Sorry. I was talkin' to Ky."

"How's he doing?"

"Seems to be all right. They're goin' on a boat ride in the sound tomorrow, so he's pretty excited."

"How's Dad doing?"

"Miss the squirt like I lost my right arm."

She continued to stare out the window. "This is such a beautiful view."

"The one good thing about this damn monstrosity." Cord placed his hands on her shoulders. She jumped. "Relax. What's got you so tense?"

"Family stuff. Jenn and the kids showed up, which I expected. I didn't expect her to tell me she'd left her husband."

Cord's hands fell away.

Was it an automatic reaction because it brought to mind the demise of his own marriage? "I'm not surprised, things have been bad for a while. Alan is constantly on the road driving truck. When he is home he's not much of a husband or father. Jenn's always pretended things'd get better, but she found out he lied to her and she's fed up. She and the kids are moving in with us while she makes some decisions."

After a while Cord said, "I'm sorry."

"Me too. She needs me tonight, so I can't stay."

Cord spun her to face him. Then his hands were in her hair and his mouth was hot and demanding on hers. She sank into the kiss, twining her arms around his neck, threading her fingers through his damp hair. He herded her until her spine hit the counter.

"Wait, I have to go—"

"You drove all the way over here to tell me you can't stay?" He nuzzled the skin below her ear. "You could've called. Which leads me to believe you want to stick around."

"I do. But I can't."

"You will stay."

His low sexy voice reverberated throughout her entire body. "Cord—"

"Thirty minutes." He tipped her chin up to gaze into her eyes. "You owe me, baby doll. I've been thinkin' all damn day 'bout how bad I want your hands on me. And with the way I feel right now, it's gonna last thirty seconds." He kissed the corners of her mouth. "Which still gives us twenty-nine minutes and thirty seconds to mess around."

"Is that, um, enough time?"

"With you? Not nearly." He reversed their positions and his back rested against the counter. "You want me to teach you about sex and how to satisfy a man's needs, right?"

"Right."

"Undo my pants."

"Now?"

"Right now."

Oh wow. Even though she'd been waiting to get her hands on him forever, AJ's hands shook as she unbuckled his belt. She fumbled with the top button of his jeans. After several frustrating attempts, she pressed her forehead to his chest, feeling embarrassed, feeling...virginal. "I don't know what I'm doing."

"Hey now, you're doin' fine."

She chanced a look at him. God, he was gorgeous. His rugged face defined masculine ferocity—the hard angular edge of his jaw, and his jagged cheekbones. His blue eyes burned indigo with lust. His goatee and mustache was the perfect frame for his perfectly kissable full lips. She wanted him so much. How could she prove it? "Kiss me."

He pecked her on the forehead. "I plan to spend hours kissin' you, but I wanna see the look on your face when you see my cock for the first time."

Heat flooded AJ's cheeks.

"Ah, you are so goddamn sweet when you blush like that. It's sexy as hell."

Buoyed by his enthusiasm, she reached for the tab on his zipper and tugged it down. Her palm brushed the firm lump off to the left. She stroked it, amazed she could feel heat through the denim.

Cord sucked in a harsh breath.

AJ wrenched his pants legs until the jeans were down around his knees, leaving him in his navy blue boxer briefs. She grinned. "I expected Superman underwear like Ky's."

"The man of steel ain't got nothin' on me right now."

"Sort of looks that way." She slipped her fingers under the elastic band and stopped. "Take off your T-shirt first."

"Why?"

"I wanna see you mostly naked."

"Remember you said that when my turn comes around." Cord whipped the navy cotton over his head and chucked it on the floor.

Her eyes bugged out. "No wonder you always wear a shirt. Keeps the bulls from chasin' after you as well as the lovesick sows. Lord. I could just eat you up." AJ pressed a kiss above the brown nipple, then rubbed her lips over that smooth, warm flesh, amazed by how fast it puckered.

Rough male hands curled over her cheeks. "Focus, AJ."

"You saying the only part of you I can touch is your...?"

One dark eyebrow winged up. "My what?"

"Your...you know."

"Say the word, baby doll. You're gonna be handlin' it soon enough."

"Your cock." When he pulled his underwear to his knees her eyes bugged out again. "Whoa."

Cord didn't say a word. He just watched her.

AJ ran her finger up the pulsing vein from root to tip. She drew circles on the purplish head and the whole shaft jerked against his flat belly. A bead of clear liquid covered the slit. She wrapped her hand around the girth and squeezed. Hard, not unlike steel, but smooth. And hot. Heat singed her palm, zinging from his cock right to her core as if an electric current flowed between them. She moved her fist down to the thick base and back to the top.

He hissed.

She looked up at him.

"Jesus. You should see your eyes."

"Do they look scared? I don't know how to tell you this, Cord, but I don't think this is gonna fit in me."

He laughed softly. "Oh, it'll fit. It'll be the perfect fit, trust me."

AJ released him, letting her fingers lightly trace the length from tip to root. Touching him was making her wet and squirmy. She reached down to feel his balls. "Are they always this hard and tight?"

"Only when I'm about to blow."

She wanted to see him blow. "Show me how to make you do that."

"With pleasure." Cord kissed her first, encouraging her to keep touching him by kissing her harder when she did something he liked. Then he broke his mouth free, reaching along the countertop for a bottle of olive oil and uncapped it. "Hold out your hand." He dribbled a few drops on her palm. "Saliva is a better lubricant, but this'll do."

Another wave of heat blasted her as she imagined tasting him, feeling the velvety skin of that stiff rod sliding between her lips and across her tongue.

"You're killin' me. You wanna know what it'll be like to have my cock in your mouth, don't you?"

"Is that bad?"

"Hell no."

AJ gripped the base of his shaft and stroked up with her whole hand. "Tell me what to do."

"You're doin' it. Go a little faster. Yeah. Like that. Don't squeeze too hard unless you're tryin' to keep me from comin'."

"Umm. Why would I want to do that?"

"You don't. Not this time anyway. Keep it a steady pace until I tell you to move faster. Sweep your thumb over the spot below the slit."

"This spot?" She rubbed back and forth over the spot where the cockhead split into the shaft.

"Baby doll, that feels good."

What a heady sense of power; her hand could make him whimper. Could make him thrust his hips at her for more. Why, she could probably make this big bad cowboy...beg. Ooh and she'd take such pride in cracking his tough-guy mask.

"Gimme that mouth," he growled, swooping down to inhale her in a sizzling meeting of lips and tongues.

Somehow she kept a uniform rhythm as he scrambled her brain with his tongue-tangling kiss until he groaned.

"Faster." Cord tipped his head back. "More. Like that. Jesus. Don't stop."

AJ alternated between watching his face and her hand.

"Here it comes."

His cock spasmed and thick creamy liquid streamed out, landing on his belly. He arched his neck, losing himself in the moment. His fingers gripped the counter behind him until his knuckles turned white as the last spurts flowed over her hand.

She thought she might be embarrassed by the nitty gritty bodily functions of sex. But she was awestruck by the primal need his climax had brought out in *her.*

Cord opened his eyes. "You okay?"

"Uh-huh."

"You can let go of my dick now."

"I don't want to." AJ squeezed his shaft and he hissed again. "You're still hard. I want you to teach me some more. Show me some more. God, Cord, show me everything."

"AJ—"

"We have time. Please. I have this ache low in my—"

His mouth slammed down on hers. He kissed her until she was woozy. "Clothes. Off. Now."

Her tank top hit the floor. AJ unhooked her bra, kicked her boots away, slid out of her jeans and panties.

Cord was as naked as she was when he reached for her. Then they were on the floor with Cord on top.

Oh yes, this was what she wanted, his need as escalated as hers. That heady give-it-to-me-now sensation of lust.

As his hungry mouth suckled her right breast, his hand swept over her mound and he thrust two fingers inside her pussy.

A low groan rumbled from him and vibrated against her chest. "You're so ready."

"Then put it in me."

"No."

"Cord. Please."

"No. I will get you off, but I am not makin' love to you for the first time on the goddamn kitchen floor, AJ. You've waited this long, you can wait another damn day."

"Do something!"

He pinned her hands above her head. "Spread your legs."

The second she was in place, he dragged his cock from the root to the tip down her cleft, keeping constant friction on her clit.

"Oh. Yes."

"Like that? How 'bout this?" He thrust faster.

"Oh-man-oh-man-oh-man."

Cord kissed her as he steadily rocked. And rocked. Sliding. Gliding. Changing the tempo until she was begging without saying a word.

The sensation of his solid weight, his scorching body heat and his seductive mouth, coupled with the exquisite pressure between her legs, overwhelmed her and she exploded.

When the last pulse in her clit slowed, Cord stilled. His cock jerked against her stomach leaving behind a pool of warmth.

She tried to level her breathing, but it was impossible with two hundred pounds of amorous cowboy squeezing every bit of air from her lungs.

Not that she was complaining.

Cord raised up on his elbows only high enough to suck on her nipples. "Have I mentioned how much I like your tits?" Using his teeth to pull her nipple into a long point, he watched it shrink and repeated the process on the other side. "I could suck on them, play with them, fuck them all day long."

"How does that work?"

He looked at her. "What?"

"Umm. How would you..."

"Fuck them?" He grinned. "I could tell you, but I'd rather show you." He smooched her nose. "Once you get goin' you really ain't shy at all, are you?"

"No." AJ trailed her fingers over his chin. "Lord you have a sexy mouth, a sexy everything, Cord McKay. I like the way your facial hair feels on my skin."

"Think of how good it's gonna feel rubbin' between your thighs as I'm kissin' your sweet spot, baby doll."

She shivered with want.

"Maybe we oughta get off the floor, huh?" Cord eased back, snatched a kitchen towel and cleaned them up. Neither spoke as they dressed.

As AJ passed the hall mirror she caught sight of her reflection and nearly shrieked. Tangled hair. Red and puffy lips. Bright eyes. She was an absolute mess.

Cord tugged her away from primping. "You look like a woman should, tousled and sexy, satisfied from good lovin'."

AJ froze at the word "lovin'".

Using that word doesn't mean he loves you.

"What?"

"Nothing." Her eyes studied his. "No regrets? You don't look at me and feel guilty for messing around with the Swiss Miss Instant Cocoa Girl?"

He scowled. "No. Who the hell ever said that about you?"

"Your brother Colby called me that one time."

"Consider the source. Colby's a bonehead. That ain't what I see at all when I look at you."

"So, what do you see when you look at me?"

"Not Amy Jo, my son's babysitter. When I noticed you dancin' at the Golden Boot in that shamelessly brazen miniskirt and them naughty red panties, I started thinkin' of you in terms of us naked together. A lot."

Better than she'd hoped.

"What do you see when you look at me?" he asked.

"A hot rancher with a killer body, a wicked smile and even more wicked hands. A good man I trust." *A man I've been in love with my whole damn life.*

"You know I'm too old for you, right?"

"I'd say experienced, not old."

"Right. But I'm such a selfish prick I ain't lettin' no other man touch you until I've had my fill of you."

May that day never come, Cord McKay.

Cord framed her face in his hands. "I haven't had my fill of you tonight, that's for damn sure. But your thirty minutes are up, so it'll have to wait until tomorrow night."

"What if I can't make it?"

"You will be here. We have a deal. Your nights are mine, AJ. If you miss a night, you will owe me a day. And don't kid yourself for a single second that I won't chase you down to collect."

"I might enjoy you chasing after me for a change."

"What?"

"Never mind." She kissed the lines between his eyes. "Don't scowl. It'll give you wrinkles."

"They'd go with the gray hair Ky's givin' me."

She put her fingers over his lips. "Not another word about being old."

Chapter Eight

Kade volunteered for all the shit jobs around the McKay ranch. He'd avoided his brother and Colt when they weren't working, even crashing at his folks' house because sleeping at the Boars Nest made him uneasy.

Part of him wondered if what he'd seen really happened or if it was just another weird-assed dream fueled by alcohol.

Resting his forearm on the pitchfork, he took a breather and allowed his mind to drift. The night after the threesome with Jazz, he'd gone out with his cousin Dag and they'd returned to a house filled with drunken strangers. Dead tired, he'd dropped into bed. Dag had decided to stick around.

A few hours later Kade had stumbled to the kitchen for a bottle of water when he saw two naked bodies fucking on the living room floor.

Guys. Going at it like animals.

A skinny man was on his knees with his bony white ass hiked high in the air, his arms stretched above his head on the floor, wrists tied with a bandana and a gag shoved in his mouth. It was so dark Kade couldn't see his face.

A bruiser with a crew cut was jacking off the skinny guy as he fucked his captive in the ass so savagely they both skidded across the carpet with dual groans of satisfaction.

By that time Kade decided he wasn't so thirsty after all. He returned to bed. No sign of the horny guys in the morning, so he wondered if it hadn't been some kind of homosexual dream. He sure wasn't gonna ask Kane or Dag or Colt if they'd seen it and have them tease him for fucking ever about it.

Not that he could give a shit what went on behind people's bedroom doors in their own houses. But if what he'd seen had been real? And going down front and center in his house? Different story.

His family would be appalled if they knew about the circus-like sexual situations happening at the Boars Nest on a regular basis. His cheeks burned with shame. What had he been thinking, fucking a total stranger? Then a threesome? Followed by another threesome with his twin? He didn't want to live his life being just another "wild McKay boy" and the butt of jokes in four counties. Kade worried no decent woman would want him if she ever got wind of his previous sexual antics.

If he was completely honest, the debauchery had stopped being fun a while ago. And it seemed the chances of him ever finding a decent woman in this small community, who not only didn't know about his every past sexual conquest, or who wouldn't automatically mix him up with his twin brother, were slim to none. He'd learned enough from Cord's failed marriage that a city girl wouldn't fit here either. Basically, he was screwed on the relationship front. Not that any woman would probably believe him if he admitted he was more than ready to settle down.

With a sigh, he got back to work. There was always plenty of work on the McKay ranch.

An hour later his brother Kane called in his favor, sending him on an errand to the next town thirty-five miles from home for some special kind of lotion their mother used.

Kade parallel parked in front of DeWitt's Pharmacy. He wandered around until he found the display—Sky Blue—all natural ingredients—locally made.

Right. Another freakazoid, Birkenstock-wearing, organic type who invaded Wyoming to bilk gullible ladies like his mama into buying beauty junk they didn't need. He picked up a bottle of lotion. Nineteen bucks? Holy crap. He was definitely in the wrong business.

He noticed a bar of soap with the same scent as the lotion. After a quick look around to make sure no one was spying on him, he picked it up and sniffed. Not bad. Kind of tangy. Lemony. He added a can of motor oil and a package of mousetraps to the cart just so he didn't look like a total fucking pussy to the cashier.

Kade stood on the sidewalk debating on whether to have lunch first before heading home. *Click click* sounded and he turned to the woman in heels storming toward him.

Mercy. She was all curves: hips, ass, thighs, and breasts. He loved women who looked like women and not a skeleton with skin. Her straight brown hair had a hint of red in the bright sunlight. Kade stepped out of her way, figuring she'd pass right on by.

Wrong.

Miss Sexy Curves bumped her pointy-toed purple shoes against his shit-covered boots and glared. "You were a total jerk to me the other night, Kane McKay. I don't appreciate you ditching me at the restaurant. What kind of shithead—"

"Whoa. Wait a second. I'm not—"

"—the least bit sorry, yeah, I can tell. Why are you here? Trolling for some woman who'll give you a piece of ass on the first date since I wouldn't?"

That fucker Kane was such an asshole. Times like this it plain sucked they were identical twins and few people could tell them apart. This woman must be Kane's date from the other night.

His brother was an idiot too. How had he walked away from such a smoking hot firecracker?

"Got nothing to say, McKay?"

And he had a really good idea on what he wanted to say, and how to make this right.

No. It was a bad idea. A terrible idea.

The devil on his shoulder said: *Do it. You and Kane used to switch places all the time. You're not misleading her; you're protecting the McKay name from another bit of damaging gossip.*

"Actually, I do have somethin' to say to you." What the hell was her name again? Something hippyishly weird. Aha. "Skylar."

"I'm listening."

"I'm sorry. I lost your number or I woulda called to apologize for bein' a first class jerk. But I'd taken some allergy medicine and lordy, did it do a number on me. Normally I don't act like that. Not that I remember a whole helluva lot besides goin' home and crashin'."

Skylar looked at him skeptically.

"Can I make it up to you? Buy you lunch? I swear I won't run out again."

"When?"

"How about now?"

"Sure. You don't mind vegetarian?"

Fuck. Kade slapped on a fake smile. "Not at all."

She laughed; it made him think of bells. "You are such a liar. Your family raises cattle. You probably shoot vegetarians."

"Only if they're part of PETA protestin' inhuman treatment of our stock. That pisses us off."

"I can imagine."

"Besides, I eat salad. Not crazy about tofu. Or beans ground up and passed off as burgers. A burger is supposed to be meat. Beans are only good in tacos and chili." Kade looked up. Damn. He'd been babbling.

Her lips curled in a cat-like smile. "Too bad you weren't this honest the other night. I know just the place. Let's go."

Later that same afternoon Cord pushed back his hat and wiped the sweat from his brow. He looked over at his brother, who was doing more leaning in the back of the truck than working.

"Pull the lead out, Colt. I ain't got all goddamn day."

"Cut me some slack. I'm whupped."

"Only reason you're whupped is because you were up late last night fuckin' around."

"Jealous?"

Not since he'd been doing some fucking around himself, but no way would he share that with his smartass brother. "No. I'm pissed. You've been draggin' ass more than usual lately. I'm sick of carryin' your share of the load."

"Some of us have a life."

"Maybe I could have a life if I wasn't so busy workin' my ass off so you don't have to."

Colt straightened up and rested on the pitchfork. "Got somethin' to say to me?"

"I'm sayin' it. Show up for work on time, Colt. Not hungover, not fuckin' whinin' like a toddler. And while you're at it, maybe you oughta think about the fact this is a small county. Some of the sex shit you and Kane and Kade are doin' with every woman in the tri-county area is gettin' around and before long it'll get back to Ma."

"Right. Like you have a right to talk. Why do you think everyone says 'them wild McKay boys'—you and Colby and Quinn wrote the damn book on bad behavior. I'm just sowin' my oats, same as you guys done."

"Wrong. I was *done* by the time I was your age."

"Well, la-di-fuckin'-da. I think you're pissed off because Jasmine didn't invite you to join in the fun and games the other night because you're old and cranky."

Furious, Cord jumped off the tailgate. "I'll show you old. I'm gonna kick your smart ass, punk."

Colt tossed the pitchfork aside. "Come on up here and try it."

Just about that time, Colby galloped up on his horse. He reined between the two pickups and the two angry brothers. "What the hell is goin' on here?"

"Ask Colt. Better yet, why don't you ask him what he's done today? Or yesterday? Or all goddamn week?"

"Accordin' to Cord, if you ain't workin' twenty-four hours a day, you're a fuckin' slacker."

"You'd know all about bein' a slacker, Colt."

"Enough. Both of you." Colby's horse stuck his head in the back of the truck bed to sniff for food.

"Fine. I'm done anyway." Colt climbed in his truck and roared off.

Cord stared after his shithead brother, mentally cataloging half a dozen crappy jobs for him to do tomorrow.

"What's really goin' on with him? Why's he bein' so damn ornery?"

Cord relayed what he'd seen in the Golden Boot. "Only thing he cares about is gettin' laid and gettin' drunk. And if you think I'm exaggeratin', ask Dad. He knows what Colt ain't been doin' around here."

Colby sighed. "I did. That's why he sent me. He says you're workin' too hard."

"Dad said that? He oughta talk. I ain't doin' any more than what I usually do—which just proves that Colt ain't been doin' his share. Not just this week, either. Ever since calving season."

"Didja try talkin' to him 'bout it?"

"Yeah. I even talked to Kade since he lives with him, see if he noticed anything. Kade don't see nothin' wrong, so I dropped it."

"You done here?"

"Was 'bout to head home. Why?"

"Channing told me to ask you to supper."

"She feelin' better?"

"Nope. Still sick as a dog. Doc says it'll pass next month. Ma says it'll pass next month." He scrubbed a hand over his jaw. "Hard to be excited when she's so miserable."

"It gets better. And I'll bet she's happy even when she's throwin' up."

Colby smiled. "True. Anyway, she knows you're missin' Ky, we're missin' him too. So you wanna come over?"

"Nah. Tell the mama-to-be thanks and I'll wait 'til she's feelin' up to company."

"Good enough. You care if I hang around tomorrow and keep an eye on Colt?"

"I'd appreciate it. I'm runnin' behind. Again."

Cord threw his tools in the back of his truck and started the drive home. The summer air was heavy with heat. Gnats buzzed around his head. Burrs stuck to his clothes. He was hungry. Dirty. Still, this was his favorite part of ranching, gazing across his spread, knowing he'd accomplished something important during the long hours he'd spent outdoors.

About this time he looked forward to cleaning up. Having a bite to eat with his son. Playing games or watching TV before wrestling Ky into bed.

But after he'd tucked Ky in for the night...that's when he felt lonely on occasion. Not a constant ache, more along the lines of a distant memory of the throb of a broken finger. Seemed he'd been alone so long he was used to it.

Yet, Cord wouldn't be alone tonight. AJ would be rolling in. AJ with her big silver eyes. AJ with her sweet smile and inquisitive nature. AJ with her hungry kisses and look of wonder.

How could she be both innocent and daring? Why had she picked him, a cranky old man with no life, according to his brother, to initiate her into the pleasures between the sheets?

Why hadn't AJ chosen Colt? He was closer to her in age. More charming. Probably had a lot of experience breaking in virgins.

But Cord knew if his brother so much as looked at AJ with lust in his eyes he'd beat the living shit out of him.

Lord. Part of him was plain nervous. Just how was he supposed to pop her cherry? Candlelight, soft music, champagne and a slow seduction? Did he have the patience to create an elaborate scene?

No. But what if that was how she'd dreamed it would be?

He'd never been a romantic guy. Maybe he oughta take her hard and fast in the heat of passion. Then they could try some of the more interesting scenarios he'd been thinking up when he'd been alone out on the range all day.

No matter what cues she gave him, Cord knew tonight was the night and he better get a move on.

Chapter Nine

After Cord returned home, his dad swung by. They talked about the worsening situation with Colt. Discussed plans for the rest of the workweek. Ranch stuff Cord lived and breathed. Usually Cord convinced his dad to stick around for another beer, but tonight he couldn't wait for the man to leave.

And didn't that make him a selfish bastard? Did it make him a nancy boy that he'd spent extra time on his appearance? Trimming his mustache and goatee. Giving himself a close shave. Plus he'd changed the sheets on the bed, cleaned the bathroom and generally tidied up the rest of his house.

So where was she?

The phone rang and Cord was half-afraid to answer it, thinking AJ might be calling to cancel. But it was his mother, grilling him on Colt. As he listened to her chatter, he saw dust plumes on the main gravel road. AJ had arrived.

"Ma. My cell is ringin'. I'll talk to you tomorrow." He hung up and watched AJ's metallic black Jeep park in the hidden alcove next to the barn.

His heart kicked into double time. He'd never been the type for unbridled affection with anyone besides his son. Why didn't he rush out to meet her? Swing her into his arms, pepper her sweet face with kisses just to hear her laugh?

Because you'll appear too eager. Too desperate.

So instead, he slouched against the newel post at the bottom of the staircase, waiting for her to come to him.

Light footsteps echoed across the porch and then two solid raps on the screen door. Cord counted to ten and walked to the front entryway.

He smiled and opened the door, giving her a hot head-to-toe appraisal. Short pink skirt, skin-tight white T-shirt proclaiming "Cowgirls Ride Better Dirty" and rhinestone-dotted flip-flops. He experienced a twinge of guilt because she looked so young and innocent. But the guilt vanished when he saw the lust brimming in her eyes, making them as hot as liquid mercury.

"Hey, baby doll. Don't you look good."

AJ stared at his mouth. "Thanks."

"Can I getcha a beer?"

"Ah. Sure."

"What's wrong?"

"Nothing. But aren't you gonna kiss me hello?"

Cord bent down to press his lips to hers, gliding over the plump softness of her mouth a couple of times and retreated to lick his lips. "Mmm. You taste like lemons." He gauged her disappointment. "If I start kissin' you proper, I won't wanna stop and I ain't gonna maul you in the foyer."

"I wouldn't mind."

"Playin' with fire, AJ. I'll grab the beer and be right back."

"Don't you want me to come into the kitchen? I could help."

He spun back around and shook his finger at her. "You stay right there. We get into trouble in the kitchen."

"I'm hoping we get into trouble everywhere else too." AJ smiled coyly and wandered away.

Cord popped the tops on two Budweisers and tracked her to the living room. Damn, she was a bright spot of color against the dark wood and formal furniture. "Here."

She grabbed the bottle from him. "Thanks. So, what did you do today?"

"Fixed equipment. Hauled water. Dumped manure. Chewed Colt's ass. Everyday ranch stuff." He sat on the couch and put his beer on the coffee table. "What about you?"

"Dealt with Jenn after she went to the lawyer's office."

"She's really goin' through with it?"

"Apparently. She talked to Alan this morning. He doesn't seem too upset about the divorce, which is upsetting to her. It's upsetting to me too."

Several minutes passed and she didn't say another word.

"C'mere."

AJ abandoned her spot by the floor-to-ceiling picture windows and moved to the couch. As she attempted to plop down next to him, Cord tugged her on his lap.

"I said come *here*."

She twisted until their bodies were matched pelvis to pelvis. She draped her arms over the back of the couch behind his head. "Now that I'm here, what're you gonna do with me?"

Fuck you until you scream my name.

He took her mouth like he wanted to take her body—a slow build up, then wham! A no-holds-barred, hot, wet, hard swamping of her senses until she couldn't breathe.

AJ rubbed her chest to his, returning his demanding kiss—her enthusiasm a contradiction to her innocence.

Cord slid his palms up the back of her sleek thighs and found only bare skin. The little minx hadn't worn panties.

He clamped his hands to her butt and lifted her slightly, changing the angle of her hips. His middle finger traced the seam of her ass down to where she was wet. He circled the opening to her sex and pushed his finger deep, feathering his thumb over her clit.

Her sexy whimper reverberated in his mouth.

As much as he loved hearing her muted surprised sounds of pleasure, he needed more. Cord moved his hand to the small of her back, scraped his teeth across her bottom lip and broke the kiss. "I'm gonna put my mouth on you. I wanna feel you come against my tongue."

"Oh. I, ah. Um. Okay."

He held her hips as he rolled them until AJ's back was against the cushions. Cord slid to his knees on the floor. As he kissed her, he shoved the velvet square throw pillow underneath her ass. He tucked her skirt out of his way, baring her completely from the waist down.

"Keep your hands right there and hold on."

As his palms traveled down the center of her body, Cord wished he'd made her strip so he could feel every inch of her skin.

"Cord, I'm not sure—"

"You want this." He dragged openmouthed kisses from her left knee up the inside of her quivering thigh and licked the crease where thigh met hip.

She jumped.

Smiling, Cord brushed his mouth down the top of her leg, using his tongue to trace the musculature of her thighs, courtesy of the years she'd spent on horseback. He used the same thorough treatment on her right leg. By the time he finished, AJ trembled.

Her glistening sex was at his mouth level. He pressed his lips to the top of her pubic bone. The soft curls covering her mound were so light blonde she appeared bare. Damn humbling to think he was the only man who'd ever seen her delicate femininity. It also increased the pressure on his performance when he considered she'd remember him loving her with his mouth first.

He lightly rubbed his lips above the sweet cleft and inhaled deeply. "Goddamn you smell like sunshine here too. I oughta be tellin' you how pretty this pussy is, all pink and wet and soft and untried, how sexy that it's weepin' for my attention. But I can't wait." He lowered his chin and licked straight up her slit.

AJ made a strangled moan.

Cord licked her again. And again. His fingers spread her open and he burrowed his tongue deep, tasting her from the inside out. He used the very tip to trace every delectable crease and hidden fold. He suckled her lips, intentionally avoiding her clit. Then he circled kisses from the top of her pubis down and back up.

She whimpered and bumped her pelvis closer to his face.

He grinned even when his cock was so hard it hurt.

Cord savored her sweet essence, prolonging her pleasure until thick cream poured from her sex.

"Oh God, please, Cord."

"Do you like this?"

"Yes! I never thought..."

"Never thought what?"

"That anything could feel this good."

"Mmm. And I'm not even to the good part yet." The vibration made her gasp. So he did it again. Then Cord placed his mouth on her clit and sucked.

AJ nearly shot off the couch.

He alternated little whips of his hot tongue across that inflamed pearl with deep rhythmic sucking. It didn't take long before AJ arched; he gripped her hips as her orgasm exploded in his mouth.

She screamed. And thrashed and tried to get away even as she tried to get closer.

He didn't release her until the very last pulse.

With his mouth still connected to her throbbing sex, he looked up and saw her gazing at him. Not with embarrassment, but with awe. With hunger.

"Cord."

The hoarse, needy way she'd whispered his name sent every last bit of blood to his dick.

He gave her clit one last hard suck before he pushed back and stood. "In my bed, AJ. Now."

Cord clasped her hand and led her upstairs.

AJ's whole body shook. With need. With surprise. With fear.

The sun was setting, softening the light filtering through the blinds to a hazy purply pink. The king-sized, four-poster bed was the centerpiece in Cord's masculine bedroom—the only room he'd redecorated after his wife had left. A heavy mahogany nightstand with a stained-glass lamp on top was shoved in one corner, a matching bureau took up the largest wall and an antique wooden rocking chair was in front of the bay window.

She leaned against the doorjamb to the master bath and watched Cord toeing off his Tony Lamas. He folded the comforter to the end of the bed, exposing plain white cotton sheets.

Cord faced her as he unbuttoned his crisply ironed navy blue shirt.

"Should I be doing that?" she asked.

"Next time. If you put your hands on me anywhere right now, I guarantee I'll be on you and in you before you can blink."

"Sounds good to me."

He growled and tossed his shirt on the dresser.

AJ stared at his chest. Man. Talk about perfect. She wanted to sink her teeth into his hard pecs. Lick his bulging biceps. Suck the flat disks and see how fast his nipples hardened. Trace the ridged lines of his ripped abdomen with her tongue. Follow that intriguing trail of dark hair from his belly button down...way down to see exactly where the hair ended. She bit her lip as he lowered the zipper on his jeans.

"AJ, I'm warnin' you."

"What?"

"Stop lookin' at me like you wanna eat me alive."

"If you didn't want me to look, Cord, you shouldn't look so damn good."

That slow, sexy grin appeared. "Like what you see?"

"I've always liked it." *Even when I was a little girl and I didn't know* why *I liked it so much.*

His jeans hit the floor and he was buck-ass naked.

Her gaze zeroed in on his groin and her heart rate quadrupled. "Umm. Wow. Did it grow? Because it looks bigger."

"Kissin' your red-hot love flower made this stem grow big and hard just for you, baby doll."

AJ managed to meet his eyes. "Love flower?"

"Thought maybe you wanted some kinda sweet-talkin' love words first."

"Is that the next step? Because I thought we'd just get naked and you'd put your stem—"

Cord's mouth cut off additional comment. He fiddled with her rhinestone belt and her skirt thudded on the floor. He released her mouth long enough to say, "Lift," and yanked her T-shirt over her head. *Snap*. Her bra opened and he slid it off her arms. He walked her to the bed until the backs of her knees hit the mattress.

His hands kneaded her breasts and then his hot mouth enclosed her nipple.

AJ let out a squeak.

"I wanna fuck you fast and get this first time out of the way so I can fuck you slow next time. Then fast the time after that. Then slow. I want to fuck you so many times in so many ways that you won't be able to sit on a horse for a goddamn week, AJ."

Liquid heat pooled between her thighs, her pulse pounded and every part of her that wasn't touching him ached to be touching him. "Cord—"

"Get on the bed. In the middle."

She scooted back on her elbows until her neck brushed the pillows. The cotton sheets were cool beneath her feverish skin.

Cord stood at the foot of the bed, stroking himself, eyeing her like she was the lottery, a gourmet meal, a prize-winning Thoroughbred—and he held a winning ticket to all three.

As he stared at her, she wanted to tell him to hurry up; she wanted to tell him she was scared and to go slow. When he crawled across the mattress, stalking her with his big body and smoldering eyes, she knew she'd made the right decision waiting for this man to introduce her to the carnal delights of sex.

He put his callused hands on the inside of her thighs and pushed them open.

The tips of her nipples tightened when Cord lowered his head and licked a path from her clit up to her mouth. Even his kiss tasted darker. As he nibbled on her lips, she heard a *click* and then his fingers were pushing a cold, sticky substance inside her.

She gasped softly.

"Just lubrication. You're wet, but I don't wanna hurt you. Ready?"

She nodded, hoping he attributed her racing heart and shaking limbs to excitement and not fear.

Cord levered himself over her and reached between them. He circled the blunt tip around her opening and then started to push his cock in.

And in.

And in.

And it still wasn't in. And what was in—hurt.

His hot breath teased her ear. "AJ, don't tense up."

"I'm not. I told you it wouldn't fit."

Cord half-laughed/half-groaned. His lips feathered across her jaw to her mouth. He began to kiss her in that bone-melting way of his.

AJ slid her hands up his strong arms and into his hair. She concentrated on the feel of his silky tongue in her mouth. The glide of his rougher skin on hers. The delicious way he smelled. The cool sheets on her back. The heat of his muscled body on her front. The sounds of their labored breathing. The muted lighting and the soft mattress. The fierce need but unbelievable gentleness pouring from him.

He was rocking into her in short bursts when all of a sudden the kiss intensified. His hands pushed her hips down as his pelvis thrust up.

She gasped. "Oh God. That hurts."

"Ssh. I'm in all the way. Just relax around me. It'll get better."

Then Cord bent his head and suckled her nipples. And kept sucking until some primitive instinct told her to move under him. He kissed her neck, returned to her nipples, nuzzling her cleavage, breathing over the damp spots he'd created on her skin, kissing wherever he could reach, muttering nonsensical words against her skin. Dragging his rough fingertips up and down her shaking thighs.

He murmured, "Baby doll, I've gotta move. Wrap your legs around my waist. Trust me."

AJ was feeling less panicked but nowhere near comfortable. The second she lifted up, all the hot hardness slipped out and plunged back in.

That wasn't bad. That felt kinda...good. "Do it again."

Cord pumped his hips, slowly sliding in and out. "Okay?"

"Yeah. Is it okay for you?"

"Hot." He pulled out. "Wet." He pushed in. "Tight." He eased out. "Not just okay. Perfect." He thrust in a little harder. "See? You are a perfect fit for me."

AJ closed her eyes, feeling the thick male part filling her, sending tingles from her core throughout her whole body. "I like that."

He increased the pace. The strokes were shorter. Deeper. His breaths near her temple were unsteady and fast.

"AJ. Look at me."

She opened her eyes. Sweat trickled down Cord's face. His jaw was tight. She traced his profile, amazed by him, by this intimacy. "What?"

"This." Cord squeezed his hands on her butt, buried his face in her throat and drove his cock inside her to the hilt.

As he groaned, her inner tissues were so swollen and sensitized that she felt the tip of his sex twitching as he bathed her insides with his hot seed.

She couldn't think of a more ideal way to lose her virginity.

Chapter Ten

Cord raised his head and gazed at AJ's face. Her long black lashes fanned her flushed cheeks. Her well-kissed lips were curved into a smirk.

He tickled that sassy little mole with his beard.

She sighed. "A virgin no more."

"You sore?"

"A little."

"Then I'm not pullin' out because I can't wait to have you again."

AJ blushed.

"Hang on." Cord rolled until his back was flat on the mattress and she was on top. "Better. Now I don't hafta worry I'm squashin' you."

"I don't mind." She laid her head on his chest and sighed again.

Such a heartfelt sigh. He knew the feeling as he let his palms drift up and down her naked back from her ass to her shoulders.

"What was your first time like?" she asked.

"Fast. Happened in the back of a car out past the rodeo grounds when I was fifteen."

AJ looked up at him. "I'm glad I waited. Thank you. This was...spectacular."

"Except for the fact you didn't come."

"I did before when we were in the living room."

"That don't count."

"Why not?"

"A good lover will always see to your needs first. Besides, I wanna feel you come around my cock. I wanna watch your face when you feel the difference."

"There's a difference in orgasms?"

Right after she said that, his dick twitched to life.

Her eyes widened. "Whoa. I can feel that. I thought it'd take like fifteen minutes for you to get hard again."

He lifted a brow. "Why? Because I'm old?"

"No. That's what it said in *Cosmo*. Besides, you're not old, stop saying that. God, you're twice as sexy and hot as any man..." Embarrassed, she averted her gaze.

"What? I was likin' the way the conversation about me was goin', baby doll," he teased.

"I can't believe I'm really here with you, Cord McKay. I've had a crush on you for so long."

Cord grinned. "Really?"

"Yeah. But you've never noticed me."

"Not entirely true." He twisted a section of her baby fine hair around his index finger. "What would you have done if I'd chased after you down at Carter's wedding last year and taken you up on your offer after kissin' me so sweetly?"

"Probably would've lost my virginity in a car with you at the Bar 9."

"Jesus."

"And as long as we're confessing things...a couple of times when I babysat Ky? After I put him down for his nap, I came in here and laid on your bed. Wondering what it'd be like to be in this bed naked with you."

"Don't tell me stuff like that." He paused and studied her face. "Did you touch yourself when you were layin' on my bed?"

"Geez, Cord, *no.* I was babysitting. I imagined you touching me though. I gotta admit my imagination didn't do it justice."

He captured her face in his hands. "No need to make your imagination work when I'm here. I'll admit I've been fantasizin' what you'd look like on top of me. Naked." He nudged her upright and murmured, "So, ride me, cowgirl."

Panic flashed in her eyes. "But I don't know how—"

"Your body will guide you better than I can. Bring your knees by my hips."

She maneuvered herself around.

"That's it." Cord placed her hands on his shoulders. "Fast or slow as you wanna go. You're in total control."

"But what if I do it wrong?"

"No such thing as wrong. Do whatever you want. Do what feels good. I ain't gonna complain or say no."

AJ's eyes met his. "What will you be doing?"

"Watchin' you."

She was so tentative, hardly moving, unsure where to put her hands. Not trusting her body to find a natural rhythm. Again, her innocence was more arousing than he'd expected. His thumbs rasped her nipples. He was dying to suck them until she screamed, but he worried his attention would be a bigger distraction to her sense of imbalance.

When AJ leaned over to kiss him, her clit rubbed the top of his groin. She blinked with surprise. "Oh. That feels good."

"Then keep doin' it."

"But I wanna touch you. I've been dying to get my hands all over you for so long. Too long."

AJ ground her pelvis into his, keeping his cock deep inside as she rocked over her clit. Her hot tongue made circles around his nipples. She licked and sucked his neck and collarbone until he wanted to explode. His thighs went rigid when she bounced faster.

He clenched his ass cheeks to keep from thrusting into her, letting AJ learn how to get what her body needed.

She threw her head back, closed her eyes and gasped with surprise as she came without warning.

Cord gritted his teeth as he felt the spasms tightening around his cock. *Hold off hold off.* The second her eyes blinked open after the last orgasmic ripple, he flipped her on her back.

"Now I'm gonna ride you." He pinned her arms above by the headboard and drove into her.

Stroke after stroke they were spiraling higher, both covered in sweat. Both breathing hard. Both lost in the moment.

He put his lips below her ear. “So fuckin’ wet. So fuckin’ tight. Feel how hot and hard you make me burn.”

“Cord—”

“Come with me this time.” He changed the angle of his hips and hammered into her.

She shrieked and he shot his load. His vision blurred, his throat closed. Her greedy sex milked every drop from his cock until he was completely inert.

Still, he sought AJ’s mouth. She pressed her chest to his, breaking free of his handhold to run her hands all over his body.

Cord rested his sweaty forehead to hers. “Whoa.”

“Yeah. I think you blew out all the pleasure receptors in my brain.” He shifted his weight to pull out of her and she hissed.

“I got a little carried away. You’re probably sore.”

“I like that you got carried away.”

“I’m glad you don’t mind. I can be rough.”

“I’m not nearly as delicate as you think I am.” AJ looked at the alarm clock on the nightstand. “Is that really the time?”

“Yeah. Why?”

“Because I’ve gotta go.”

“Why?”

“Caring for my mom, remember?” She bounced off the bed and snatched her clothes.

Cord returned from the bathroom with a washcloth. “Let me clean you up first.” He wiped between her thighs and tried not to wince at how swollen she was. “That’s weird, you didn’t bleed.”

“You questioning whether I was a virgin?”

“Not at all.”

“Good. Because I’ve been on horseback my whole life, which has been known to break a hymen. Plus, I’ve been using tampons for years—”

“No need to get defensive.”

Cord tugged his wrinkled Wranglers over his naked flanks.

Part of him wished she could stay in his bed all night. Another part was glad to see her leave. A lot of shit had happened in a short amount of time and he needed some quiet time to process it all.

He followed her downstairs, flipped on the yard light and gave her a long kiss. “Drive safe. I’ll see you tomorrow night.”

“But—”

“No buts. You *will* be here. Period.”

Chapter Eleven

"What would you say if I told you I was thinking about selling the ranch?"

The knife in AJ's hand froze above the cutting board.

You knew this was coming.

She sliced the ham sandwich, arranged it on a plate alongside a home-canned dill pickle, tossed on a handful of potato chips and slid it in front of her mother.

"I'd say the future of the ranch is your decision."

"Telling me what I want to hear and honestly answering the question are two different things, Amy Jo."

"I know. But Daddy left the ranch to you. Do I hope you sell it? No. But do I understand why you'd want to? Yes."

AJ made her sandwich and sat down, wondering if she could swallow bread through a tight throat.

Lunch was a somber affair.

Table cleared, coffee poured, the last of the sugar cookies between them, her mother addressed the issue again, just as AJ expected she would.

"Neither Jenn nor Alan showed interest in ranching. If you were married—not that I'm wishing you were—and this place was supporting you and a husband, I wouldn't even bring it up. But with you off at school, Jenn looking at starting over someplace else, and me half-crippled, it's past time to talk about it."

"Which means you've made your decision."

"I have. After your daddy died, I promised Carson that the McKays would have first crack at buying it. No doubt they'll give us a fair price, plus they have the same philosophy about ranching, so I don't worry the land will be well cared for."

AJ stared out the window at the place she called home. The elm and cottonwood trees beyond the driveway wavered in the blustery summer wind. The midday sun bleached all color from the blue sky, but the dazzling brightness would return before sunset.

How many times had she done dishes at this old enamel sink? She'd never once wondered if it'd be the last time she'd listen for the melodic coos of the mourning doves, or see the golden finches pecking at the bird feeders blowing in the sage-scented breeze.

"Sweetheart?"

"Where would you go?"

"Probably tag along with Jenn to wherever she's going. Not to live with her, but I can't imagine not seeing Krista, Mason and Ariel regularly. Does that bother you?"

"Why in the world would it bother me? I know that if I had three kids and an iffy future you'd be right there with me, instead of with her."

"Instead—"

"Instead, I have school to finish." AJ faced her mother and smiled. "I won't pretend this is gonna be easy on me, Mama, because unlike you and Jenn, this is the only home I've ever had."

"I know."

"Have you called Carson yet?"

"No. I wanted to talk to you first, since it affects you the most."

"I appreciate it. Call him after you rest."

Florence squinted at the clock. "He's probably having lunch, so I believe I'll call him now." She grabbed the cordless phone and dialed.

AJ half-listened to the conversation, wondering if Cord was chowing down at his folks' house, but she suspected the man forgot to eat if he wasn't cooking for Ky.

The phone beeped when her mom hung up.

"Well? What'd he say?"

"Carson will swing by around three."

"You relieved?"

She nodded. "And tired. This decision has been weighing on me, girl."

"I can see that."

"I assume he'll bring Cord along, since he runs as much of this part of the ranch as Carson does these days."

At the mention of Cord's name, a wave of heat flooded her body.

"Amy Jo, you okay?"

"Ah, yeah, why?"

"Your cheeks are red."

"Oh. Don't you think it's hot in here?"

"Not particularly. Feels good. Always a bit cold in the front room."

"You want me to adjust the air conditioner?"

"No. It's fine, I'm used to it with the way the heating system in this house has never worked the way it's supposed to. Stop fussing. Get some fresh air. Work with Lucy for a few hours."

"I'm not gonna ditch you to hang with my horse, geez. I'm taking care of you, remember? I'll deal with Lucy when you wake up." AJ helped her mom back into bed. She stirred up a batch of oatmeal raisin cookies. While they were baking, she sat on the back porch and called Keely.

"So?" Keely answered. "Did you do the deed?"

"Yep."

She squealed. "And?"

"Oh. My. God. Why didn't you tell me it'd be like that? He was everything, so amazingly perfect, romantic, hot, sexy. Sweet. Intense. God is he intense."

"Okay, I don't want down and dirty details, because, eww, he's my brother, but he treated you right?"

"Unbelievably right. A couple of times."

"Too much information, AJ. So now that your cherry's been popped by your dream man, you'll be moving on?"

"Literally moving on."

"Why? What did he do?"

"It's not what you think—"

"I'll come back there and kick Cord's ass if he pulled that typical McKay love 'em and leave 'em bullshit—"

"No, calm down. It doesn't have anything to do with Cord."

"Then what?"

AJ told Keely about her mom deciding to sell the ranch and found herself sobbing out the fears and frustrations she couldn't tell anyone else.

"Come on, AJ. Dad and my brothers will take good care of it, just as good as you did all those years no one knew about you being the youngest ranch hand in the county. You can stay with us whenever you wanna visit, so it's not like it'll be in the hands of total strangers who're putting up a gate and keeping you out forever."

"But when we leave Denver for Christmas, I won't be coming back here. You will be. Where will I go?"

Keely was quiet. "I'm having a blast living in Denver, but I know I can always go home. There's never been any doubt I'll move back to Wyoming as soon as I'm done with school. And I can't imagine that I won't be able to hop on a four-wheeler or a horse and high-tail it over to your place whenever I want."

"You're supposed to be cheering me up, Keely."

"Sorry. Back to my favorite topic: sex. So you officially seeing Cord now?"

"In secret. We won't be two stepping at the Golden Boot. Or eating supper at the Twin Pines."

"Probably for the best. You'll get to live out your sexual fantasies with a wild McKay man and no one will be the wiser. Not that you'll have to worry about your reputation in Crook County because you won't be livin' there much longer."

"True. Tell me about your date with Lex the other night."

"I'm afraid he's a serial killer. No. Don't laugh, I'm serious." Keely regaled her with another dating horror story. "That's the last time I date a guy who's not a cowboy. Next time I say yes to some doofus in a three-piece suit, remind me about Lex, the letch."

"And Adam, the arrogant asshole?"

"Yes. And Pete, the prissy prick."

"And gorgeous Giovanni?"

"Mmm. No. He was worth it. Being a hot, hung Italian stallion and all."

"Bet he doesn't have anything on your brother."

"Eww! AJ, that was just...eww!"

AJ laughed. "You deserved that for all the years you've tormented me with too much information. Gotta run. The timer on my cookies just dinged."

Keely expelled a disgusted sigh. "You're already making cookies for Cord?"

"Nope. They're for your dad."

"Dad? He'll probably adopt you and disown me."

"His precious baby girl who drives him insane? Wrong. I'm sure daddy-o will grill me on what you've been up to. Studying, right?"

"Absolutely. Speaking of, when you get time off from playing Betty Crocker, I wanna run something past you."

"Sure. Thanks, K."

"Later."

AJ finished a couple of things before she woke up her mother. By the time Carson McKay's pickup pulled into the yard, AJ realized she hadn't bothered to look in a mirror all day. She peeked out the window. Sure enough, Cord hopped out of the passenger's side.

Great.

"Amy Jo, will you put out the creamer and sugar? Cord might use it in his coffee."

It was on the tip of her tongue to say Cord drank his coffee black, but she didn't want her mother getting curious about why AJ knew such things about him. Why she'd always known how Cord took his coffee—and every other little thing about him.

AJ welcomed the McKays into the kitchen, including Carolyn, and settled everyone with coffee and cookies. Chatting about Keely and school in Denver was easy enough. It wasn't so easy not to act stiff around Cord or overly friendly. When she sensed they wanted to get down to business, she made a break for the barn.

She saddled Lucy and took off, riding her hard. It was bittersweet; she loved the freedom of the horse zipping across the open plain as much as she hated the idea she wouldn't have the luxury much longer. What was she supposed to do with Lucy after the ranch sold? She couldn't imagine living her life without a horse. Heck, she couldn't imagine living anywhere but on a ranch.

After treating Lucy to an extended brush down and a bucket of oats, AJ dragged her tack into the barn. She'd hefted the saddle on the hook when the door creaked. She spun around. A shiver went up her spine—Cord stood not ten feet away from her. Burning away every stitch of her clothing with his molten eyes.

AJ wiped the sweat from her brow and straightened the blanket draped over the stall railing. She stood on tiptoe, lifting her arms to hang the halter and bridle. The motion made her shirt ride up and she felt his searing gaze roving over the exposed skin.

Then he was behind her. "Need some help?"

"No. I've got it."

"Yes, you definitely have it all."

She pivoted. "What are you doing here?"

"Hopin' to steal a kiss from my girl while they hammer out the rest of the details."

"Cord—"

"AJ." He stalked her until her back hit the post between the stalls. "Your cookies were sweet, but not as sweet as the taste I've had of you."

His lips were so close. So warm and full. And tempting. Her tongue darted out and licked the seam of his lips. Mmm. Coffee. Cookies. Cord. His breath caught, but he didn't take over, as she expected. He allowed her to explore. She slid the tip of her tongue over his teeth. Nibbled on his lower lip, then his upper lip. She kissed the corners of his mouth until he smiled. She stopped teasing and slipped her tongue inside the warm cavern.

Cord kept a firm grip on her wrists, almost as if he didn't trust himself not to touch her. The kiss went on and on, both sweet and hot, and intense and lazy.

Reluctantly she eased her mouth away. "You make my head spin."

"That's bad?"

"Right now? Yes, because my body craves the rest of that headlong rush. I want to tear off your clothes. I want you to tear off my clothes. Then we can race up to the hayloft—"

"Stop. Jesus, AJ."

"See what I mean? Quit kissing me like I'm nekkid." She looked at the bulge in his Wranglers and a tiny surge of pride arose. "I'll walk out first. Give you time to think about baseball or something."

"You really have to stop reading *Cosmo*."

"But now I can finally utilize some of those sex tips I've been saving up." She ducked out of the barn to the sound of his frustrated male groan.

A few minutes later, Cord propped his boot on the fence next to her, which looked casual to the casual observer, but wasn't casual in the least.

"Better?"

"No. I want you so fuckin' bad, I'm thinkin' takin' you for a roll in the hay in the barn in broad daylight might be worth someone discoverin' us."

Her hopeful sex sent a rush of wetness south.

He pointed to Lucy. "Ever think about breedin' her?"

"I wanted to this year. But it'd be too much work for Ma."

"You upset about Flo sellin' the ranch?"

Yes. "I'm not really surprised. She isn't spry enough to run this place on her own, she wasn't years ago when they made me do it after Dad..."

"What? After he died?"

Damn. No one knew what'd gone on in the years before her dad died and she intended to keep it that way. "She's been struggling since I went to school, though she doesn't want to admit it. I panic when I think how things might've turned out if Jenn hadn't found her right away that day." AJ winced at the image of her arthritic mother laying in the pasture with a broken hip.

"Take a deep breath. Come on, baby doll, she's all right. So are you. Accidents are part of life. A big part of ranch life, we both know that."

A moment of silence passed.

"Sometimes I wonder if I won't be out checkin' cattle and I'll find my dad has done some fool thing and broke his fool neck. Then I'm amazed that Ky hasn't busted more bones from all the stunts he's pulled."

"Like father like son, huh?"

"Somethin' like that."

They talked about Ky. About the time AJ relaxed, Cord said, "You sore from last night?"

"Didn't bother me when I rode Lucy, if that's what you're asking."

"No, I'm askin' purely and simply because I cannot wait to have you again. Can you come to me tonight?"

AJ's belly did a little flip. "I don't know. Jenn and the kids moved in, and if she's upset and needs someone to talk to, I can't blow her off to blow you."

"Amy Jo that was just plain...raunchy." He paused. "I like that side of you."

"Not so sure you'll get to see that side of me tonight."

"Wrong. I expect to see you tonight. You'd better find a way to make our deal work."

"Or what?"

"Or I'll create a suitable penalty."

"Penalty? I didn't agree—"

"Ah ah. You agreed to whatever demands I make."

"Like?"

"Like if I tell you to bend over this fence, I'd expect you to do it. If I decided I wanted to spank your butt until it turned the same pink as your pussy, you'd let me do that too."

"But—"

"No buts. There are consequences for disobedience. I don't see you as the disobedient type, but I hope I'm wrong because dishin' out penalties oughta be interestin'."

"Have you…penalized women before?"

Cord stared straight ahead. "What if I say I've always wanted to but I've never had a woman willin' to give me that much control?"

"I'd say *no* is a much safer answer for me than *yes*."

"Why?"

"Because I'd like to give you something no other woman has. Do your ideas for kink go beyond spanking me?"

No answer.

"You want to tie me up?"

"AJ, I'm warnin' you."

"What?"

"Stop talkin' before you get yourself inta trouble."

"Hah! You can't do a damn thing to me right now."

"I can make you pay for it later."

She loved the dangerous glint in his eye. Loved that she could incite him to cut loose, to show a side of himself to her no one else knew. "You'd like to take me to that edge. Make me beg. And isn't it just a little sweeter to know that I've never begged another man for anything? No man has ever touched me like you plan to? Or done any of the things you're itching to do to me?"

"You are so in for it tonight, baby doll."

AJ faced him. "Go ahead and think up a penalty, cowboy, because I'm telling you right now, I plan on being a little late." She whirled on her bootheel and returned to the house.

She heard him say, "Big, *big* trouble," and she smiled.

When Jenn and the kids showed up a few hours later, AJ and Jenn struck a deal. As AJ was the daytime caretaker, she wanted her nights free. Jenn didn't argue, although AJ sensed her disappointment that she wouldn't be around in the evenings.

Only within the safety of her room did AJ wonder what she'd gotten herself into taunting Cord McKay.

You're getting exactly what you want: the full scope of his passion. You aren't a little girl or a shrinking violet; you are a woman going after what she wants. This might be all you ever get from him, so be greedy and take it while you can get it.

No fear, no apologies, and no regrets.

Words to live by.

Chapter Twelve

Cord half-listened to his parents discussing the purchase of the Foster place. Yeah, it was exciting to transition from leasing the prime grazing land to owning the whole kit and caboodle. The amount they'd offered Florence meant they'd have to borrow money from the bank to cover the associated costs. Usually that sort of financial issue concerned Cord, but he couldn't seem to focus beyond the thought of AJ taking the penalty he planned to mete out.

To hear her talking so boldly...it'd been more than he could stand. She about got her first lesson right there against the fence.

Luckily his folks chalked up his distraction to worry, which was fine by him. Better that than them seeing how desperately he wanted little Amy Jo Foster naked, tied up, trussed up, at his every wicked whim, right there in public—to hell with any kind of decorum.

Chores kept him from going crazy the last few hours.

Cord sipped his beer and messed with the recording on the TV screen. He heard her tires crunch on the driveway and he couldn't help but grin with anticipation.

AJ knocked. He yelled, "It's open."

The screen door slammed and she stood in front of him looking sexy and...wary.

"Evenin', baby doll. You're late."

"I thought you'd be happy to hear that my chat with Jenn went well and she's agreed to take over caretaking duties when she gets home from work."

"Which leaves you where?"

"Here. Starting at around 6:00 every night."

"It's 7:00 right now. Where you been?"

Two spots of color dotted her cheekbones. "I told you."

"You owe me an extra hour. Now c'mere and kiss me."

Her face relaxed. She bent down to brush her mouth across his. Not in a teasing manner, but tentative.

Cord kept the kiss easy. When AJ began to get more demanding, he backed off. "Did you shut the front door?"

"No."

"Go shut it, make sure it's locked and come back here."

By the time she returned he'd finished the beer. "Take off your clothes. I wanna see nothin' but that gorgeous bare skin."

Her fingers started at her throat and worked the buttons on the sleeveless blouse until it fluttered open revealing a bra the color of sun-ripened peaches. *Pop pop pop* and the fly of her jeans showed a slice of skin and matching peach panties. She shimmied the jeans to the floor and stopped.

"There a problem?" he asked.

"N-no. I just didn't know if you meant completely naked."

"I did."

AJ's whole body flushed a rosy pink as she stripped. Her platinum hair fell across her face, obscuring her expression.

"Baby doll, look at me."

She tipped her head up and met his gaze.

"Come sit on my lap."

"Aren't you gonna take your clothes off first?"

Cord shook his head. He patted his thighs.

She tried to sit sideways with her left hip pressed to his, but Cord reversed her so her ass was nestled against his groin. "Relax." He positioned his hands on the inside of her knees and urged them open.

AJ obediently stretched out at his command, but she was strung tight as a new roll of baling twine.

He stroked his hands down the outside of her legs.

"Is this my penalty? I'm naked and you're not?"

"No." He kissed the tender rise of her shoulder. "We'll get to the penalty portion later. Right now, I'm gonna touch you however I want while we watch TV." Cord grabbed the remote and hit PLAY.

The image on the screen solidified. A naked woman. On her knees and unzipping a man's pants with painstaking precision. Oohing and ahhing over the bounty she'd discovered as she fondled his cock with her hand. Then she rubbed the length over her enormous tits, wiping the tip of his cockhead on the tips of her hardened red nipples. She teased his dick over her cheeks and jaw in complete ecstasy, finally stroking her full, glossy lips across his stiff prick.

AJ's breath caught.

"Ever watched porn with a man?"

"Umm. No."

"Good."

"Why are we—"

"You've never given a real blowjob, have you, AJ?"

She shook her head.

"Watch. Learn." He nipped her earlobe. "There will be a test later."

"Oh. Wow. Okay."

The woman onscreen licked up and down the man's shaft with the flat part of her tongue. Then her pink tongue flickered from root to tip in a zigzag pattern. Up and down. Faster and faster. The camera moved from her tongue to the ecstasy on the man's face and everything switched to slow motion.

AJ squirmed.

Cord cupped AJ's breasts, rasping his thumbs over her nipples until they were hard peaks. He dragged wet kisses up the side of her neck.

She turned her head to reach his mouth.

"Huh-uh. Eyes on the screen. The best part is just about to start."

"You touching me is the best part."

He chuckled. "True."

The woman on the TV worked her hand from the guy's balls

to the tip in a twisting motion while suckling the purple knob. She took a break to scrape her teeth up the vein.

AJ whispered, "Doesn't that hurt?"

"Only if you bite down."

"I'll remember that."

Cord placed AJ's hands on her bare breasts and said, "Touch yourself here. Show me whatcha like." He trailed his fingers down her belly, loving how the taut skin quivered in anticipation of his touch.

"Cord—"

"Don't close your eyes. Keep watchin'. See how she takes the whole cock in her mouth? Opens her throat? Tightens her lips as she's pullin' back? See how her saliva makes his cock shiny? How much easier keepin' her mouth wet makes it glide in?"

She nodded.

"Is your mouth waterin' to taste me like that?"

AJ squeaked when his fingertip slid over her pubic bone and down her cleft.

"Does porn turn you on? Or is it the thought of me makin' you come that's got you all hot and bothered?"

"Both. Just being with you turns me on."

"You think that sweet-talkin' will get you what you want?"

"I'm hoping."

Cord lost any guilty feelings about AJ picking him to take a bit of the shine off her halo. She wanted this, wanted him, she wouldn't be here otherwise. Truth be told, he was looking forward to the next few weeks in a way he'd never imagined.

He coated his finger with her wetness before pushing it inside her. She moaned softly. "You like that." He used the heel of his hand to slide side to side over her clit. "What about this?"

"Yes."

"Watch. He's about to come." Onscreen the guy plunged his cock into the woman's mouth and Cord matched the rhythm with his finger inside her. "This flick is a favorite of mine. Here comes the money shot, seein' him blow all over her tits."

"It that what you're gonna do to me?"

"Yes." He stroked the spot behind her pubic bone with the tip of his long middle finger.

She undulated her pelvis. "Cord, please."

"Please what?"

"Get me off...make me...I-I—"

Cord breathed in her ear. "Like this?" He increased the friction on her clit and fluttered his finger and her interior muscles quivered.

AJ flew apart.

When she drifted back, he shut off the TV. She turned and plastered her chest to his, grinding her wet sex against his crotch as she made him mindless with her frantic kisses.

"My turn." Colt looked into her eyes. "I can't wait to see your lips stretched around my cock. On your knees."

Without further prompting, she slid to the floor between his legs. He lifted his hips so she could tug off the fleece workout shorts. She traced the edge of her thumb over the thick vein running up his cock, sweeping it across the tip to spread the pre-come around, just as he'd shown her how he liked it.

"You okay?"

"Nervous."

"Why?"

"I don't want to get a failing grade on this test."

Cord laughed. "I'm not grading you, AJ, I was kiddin'."

"Good." She sucked him into her mouth.

"Holy shit."

AJ released him. "What? Did I do it wrong?"

"No." He cupped his hands around her face. "Feels so damn good, baby doll, it just startled me."

"How will I know if I'm doing it right?"

"There is no right. Just do whatever you want."

So she did. She sucked and licked and experimented with her hands, lips, teeth and tongue until she'd worked him into a frenzy of need.

Cord's body shook. His legs twitched. His nuts were as hard as rubber balls. He couldn't take his eyes off the erotic scene—this beautiful woman on her knees before him, an intense look of concentration and innocent wonder on her face as his cock disappeared between her lips.

"Enough," he said hoarsely. "Finish me."

Her mouth bobbed and she sucked harder, she circled her fingers loosely at the base of his shaft and moved in rapid, short strokes.

"Faster. Yeah. Like that. There it is."

Cord pulled his cock out of her mouth and curled his big hand around her smaller one, pumping them together as he aimed and came on her chest. He groaned and closed his eyes, lost in bliss, but he sensed her studying every spurt, gauging his every reaction. Not clinically, but with the intention to learn exactly how to please her lover.

His hand fell to his thigh. He sagged to the cushions. Talk about a fucking mindblower.

AJ licked the come from the tip of his cock.

"Jesus."

"Did that hurt?"

"No. It's just ultra-sensitive."

"Mmm." She licked him again. "Tastes kinda salty."

Cord managed a grunt.

She kissed his hipbone and rubbed her sticky breast on his thigh. "That was really hot, making you come with my mouth. You really like blowjobs, huh?"

"Uh. Yeah."

"I liked watching you. Seeing you lose control. Made me feel...powerful."

Not a coy thing about AJ. "You can prove your power over me any time you want."

"How long until...?"

He laughed. "You're gonna be the death of me, woman. C'mere. Let's see if I can't take the edge off while my dick recovers."

She crawled on his lap. "Lose the shirt. I love your chest."

He whipped the T-shirt over his head and used it to wipe off her breasts.

"Look at you." Her fingertips trailed over his pecs, tracing the delineated line to his navel. "You're so perfect. I can't believe I'm here with you. Naked." She pressed her mouth to the scar below his collarbone and sucked. "Having you look at me like that."

"Like what?"

"Like I'm a porn star rodeo queen."

"You are."

"Like you can't wait to put your hands on me."

"My hands are on you."

"Like you'll do whatever I ask you to."

"What do you want me to do to you, AJ?"

She licked his Adam's apple. "You smell good. Like the Wyoming sun and wind left a permanent scent on you."

"That doesn't answer my question. Tell me what you want."

Silence echoed, except for the ragged sounds of her breathing against his throat.

"You're not goin' all shy on me now, are you?"

"Maybe."

Cord tilted her face up. "Don't. I like your curiosity. Be honest about what you want. You've gotta know that I won't deny you a damn thing."

Her mouth drifted to his ear and her soft, breathy voice sent chills across his skin. "I love your mouth on me. I think you can make me come just by sucking on my nipples. When you use your teeth? Lord, it gives me goose bumps on goose bumps. I get all wet and achy."

"I can work with wet and achy." His hands slipped down her neck to cup the generous mounds. He held her breasts together and lapped at her nipples, one at a time, then at the same time. Suckling the tips hard, then barely at all. Tickling every sensitive inch with the soft hair of his goatee, with his hot breath, with his lips and wet tongue. Drawing out her pleasure, trying to fit as much of her glorious tits into his mouth as possible.

Her head fell back and she moaned.

Cord teased her until his cock was ready. Until he smelled

the sweet cream gathering between her thighs and *she* was ready. He rubbed his face against the upper swells of her chest and picked her up to position her on the plush rug in front of the couch. Pinning her arms above her head with one hand, he urged her legs around his waist.

"I don't wanna hurt you. Take a deep breath, baby doll, and let me in."

"I'm ready. Don't wait. Please."

Cord gritted his teeth, aligning his cock to slide into her tight, warm channel an excruciating inch at a time. Once he was fully seated, sweating, breathing like a winded horse, her hands broke free from his hold and clutched his ass.

"What? Stop?" He eased back to look at her face.

"Don't go slow for me."

"AJ. I don't know if you're ready for—"

"You said you wouldn't deny me anything. I'm asking you, no, *telling* you, Cord McKay, give me that dark passion I see burning in your eyes. I've earned it."

He leaned down until they were nose to nose. "You remember you said that when I'm ridin' you hard. When I won't let you up until I've had my fill."

She slapped his ass. Twice. "Stop talking."

A snarl left his throat. He plowed back into heaven. Plunge. Retreat. Sweat poured down his body as he fucked her. His eyes never left hers. "Too much?"

"More."

"You little minx." Cord unwrapped her legs from his hips, placing her ankles on his shoulders, so the backs of her thighs were pressed up his chest. He rolled his hips and drove deep.

AJ gasped.

He trapped her hands above her head, forcing a deeper angle. The sounds of slapping flesh ricocheted as Cord pushed her harder and higher. When her orgasm loomed, he twisted his pelvis so his pubic hair abraded her clit. She began to whimper. "Send us both over the edge."

"Then kiss me."

"After. I'll knock your teeth out if I kiss you now."

"Do something," she wailed. "I need your mouth on my skin."

Her plea nearly undid him. Without decreasing his strokes, Cord brushed aside the damp hair by her cheek with his chin. He placed his mouth over her ear and sucked.

"Oh God. Oh God. Oh God." Her whole body stiffened as her pussy crimped around his cock like a metal vise.

His balls tightened and long, hot pulses shot out, pulses that didn't seem to end. A tingle raced straight up the center of his torso from his dick to where he felt her teeth sinking into his throat.

When he quit moving she moaned, "Don't stop, I'm coming again, there, like that."

Cord felt another set of rhythmic pulls and stayed with her until the final vibration. He brought her legs down to the rug and lost himself in the sweetness of her kisses.

AJ didn't push him away. She seemed content to kiss him, caressing the planes and angles of his face. Running her fingers through his damp hair. Squeezing the muscles in his back and arms. Not only did she enjoy touching him, she understood he craved the closeness in the aftermath of loving.

When his sweaty skin began to cool and she shivered, he looked at her and saw a smirk. "What?"

"If that was my penalty for being late, I can pretty much guarantee I won't be on time ever again."

Cord laughed.

She outlined his mustache and goatee. "Can I ask you something?"

A tiny bit of unease made him tense up. Was she going to grade him on his performance? "I guess."

"Is sex always like this? Needy, hot and out of control? Because I've had three outstanding orgasms and I'm sore, but I can't wait to do this with you again. Does that make me some kind of a slut? I look at you and want you like a drug?"

No. That makes you perfect.

Shaking aside that thought, he said, "If there was a line of men outside the door waitin' for their turns with you, maybe that'd be considered slutty behavior. However often you and I are naked together or what we do behind closed doors ain't nobody's business but ours, AJ."

"That's a relief."

"Glad I can ease your mind on that account. Anything else?"

No answer.

"What?"

"You said there's some other things you're interested in trying that might be considered, well, kinky."

An image arose of her naked. Her arms bound behind her back with his favorite bright blue nylon rope—a vivid slash of color against her pale skin. She'd be bent across a hay bale in the dim light of the barn, wearing those "fuck me Big Daddy" high-heeled silver boots and nothing else. Her feet spread-eagled, her ripe mouth, her juicy pussy and the tiny rosette of her ass at the ideal level for his cock.

He'd stroke his erection as he circled her, deciding which hole to try first. She'd whimper with want, plead with her eyes, and he knew she'd love whatever he did to her. First, he'd fist his hands in her baby soft hair and fuck her mouth. When his cock was good and saturated with her saliva—all the lube he needed to fuck that tiny virgin portal—he'd move behind her. Separating those pearly white ass cheeks to watch the thick head of his cock and his blood-darkened shaft disappearing into that tight, hot hole until he was buried balls deep and her untried muscles clenched around his dick like a fucking wet dream.

"Cord? You gonna teach me what they are?"

He blinked. "Not yet. You're already earnin' an A-plus-plus-plus, baby doll, you're surpassin' all my expectations, but I don't wanna do too much too soon."

"I expect you'll need to feed me soon. I didn't have time to eat before I left home and I'm starved."

When he pushed back, his sated cock slipped out easily. Lord, it turned him on to see her sex shiny-wet with the mix of their juices, knowing her pussy was all pink and puffy from him loving on her.

Fucking her. Get it right. No love involved here, old man.

"I'll use the bathroom upstairs to clean up if you wanna use the one down here."

AJ snatched her clothes and hustled down the hallway, leaving him to wonder if he'd said the wrong thing.

ᏍᏕ

AJ scrutinized her reflection. Swollen mouth. Swollen nipples. She wiped between her legs and winced. Yep. Swollen there too. She'd brought that overwhelming show of sheer strength and power of Cord's lovemaking on herself. Not that she had regrets.

Did he? Did he know she was crazy in love with him? Why else would he send her to Ky's bathroom? The last two nights he'd been so thoughtful, cleaning her up.

You're worrying too much. Cord doesn't believe in love, he believes in lust and that's all he'll see when he looks at you because he can't offer you anything else.

Cord knocked on the door. "AJ? Baby doll, you okay?"

"Yeah. Be right out."

She used another cloth to swipe her face and neck before she put her clothes back on.

He'd slipped on a pair of jeans and a clean T-shirt. She found it incredibly intimate his feet were bare. The man rarely exposed his body or his thoughts, so maybe he was opening up to her a little. A tiny bit of hope surfaced again that she was making progress with him.

"You want scrambled eggs? Or a sandwich?"

"Eggs are fine, but you don't have to cook for me. I can make it myself."

He walked over and kissed her nose. "Sit. It'll be done in a minute."

AJ knew Cord was completely at home in a kitchen. Her father never had been. She suspected Carson McKay wasn't either. But up until a couple of weeks ago Cord had been mother and father to Ky and he'd had no choice.

He slid two steaming plates piled with eggs and toast on

the breakfast bar, then came around to sit beside her.

"Looks good. Thank you."

"No problem. You need ketchup?"

"Yuck."

"Ky won't eat eggs without drownin' them in red goo."

"Hopefully my palate is more developed than a four-year-old boy's."

Cord's fork stopped above his plate. "I didn't mean—"

"I know. I was teasing."

They ate the rest of the meal in silence. Cord picked up the plates and shoved them in the sink next to the frying pan and the breakfast dishes.

"Since you cooked you want me to do those?"

A strange, tight look crossed his face. "That's not necessary."

"I don't mind." AJ squirted dishsoap in the sink and turned the water on. "So I know it's probably too soon, but did you and your dad talk about what you're gonna do with our ranch?"

"Some. We've talked about plantin' buffalo grass in the north pasture to see if it'll take."

"Smart. I've always been worried about overgrazing in that section. My dad wasn't vigilant as far as rotation. Before you bought us out I'd planned on having mom talk to you about resting the grazing field to the south this fall anyway. Looks a little rough for the wear."

Cord seemed unusually quiet, in a considering way, and AJ realized she'd revealed she knew too much. She scrambled for a subject change. "As far as plans for our house? It needs some work. Major work."

"Guess we won't make any decisions until..."

"We're gone, right?" She scrubbed the plates and placed them on the left side of the sink.

"Sorry, that was kinda thoughtless."

"It's okay. I haven't really wrapped my head around the fact it won't be my home anymore." She dropped the cleaned forks next to the plates. "Keely said I could come home with her whenever I wanted, which was sweet, but visiting won't be the same as living here."

"You talked to Keely?"

"Of course I talked to her." AJ rinsed the soap from the dishes. She reached for the dishtowel, but Cord had it in his hand and plucked up a plate to dry.

"What else did you talk to my little sister about?"

"Why don't you come right out and ask me if I talked to her about us making mattress angels?"

"Fine. Does she know?"

"Yes."

"That's just fuckin' great."

She whirled around. "I trust her. I don't care if you are pissed off about it. She's my best friend and I talk to her about everything that's going on in my life. The fact you're her brother doesn't matter and if it bothers you—what the hell are you staring at?"

"Put down the fryin' pan, AJ. Unless you plan on smackin' me upside the head with it?"

"What?" AJ looked at her hand and saw she'd been shaking the soap-covered cast iron pan in his face. "Sorry."

Cord took the pan and rinsed it. He dried it before speaking again. "Would it bug you if the situations were reversed and I blabbed to your sister about everything goin' on between us?"

Attempting to stay calm, AJ unplugged the sink. Rinsed out the dishrag and twisted it, spreading it out to dry over the edge of the counter before she answered him. "A—I don't blab; neither does Keely, so you can rest assured no one in the McKay family will find out that you and I are boinking like bunnies. B—If I have to choose between screwing around in secret with you for a few weeks or having Keely as my friend for the rest of my life, then no contest, because she wins. Hands down."

AJ made it to the door before Cord caught her.

"Wait a minute, that wasn't fair."

"You're right. It wasn't."

He stared at her, that brooding expression darkening his handsome face, as if he expected her to say something else. To apologize for something that wasn't her fault.

"Thank you for tonight, Cord, it was...great. It's been a crazy day and I'm a little on edge. I'll see you later."

She wasn't particularly surprised he let her go. But she was surprised by how eager she was to get away from him.

Chapter Thirteen

"Where the hell is Colt?" Cord barked at Kade the next morning over the phone. "Yeah, I know it ain't your day to watch him. No. I'll do it myself. I don't got time to ride over there and haul his drunken carcass outta bed again."

Cord clicked his cell phone off. "Goddamn, he's lookin' to get his ass whupped." He threw his mug in the sink, noticing he'd forgotten to dry the silverware after AJ had left.

That was another screwed up situation. Things'd been going great guns last night. He hadn't blamed his sudden tension on AJ's admission that Keely knew about them. No, doing dishes together was what sent him into a belligerent retreat.

Cooking for her hadn't been a big deal. But the second she started washing plates, knowing exactly where he kept his dishrags and dish soap, a funny feeling, sort of like hope had spread inside him. Had he tossed her out? No. He'd automatically reached for the dishtowel to dry. Like they'd done that household task together all the time. Like it was natural. Like it was the first of many times.

Damn. That kind of easy camaraderie could get a man in trouble. Big trouble. Especially when he'd gone out of his way to avoid anything with any woman that smacked of domesticity.

Still, logic made him question how AJ's thoughtfulness was a fault. She'd been raised that way. No different than her baking cookies and serving coffee to him and his folks at her mom's place. Cord knew if his ma had been here after supper, she would've run a sinkful of soapy water and cleaned up too.

So why did it seem so much...more?

Because you could want more with AJ. She knows you, your son, your ranch, and your family. It'd be easy for her just to slip into your life, swoop into your house and want to play house for keeps.

"Like hell," he said out loud. "She's leavin'. End of story."

When he returned home that night to a message from AJ telling him she wouldn't be over for a couple of days, he was relieved.

As Kade pulled up in front of his house after another fantastic date with Skylar—albeit, another date in which he hadn't told her who he really was, Kade, not Kane—the blue and white lights of the TV flickered on the big picture window. Kade parked in his spot at the Boars Nest. Four other cars he didn't recognize lined the drainage ditch. Colt's truck was there. Kane's was not. Dag's was there too.

He kicked off his boots at the door and looked around. Jasmine and Colt were buck nekkid and passed out on the couch. The place was dirtier than ever. More beer cans. Liters of the hard stuff, vodka, rum, whiskey, tequila, more whiskey, Jägermeister—all empty.

Pizza boxes were stacked on the floor. Bags of garbage overflowed in the kitchen. Stinking clothes were piled on top of the washer. He sniffed and smelled pot smoke.

Fuck. Enough.

He tiptoed down the hallway to Colt's bedroom—tiptoeing not out of a need to be quiet—but tiptoeing because of the bags of shit piled everywhere. Plus the hall light had burned out so he couldn't see where the hell he was going.

The door to Colt's room was cracked open and Kade poked his head in.

Holy fucking Christ.

Kade blinked because he couldn't believe his eyes. If he'd imbibed tonight he'd blame it on booze, but he hadn't had a single glass of wine or beer with dinner.

So what he was witnessing wasn't a weird-assed dream. But his cousin Dag on his hands and knees, bare-assed, with another guy, spreading his cheeks wide and riding Dag's ass like Dag was a pony.

Right then he knew the skinny guy he'd seen getting hammered the other night was Dag. And he knew it hadn't been a damn dream.

A Goth kid—tattooed, hair dyed jet-black, couldn't have been more than nineteen and resembled a girl more than a boy, but the big cock shuttling in and out of Dag's butt definitely belonged to a guy.

And if that image wasn't bad enough, another guy was on his knees in front of Dag, sliding his cock in and out of Dag's mouth, holding Dag by the ears as he fucked Dag's face.

Not that Kade wanted to look, but sweet Jesus, that wasn't all that was going on. The crew-cut dude was in on it too. He'd somehow contorted himself to noisily suck Dag's dick while the other two guys were doing their thing.

To his cousin.

Shit. Maybe Dag was drugged. He was blindfolded. Maybe he had no fucking clue what he was doing.

Kade made up his mind to break up the foursome, when the guy with his cock in Dag's mouth whined, "I wish I could come on your face. You've got such a pretty face."

Dag pulled back and slurred, "You say that every fuckin' time, Max, and you know I'll never blow you again without wearin' a fuckin' condom."

"I'm blowing *you* without a condom," crew-cut guy said, then returned to Dag's cock, twisting his hand firmly from root to tip as he suckled the knob.

"Fuck him harder, Leroy. Dag's a bad boy who likes to pretend he isn't one of us. We all know he likes it hard. And rough." Max rammed his meat back into Dag's mouth with a childish pout. Dag groaned his approval when Leroy started hammering his hips harder into Dag's ass.

Kade retreated.

He knew Colt was out of control, but to see Dag like that? Totally out of control too? Maybe Dag was drugged, or drunk, or maybe he just liked being fucked and blown by a guy and sucking cock once in a while. Didn't change the bottom line: Kade couldn't live here anymore. The thought of moving back in with his folks at age thirty was more than a little humbling. Yet he preferred it to knowing what was going on down the hall.

Preferred it to wondering what the hell kind of kinky scene he'd stumble across in his living room in the middle of the night the next time.

He threw his clothes, boots, hats, CDs, electronics, and the few toiletries he owned in three suitcases. After grabbing his bedding, he stormed out, slipped on his boots, climbed in his truck and didn't look back.

Two days later Cord clapped on his hat, loaded his pickup and drove out to check cattle before he started the dirty, daylong chore of haying.

But once he settled on the tractor, the problems of the day melted away. He focused on his task, allowing himself the secret joy of witnessing another cycle of Mother Nature. Months back the winter snows melted, leaving what looked like barren ground. Then tiny shoots of grass poked up through the brown earth to make a living sea of green. Now he was cutting the first field of hay. He inhaled the pungent scent of alfalfa. Of hot dry dirt. The smell of diesel and oil and overheated machinery and his own sweat.

This chunk of land was heaven on earth.

And the view. Lord, he'd never tire of the scenery displayed before him. White tufts of prairie asters and clumps of silver-green sage interspersed with cheat grass. The big sky ranging in hues from powdery blue to sapphire. The crested mountains in the background—towers of gray and black rock, shadowed stone. Ominous. Unyielding. Constant. Comforting.

His gaze encompassed the treeless horizon only broken by scattered clouds and disappearing fences. This place was home. The only home he'd known, in truth, the only place he'd ever wanted to hang his hat. Took two long years of working on a fishing boat in Seattle to swallow his pride, mend fences with his dad and admit he longed to return to Wyoming where he belonged. The workdays were long. The winters were harsh. He'd never be rich even when he slaved every damn day. But he wouldn't trade this life for anything.

Was AJ counting down the days to escape ranch work and the never-ending sink of time and money? Hours and days and years of being beholden to the weather and then to the cattle market?

Cord had little doubt she'd miss the land, the people, and the connection to both. Folks who'd never had either would never understand that permanent sense of loss.

Once she graduated, would she settle down with a financially stable guy? Pop out a couple of cute kids? Entrench herself in the suburbs, drive a minivan and wear pastel-colored tracksuits?

He snorted disdain. AJ was a horsewoman to the core. He couldn't help but think marrying a man without her same love of the true Western lifestyle would be akin to a slow death. Would the lack of those necessary things in her life extinguish the light in her eyes and her soul over time?

Made him uncomfortable to think along those lines, but ultimately there was nothing he could do, besides offer to marry her. Right. Then she'd be more tied down than ever. Despite her sweet words, he doubted she'd welcome a permanent tie with him—a thirty-five-year-old man with a kid. AJ was just starting her life and her career. She'd chosen him for a bed partner because he was safe. Experienced. And handy. It was inevitable their paths would diverge and veer different directions.

Somehow he managed to put AJ out of his mind for the rest of the grueling day's work. Dissecting Colt not showing up again was pointless too. By the time he'd run the John Deere out of gas and bumped his way across the various pastures to the house, Cord admitted he and Colt needed a break from each other. Working with family was tough. He and his father had been at loggerheads for years until Cord had left for Seattle.

Sometimes the best decision to keep the peace was distance. Literally. Luckily there were plenty of other sections on the McKay ranch for his brother to work.

Cord parked in the yard at seven-thirty. No sign of AJ. No message. No note. No doubt he'd think up a suitable penalty for her cheeky behavior.

After cleaning himself up, he slapped together a roast beef sandwich made from dry bread and washed it down with a Fat Tire beer. Ky was amazingly talkative and seemed to be missing him. By the time Cord hung up, he was surprised to see darkness had fallen and it was damn near nine o'clock.

He sat on his couch in his dark living room, bone tired. Knowing he had another full day of the same planned for tomorrow, the best thing would be for him to crawl into bed and rest up while he could.

Then again, morning wouldn't come earlier whether he stayed home or if he checked out the action at the Golden Boot.

Cord slipped on his going-to-town boots and dress hat, grabbed his keys and his wallet and made the trek into town, knowing in his present mood a run-in with either Colt or AJ spelled trouble.

Chapter Fourteen

"I'm thinking of hiring a stripper for my bachelorette party."

AJ spun the bar stool with an arch look. "Male?"

"Well, duh."

"Where are you gonna find a male stripper in this town?"

Liza smirked. "I have my sources."

"Come on, Liza, spill it."

"Rumor has it a couple of the male strippers who travel to the venues between Cheyenne, Billings and Rapid City have been killing time in the area."

"Killing time with who? And how come you didn't tell me this before now?"

"Because I just found out last night and you haven't been hanging out with me. A sad, sad fact, because I'm about to become an old married lady."

AJ waved down the bartender for another draft beer.

"Whatcha been doin'?" Liza stirred the Jack and Coke before taking a hefty sip from the striped straw.

Answering—*screwing around*—although accurate, was not an option. "My sister left her husband. She and her kids moved in with Ma and me. Which is ironic, because mom sold the ranch and she'll be moving as soon as she's able."

"Then you are going back to Denver?"

AJ nodded.

Liza squeezed AJ's hand. "That sucks. I'm sorry. That mean you won't be living here at all?"

"Who knows? Once I graduate I'll actually have a way to support myself, since the 'princess and knight' scenario we dreamed up in third grade hasn't panned out for either of us."

"Speak for yourself. Noah treats me like a princess even if he is welding armor rather than wearing it."

"True. I am happy for you, Liza. How did we get sidetracked from the stripper story? Who's flashing their butt for bucks?"

"Have you talked to Keely? Will she be here for the bachelorette party?"

"Shoot. I forgot to ask her." That was an odd question. Out of the blue. "Why?"

Liza started chomping on her straw, a sure sign of distress. When they'd been in school, by the end of the year everything in Liza's pencil box looked as if beavers had gnawed on it. "Along the rumor vein…I heard if Colt McKay has enough to drink he'll start stripping. Doesn't care where, or when, if it's a private gig or right out in public."

"Holy crap, Liza, you weren't thinking of hiring *him* for your party?"

"God, no. But that's the thing. He's been everywhere with that female stripper and the male stripper I'm considering is a coworker of hers. Colt is a party crasher. Keely would freak if she saw firsthand some of the rank stuff he's been doing."

AJ hadn't heard anything out of the norm where Colt was concerned, besides him hitting the bottle hard. "I'm sure she can't make it because of tests. A stripper? Really, Liza? Why?"

"Because I've always been the goody-two-shoes-girl-next-door. Just once, I'm dying to throw an outrageous party that'll be the talk of the county for ten years. I want everyone to say, 'Hey, remember Liza's bachelorette bash? Now that was one helluva wild time!' instead of tea and cookies and stupid bridal shower games."

AJ empathized. Neither she nor Liza craved the attention wild child Keely McKay garnered without trying, but once in a while—or once in a lifetime in Liza's case—it'd be fun to shatter perceptions about shy girls and cut loose in a way that'd leave Keely's mouth hanging open in shock.

"AJ?"

"I'm in. You need help planning it?"

"Some. I've rented the backroom. My sister and I are making the food." A mischievous smile appeared. "Cocktail weenies, brats, Rocky Mountain Oysters, meatballs. We're gonna have a brat sucking and ball licking contest. And we went online and ordered a bunch of really raunchy party favors."

"Ooh, we've gotta have an official drink. Something super sweet with a naughty name and you won't know you've had too much to drink until it's too late. Wyoming Doodle Whacker."

"Ooh. I like that one."

"Who'da thunk wild women lurked beneath our pigtails and bootcut 501s a few short years ago?"

"Not the guys in our class who voted us 'bland and blander'. There will be something very satisfying about flipping them the bird, and slamming the door in their faces because at this party no men are allowed."

For the next hour AJ and Liza made lists, planned and laughed. Noah finished his dart league and squired Liza away, leaving AJ to fend for herself.

Not for long.

She was dancing with Mikey when Cord waltzed in. She didn't acknowledge him, since she suspected the reverse was true. AJ danced and hung out with her friends, feeling melancholy about not having many nights like this left in her hometown.

Her cell phone rang. She hustled down the hallway away from the music to try and hear Keely, but it was pointless. She turned around and saw Cord blocking the exit.

Lord. The man defined bad-boy rancher hottie, the ultimate man, in her opinion. The real deal, not some cowboy wannabe. His muscles were earned from hours of hard, physical work, not hours spent pumping iron at the gym. His steely-eyed determination was honed from spending years fighting the elements. She suppressed a soft sigh. He wore a pressed cotton shirt the color of vine-ripened tomatoes, which emphasized his 'black Irish' dark good looks, crisp jeans and a straw hat. He probably smelled great too, like shaving cream and soap and the great outdoors.

Shoot. She had no experience with this stuff either. Did she ignore him? Play it cool? Play it like a bitch on wheels? Pretend she hadn't waited at his house for over an hour for him and he never bothered to call and cancel?

While she argued with herself about an appropriate response, he said, "You didn't show up tonight."

"Wrong. I waited for you but *you* didn't show up."

"So you came to the Golden Boot instead?"

"What's it to you what I do?" *Childish, AJ.* "I figured you had other plans so I made some of my own. No big deal. It's not like we're going steady."

His jaw went rigid. "Wrong. You broke the rules. Which means you've earned another penalty."

"Put it on my bill with the other ones."

He gestured to her phone with a jerk of his hat brim. "Who're you talkin' to?"

She blinked at him.

"Who?"

"My stockbroker. My Microsoft stock took a huge hit today."

"You're a real riot, AJ. Who were you talkin' to?"

"You gonna keep asking me until I tell you?"

"Yep."

"Fine. I was trying to talk to Keely. But don't worry, I didn't say a thing about you or the incredible sex we had the other night." Crap. That hadn't come out right.

Cord tipped his hat back. No smile, just a smug look. "Incredible, huh?"

"You know it was. You don't need to get cocky about it because there won't be a repeat performance tonight. Now if you'll excuse me."

"You ain't goin' no place. Get your stuff and be out by my truck in five minutes."

"No."

"No?"

"Is there an echo in here? I said *no*. You had your chance to be with me tonight. You blew it. Better luck tomorrow."

"Don't push me, baby doll."

"Then get out of my way. Unless you want me to really push you aside and make a scene?"

A hard expression flattened his lips.

"Didn't think so." She sidestepped him and strutted to the bar.

Nice goin' McKay. You handled that like a fuckin' pro.

Jesus. That smartypants blonde was so gonna get it when he got his hands on her. He'd stick around and see what other trouble she caused, see if she provided reasons to add to her punishments.

Cord snagged a corner table near the dance floor, where he could watch the entrance, the exits and her every move. Perverted? Yep. But if she took off, he'd know it. Just as well as he knew he'd chase her down—and guaranteed there'd be hell to pay when he caught her.

He nursed a beer, keeping a mental tally of who AJ danced with and how many times. Obsessive? Yep. A feeling which didn't bother him in the least.

A couple of his dad's friends swung by to congratulate him on buying the Foster place. He shot a covert glance at AJ to see if she'd figured out why so much traffic passed his table.

He shooed the guys off instead of discussing his plans for the new McKay acquisition. With AJ within earshot it seemed disrespectful. Not only that, he didn't want anyone in the community believing the Fosters had fallen on hard times and had no choice but to sell. Cord knew how much it'd bug him if local folks made such assumptions about him or his family or the way they ran their operation. Gossip ruled in Crook County and the men were just as bad as the ladies.

Kade strolled in, snagged a beer and slipped into the booth seat across from him. "How's it goin'?"

"Shitty. You?"

"Shittier."

"Where's Kane?"

"Who the hell knows?" Kade fiddled with the metal tab on his beer can. "Did you hear I moved out of the Boars Nest?"

"No. I was a little fuckin' busy mowin' the goddamn south

hayfield for the last couple of days to indulge in idle conversation."

"By yourself?"

Cord nodded.

"Shit. Sorry. I woulda been over to help you, if I'da known." Kade fished his can of Skoal bandits from his front pocket, shook out a pouch and passed the can across the table.

Cord jammed the tobacco in his cheek next to his molars. He only chewed occasionally, and only when Ky wasn't around.

Kade said, "Before you ask, no, I don't know where your stupid brother is either. Been busy after work with Ma's side of the family. First Uncle Darren wanted my help." He sighed. "You know how our dads are about Uncle Harland, so I couldn't exactly tell him I've been helpin' out Uncle H since Dag went on another bender. Spent the last coupla nights at his place. Early this mornin' I get to the northeast corner where we been fixin' fence and Kane tells me Dag had enough of Uncle H's naggin' and me tryin' to—quote 'be the son Dag could never be' so he packed his shit and now *he's* livin' at the Boars Nest in my old room."

"Uncle H tell you what went on to make Dag bail?"

"Hell no. Truth is, I don't know why Dag'd move up there besides the free-for-all-anyway-you-want sex. The place is a fuckin' pigsty. Kane and me cleaned it up a couple of times in the last month. Colt can't be bothered, but we ain't the ones makin' the messes."

"Who is?"

"Some of them people Colt has over every damn night."

"People like that Jasmine chick?"

Kade's gaze snapped up.

"I was there when she offered you and Colt a threesome, remember?" Cord watched his cousin closely and sure enough, Kade blushed. "Ended up bein' a foursome or more, did it?"

"Yeah. I ain't gonna lie, I thought it'd be hot as hell. Once in a while some variety is good, but it didn't turn out as sexy hot as it does in porn flicks. Besides, Jazz and her friends are..."

"What?"

"Freaks. Squatters. The place is even nastier to live in than usual. Booze bottles and cans, condoms and food wrappers everywhere. Dirty clothes, dirty dishes, bags of trash. My mama would faint if she saw it."

"Which means mine would too. How much has Colt been drinkin', Kade?"

"More'n I've ever seen. I ain't so sure he's not drinkin' before work. Been signs of drugs around too. Pot, mostly. A couple of vials of other shit I didn't want to know nothin' about."

Cord tried to rein in his temper and the underlying fear for his wayward brother. "Come clean with me, no bullshit. Is Colt doin' drugs?"

"I doan know. I jus' know he's a train wreck waitin' to happen and I doan wanna be no place around when he finally goes off the rails."

Cord drained his beer. "Too late. He's here."

"He alone?"

"Yeah."

"That's surprisin'."

He watched Colt stop at the bar and knock back three shots of something before he carried two beers over to another table.

"Think he saw us?"

"Hell yeah he saw us. I'd avoid me too." Cord stood. "Head on home. I'll handle this."

"Think I'll stick around."

The second Cord stopped in front of Colt's table Colt said, "Look. I know you're pissed off. You've got a right to be, okay? I had a rough fuckin' night. I blacked out. Woke up naked in my bed around four this afternoon, hungover as hell, no idea what happened. Don't know why my cousins couldn't bother to wake me up."

"They ain't your mama."

"No shit. But it ain't like I haven't done it for them a time or two."

Cord studied his brother's disheveled appearance. Scraggly hair, bags under his eyes, marks on his neck. Incredibly swollen lips. "Didja get punched in the mouth last night? 'Cause it's puffed up like a bee sting."

Colt brushed his hand over his lips and frowned. "Not that I recall."

"That seems to be the problem, bro. Even if Kane and Kade and even Dag would've been around to wake your drunken ass up, I'd've sent you home."

"Why? 'Cause I had a little too much liquid fun last night? It ain't like you didn't do shit like that."

"Wrong. I never once blacked out. I never once missed a day of ranch work because of drinkin' and you've missed two this week alone."

"I knew you'd be a self-righteous prick about this."

Heavy pause. "What the *fuck* did you just say to me?"

"You heard me." Colt deigned to look at him. "Precious Ky's gone so you've got nothin' else to do 'cept work. Some of us have a life outside of the ranch. Some of us are tryin' damn hard not to end up like you: cold, cruel, a bitter woman-hater, a fuckin' recluse, a workaholic loser with a stash of porn and a sore hand."

Never in all the years that he'd been dealing with his overbearing family had he wanted to kill one of them.

Until tonight. Until now.

Cord grabbed Colt by the shirtfront and hauled Colt across the table. The second he had a free hand he punched Colt in the jaw hard enough Colt's head snapped back. A beer can crashed and rolled off the table, spewing foam everywhere.

He cocked his arm and punched Colt in the mouth, feeling the scrape of his brother's teeth on his bare knuckles. Before Colt's nose met his fist, Colt landed a blow alongside Cord's temple and nearly knocked his head from his neck.

Cord staggered back, taking Colt with him.

They crashed into another table. Bottles shattered and beer splashed on the floor. Shirts ripped, flesh connected with flesh. Grunts, curses and groans of pain were intermingled with more curses, blood and crunching glass.

Kade intervened.

Cord forgot what a big guy Kade was until his younger

cousin literally picked him up and set him aside like he was an eighty-pound hay bale, not a two-hundred-pound pissed-off man.

"Cord, what the hell is wrong with you?"

"That cocksucker said some shit that don't fly with me. I called him on it."

Colt laughed. Picked himself up off the floor. Fell back down in a pile.

Cord knew Colt wasn't staggering because he'd thrown such accurate punches. His brother was hammered beyond all reason. Again. In public.

What were they gonna do? How had Colt gotten so hopelessly off track? How in the hell could he help him?

Once Colt made it to a chair, he spit a hunk of bloody saliva on the floor. "I ain't apologizin' for nothin', bro. You're a fuckin' prick like Dad and everyone knows it—"

Sympathy vanished and Cord lunged for him and they were rolling around on the floor. Punching. Kicking. Bleeding.

By that time, the bouncers showed up and separated them for good. A crowd gathered. His dad's and his uncle's longtime buddies. The guy who owned the feed store. He hoped his eyes were playing tricks on him and that wasn't the family banker back by the jukebox.

So much for not making a scene. He scanned the crowd and his gaze caught AJ's.

Hers was somber. Not full of pity or some mislaid compassion, but understanding. For the first time he wondered why he'd put up such stupid parameters of no public acknowledgment of their relationship. And like it or not, it was a relationship, a relationship based on sex, but that didn't change the basic definition of it.

Also didn't change the knowledge that he, cold, bitter, woman-hating, reclusive Cord McKay would like nothing better than to walk straight into her arms. Right here, right now, right in front of Toots the bartender, Sam the banker, Bebe the town gossip and everyone else.

Kade took him aside. "He's wasted."

"Yeah. I noticed."

"Says he wants to press assault charges against you."

"I ain't surprised."

"Toots ain't callin' the sheriff. I'm gonna take him home."

"Thanks." Cord knew that wasn't enough, so he repeated it. "Thanks, Kade. I really appreciate it."

"No problem. But I will tell you that you're gonna hafta come up with a way to deal with him, Cord, and I doan mean with your fists. I lived with the son of a bitch and I'd no idea it'd gotten this bad."

"Appears he's been good at hidin' it up until now."

"Appears so. But it's out there now. Whole damn town's gonna know about it by tomorrow. I doan envy you tellin' Uncle Carson and Aunt Carolyn 'bout this. I'd call them right away before someone else does." Kade focused on Cord's cheek. "Get someone to look at that cut. You're bleedin' pretty good."

Someone. Right. He had no one.

Cord made it to the exit when he smelled her behind him. He slowly turned around and wondered if he looked as pathetic as he felt.

"You okay?"

No. "Sore. Pissed off. Embarrassed."

"I figured. You going home?"

"Yeah. But first I get to wake my folks up and tell 'em their son's a drunk and caused a scene in public. Then I get to call my brothers and my baby sis and tell them the same damn thing." He sighed. "What the hell am I gonna do about him?"

"I don't know." AJ looked right into his eyes. "I want to come home with you. No strings. I just really don't think you should be alone tonight."

"AJ—"

"Would it be so hard to let me take care of you? Just for one night?"

Cord stared at her, wishing his hand wasn't bloody so he could touch her sweet face. Wishing he could be a man instead of a shell of one.

"Cord?"

"I'd like that, baby doll. I'd like that a helluva lot more than you could ever know. I'll see you at home."

Chapter Fifteen

Kade threw Colt in his pickup and he passed out before they hit the outskirts of town. He had that same hollow feeling in his gut he'd seen in Cord's eyes. Poor bastard.

No extra cars were parked at the Boars Nest, just Kane's and Dag's trucks.

Great. He hadn't seen his cousin since he'd inadvertently seen way more of Dag's nocturnal activities that night he'd moved out. If he was lucky, maybe Dag'd be passed out and he wouldn't have to deal with another fucked up situation with one of his cousins.

Colt managed to stumble into the house on his own. Kade still felt some perverse responsibility to make sure his brother was all right. After he checked on Kane and found him snoring in bed, he noticed Dag sat in the darkened living room, drinking cheap whiskey straight from the bottle.

"Evenin' cuz."

"Evenin' Dag."

"You pissed I moved inta your room?"

"No. Just wondered why you skipped out on your dad."

Dag snorted. "He don't need me. He's got his hired hand and Chassie's squeeze, Trevor, to whip the West homestead into shape." He saluted with the bottle. "Fuckin' place is rundown. None of the damn equipment works, and somehow the old man sees that as my fault. Even when I ain't been around for years."

"Maybe that's why he's blamin' you, Dag. He's old. He ain't been able to take care of that place for a long time. Since way before your mama died."

"He don't wanna take care of it. He ain't never wanted to be a rancher. He wanted to be a damn mechanic. But rather than stand up to granddad, he knuckled under. And instead of lettin' me pursue my dream of pro rodeo until it paid off, he done the same damn thing to me." Dag took another swig. "Makin' me quit the circuit to come home to tend to forty lousy cows and a thousand acres. I could hate him for that alone."

"You don't mean that."

Dag sighed. "I probably don't. It's just...I didn't ask for this. Ain't my fault I was born first, the only male. I ain't like you and Cord. I don't wanna spend my life a slave to the land."

Kade bristled. "So instead you're just gonna be a drunk? Carryin' on about your glorious past rodeo days? Don't you think there are times Cord and I wanna walk away? Say *fuck it* and do something easier?"

"No, I don't. You've both got too much of that goddamn McKay pride my daddy warns me about."

"What the fuck does that mean?"

"Why do you think my dad didn't want his sister—your mother—to marry a McKay? Because they don't care about no one but themselves. You ain't neighborly. You ain't aware of nothin' that goes on outside the borders of the all important McKay Ranch."

"Drunk talk. That ain't true."

"It is. You've all got too much pride."

"I'd rather have some pride than none like you."

"Fuck you too."

Here was the opening he'd been looking for. "No thanks. But I didn't know you swung that way until I got an up close and personal view of some of your nighttime activities."

"What're you talkin' about?"

"Don't pretend you don't know."

"I don't. I can't remember shit about anything."

"You've been drinkin' so much you've been blackin' out?"

"So?"

"So, do you ever wake up with a sore mouth, a sore dick and a sore asshole with no clue of how you got it?"

A hint of wariness crept into Dag's bloodshot eyes.

"I don't care if you're gay, Dag. But if bein' gay and bein' afraid to come out is causin' you to drink too much, you need help on a couple of different levels, cuz."

"Me? Gay? I ain't gay. Is this some kinda joke?"

Kade shook his head. "I came home one night and found you in bed with not one, not two, but three guys. At first I thought you were drugged and I was gonna step in and break it up, but you appeared to be enjoyin' suckin' Max off, while Leroy fucked you in the ass. Didn't catch the name of the guy suckin' you off. Then you mentioned you'd fucked and sucked both the guys before. Multiple times."

Dag's face went ghostly pale.

"Like I said, I don't care if you're gay. I do care if you're so drunk you don't know what the hell you're doin'. I do care if you put my brother or our cousins in danger because you're habitually drunk. You are out of control, Dag. Bad."

He swallowed hard several times. "You ain't kiddin'? You saw me?"

Kade nodded.

"Who knows about it? Have you told my dad what you saw me doin'...with another man?"

"You mean men?"

"Jesus. Men. Who knows? Kane? Colt? Trevor?"

"I don't know. I haven't told anyone, Dag. It ain't my business to do so." Kade stared at his cousin, who was looking more than a little forlorn.

A long pause hung between them.

"It'd kill my dad...to know I.... He's got a dream of me settlin' down with a local gal and raisin' a passel of kids on the homeplace. Like Colby done. That ain't me Kade. It ain't never been me. When I was on the circuit I was the real me. Happy. Doin' what I loved. Now, I'm stuck. I got no skills beyond rodeo. No place to go. I'm livin' a lie and I fuckin' hate it."

"Booze isn't the answer. It ain't gonna make any of this go away. It'll just make you more reckless and bitter."

"What would you do?"

"Ah, hell, Dag, how am I supposed to answer that?"

"No. I'm serious. If your life was a mess, what would you do?"

"Sober up, first. Then tell Uncle H how you feel about ranchin'. If he's a jerk, have him leave the responsibilities to Chassie. Move on. As hard as it is for me to imagine leavin' here, leavin' my family, I'd do it in a fuckin' heartbeat if I was as miserable as you."

Another bout of silence stretched.

"Thanks. I'll think on it." Dag gulped the last of the booze in the bottle.

"You do that. Any time you need to talk, you call me."

"Can I ask you somethin'?"

"I guess."

"How come you ain't married?"

That'd come out of left field. "Haven't found the right woman yet." Kade thought of Skylar. Even though he'd only know her for a short time she felt...right.

"So, as much as you disapprove of what me and Colt and Kane have been doin', it ain't any worse than endin' up like Cord."

Dag didn't offer any additional explanations as he shuffled off to bed.

And Kade knew Dag was actually right about one thing. He'd been using his responsibilities to the ranch as an excuse to keep his life stuck in a holding pattern. He just didn't have a clue as to how to go about changing it.

He climbed in his truck and headed home.

Chapter Sixteen

AJ stopped at the C-Mart for a Diet Mountain Dew and ice before she drove to Cord's place.

No yard lights were on when she started down the long driveway. She wondered if he'd be embarrassed about her offer and grouchy to be the bearer of bad news to the rest of the McKays about Colt.

Why did the responsibilities always fall on his shoulders?

Keely had had major concerns about Colt's behavior for a long time. Her intuition when it came to her family was largely unrealized in the McKay clan.

Last year at Carter and Macie's wedding reception, Keely had informed Colt he'd find happiness when he stopped looking for it in the bottom of a bottle or a condom box. Colt had laughed and patted her on the head—which was a typical response to her from her big, burly brothers and a reaction that drove Keely insane.

AJ shot a quick glance at Cord's dark house and dialed Keely's cell number. She answered on the first ring.

"Hey, BFF, you okay?"

Keely sniffed. "No. Colt is such a dumbass. I can't believe he'd do that to Cord. He worships Cord. We all do." She sniffled again. "Did you see what happened?"

"Most of it."

"Was it awful?"

"Yeah. I've never seen Cord so mad. Not his usual quiet, dangerous mad. It was his—"

"—I wanna rip someone's head off and watch me do it with one hand, kind of mad. I've only seen it once and that was enough."

AJ listened to Keely's quiet cries. "I wish I was there, K, because I know how much this stuff freaks you out."

"Thanks. But it's more important you're there for Cord. He told me you were coming over."

"He did?"

"Yeah. But I knew you'd go to him. I knew you wouldn't let him hurt alone." Keely's voice dropped to a whisper. "He is hurting, AJ, not just where Colt punched him. Don't let him push you away. Be there for him. Someone needs to be. Call me tomorrow."

AJ followed the curved walkway to the front door. She stepped inside. No sign of Cord in the living room. After putting the ice in the freezer, she heard the shower running upstairs.

He'd left the door to the master bathroom open a crack. "Cord? Just wanted to let you know I'm up here so you don't think I'm an intruder and shoot me."

No answer.

She saw the pile of clothes in front of the dresser. Not her place to wash them, but Cord didn't need a bloody reminder of the evening's events. She jammed them in the overflowing hamper and faced the bed. Not ideal, but it'd work. She peeled back the comforter and ripped away the top sheet, shoving the pillows to the floor.

AJ made a quick trip to the kitchen for supplies. She was arranging everything on the nightstand when the bathroom door squeaked and he limped out.

Cord wore a towel. A small towel. Even when her hormones did the boot scootin' boogie from the sight of all that yummy bare man flesh and bulging muscles, she noticed the dejected set of his shoulders, the swollen bump on his jaw, the mouse under his eye and the cut on his cheekbone.

He sighed. "That bad, huh?"

"What?"

"You should see the look on your face, AJ."

"This look?" She made a funny face and his faint smile

appeared.

"Like I said, baby doll, you're a real laugh a minute." He kept a hand on the towel and pointed. "The bed make you so mad that you ripped it apart?"

"No. Just getting it ready."

Cord sighed again. "No offense, but I'm not really in the mood tonight. In fact, I'll probably be lousy company so it might be best if you went on home."

"Huh-uh. The hottest man I know is stark naked right in front of me, no way am I going anywhere. Lay face down on the mattress, McKay."

"This bossy side of you is new."

"Hah. Ky wouldn't agree. He once said I was as bossy as...well, *you* if I recall."

He smiled slightly again.

"Besides, I hide my bossiness except when I'm in professional mode."

"Professional?"

"What part of 'massage therapist' is confusing to you?"

"You're gonna give me a massage?"

"Well, you already told me a blowjob was out for options."

"Amy Jo Foster, that is beyond ornery."

She laughed because she'd actually shocked him. "I like it when you get all prissy."

"I like it when you get all raunchy," he countered.

"Good." She patted the bed. "Lose the towel. Lay on your stomach and spread your arms above your head in a Y and prepare to be wowed."

Cord did exactly as he was told.

"Usually I'm standing, but tonight I have to improvise. Here."

He looked at the baggie full of ice wrapped in a towel. "What's this for?"

"Your jaw. It'll keep the swelling down."

Something beyond gratitude shone in his eyes. "Thanks."

"You're welcome. Try to relax. Remember this isn't sexual."

"I'll try to remember that," he said dryly.

"You want music playing?"

"No. This is fine."

AJ poured oil on her palms and started at the base of his skull, working her fingers down his neck. Cord remained tense, not that she blamed him. A first time professional massage was different than the well-meaning back rub from a loved one. He finally loosened up with a deep, heartfelt groan of satisfaction when she moved down to work on his shoulders.

"You are amazingly good at this, AJ."

"Thank you."

"No. Seriously, wonderfully, awesomely, astoundingly good. How much school do you have left before you graduate?"

"One trimester, which is mostly clinical work. Then I can hang out my shingle."

"You'll be overrun with customers. And marriage proposals from all sorts of men who've experienced your magic hands."

Would that last group include you?

Don't go there, AJ. She kept her mouth shut and concentrated on his biceps and triceps.

But Cord wouldn't let it go. "Where you thinkin' of settin' up shop?"

"Keely and I talked about opening our own place either in Sundance or Moorcroft, but that was before things changed."

Cord tensed up again. "What sort of things?"

"Things like Mama selling the ranch. Things like Jenn and the kids moving to Billings. Things like my potential partner/roommate/BFF Keely neglecting to tell me she'd rather not be a massage therapist."

"What? What does she want to do?"

"To continue her schooling and get a dual degree as a certified physical therapist and an occupational therapist."

"Where does that leave you?"

Lost. "In Denver. It's a real crapshoot at this point where I'll end up come January."

He didn't respond.

She allowed her brain to slide into professional mode as

she finished his upper back. On to the gluteus maximus—or the best butt she'd ever had her hands on. How could she stay neutral while rubbing and stroking perfectly squeezable man flesh? Without thinking of how she'd clutched it tightly while Cord pumped in and out of her with such passion? If she looked closely, she might even see scratches from her fingernails.

"What's wrong?"

"Here's the deal, McKay. It's up to you whether I skip your very fine butt and move on to your very fine legs."

"Why up to me?"

"In a situation where I'm not intimately acquainted with the client, it's not a problem. We both know that's not the case. I've had your tight tush in my hands. I don't know if I can massage it without remembering my death grip the last time you—"

"Are you tryin' to give me a hard-on, AJ? 'Cause it's workin'."

She bit back a smile. "No. We actually have a class entitled, 'The Male Erection: Nothing Personal' which is my favorite class."

"This one's personal," he growled, "very personal. Intensely personal."

"Okay, then I'll focus on the backs of your legs."

"Fine."

AJ tried not to look at the area between his thighs. But her gaze was continually drawn to the heavy sac covered in crinkly dark hair, a contrast against the stark white sheet.

"Stop starin' at my butt."

I'm not. I'm staring at your balls. "Sorry."

"Do you usually talk to your clients while you're doin' this?"

"Sometimes. Mostly they're trying to relax so it's minimal conversation. Lots of people wear iPods."

"Don't that bother you?"

"No."

"It bugs the hell outta me."

AJ pinched her thumbs down the center of his right calf. "Why?"

"It's like no one can stand the sound of silence. Always gotta have music playin' or TV blarin' or noises blastin' out of some handheld game. Even Colt can't work without some shit rattlin' his brain. Hell. Maybe that's his problem."

Here was her opening. "So what happens between you two now?"

"It ain't like I can fire him. Even though I wanted to today and yesterday when he didn't show up and I only got half the damn field hayed."

"That's why you were late?"

"Yeah. Sorry. Lost track of time. Worked 'til damn near dark, then I hadta call Ky. Shoulda called you too." He moaned when she hit a sore tendon by his ankle. "I was a dickhead earlier at the bar. I'm sorry."

His sincere apology surprised her. She honestly thought he'd be too stubborn to admit he was wrong. "You're forgiven."

"It ain't gonna be that easy for Colt. Thing's been goin' to hell in a handbasket where he's concerned. Yeah, he's a thirty-one-year-old adult male and he oughta know better than to make such stupid decisions, but he don't. He never learns. Makes me question his decisions about the ranch, if you wanna know the truth. We all excuse his behavior and laugh it off as him sowin' his oats. Well, no more.

"Dad's goin' over there to talk to him first thing in the mornin'. Guess Ma and Aunt Kimi are gonna fumigate the place tomorrow afternoon. Colt ain't gonna be workin' with me or anyone else for the time bein'."

"I'm sorry."

"I'm sorry too. And I sure as hell didn't need to end my long-ass day by getting into fisticuffs with my drunk brother."

"Wrong. You're ending your day with a massage."

He smiled over his shoulder at her. "Much as I appreciate it, I'm gonna ask you don't massage my feet. They're sore, they smell and they're—"

"Ticklish?"

"That too."

"Huh. The tough cowboy does have a weak spot. I'll have to remember that." And exploit it at some point. She slapped his naked flank. “It’s time for you to turn over anyway. I need to get busy on your front.”

Chapter Seventeen

Cord wouldn't survive those clever fingers.

He was in deep with this woman. Her feistiness in the bar turned him on. Her sweetness in the aftermath of the shit that'd gone down with Colt had turned him on even more. But her hands? All over him? Soothing and tempting and taking away all sorts of aches and pains externally and internally? He'd gone beyond turned on.

"AJ, I don't think I can stand havin' you touch me without wantin' to touch you right back in the same way."

"I wouldn't mind. I told you that."

Cord reached for her. He didn't speak. He just traced the back of his hand over the soft skin on her face. "You're so pretty. God, you're so pretty."

She blushed, making her even prettier, in his opinion. "You want me to finish the massage?"

"On one condition."

"Which is?"

"You have to take off your shirt."

AJ frowned. "Why?"

"You always make me take mine off. Turnabout is fair play. Might be crass, but I wanna see your tits bouncin' while you're rubbin' me down. I thought about that a lot as you were workin' on my back. A whole lot. What those beautiful perky breasts looked like swayin' free. If the tips were hard."

"You're joking."

"Nope. In case you haven't noticed I have a thing for them beauties." *In case you haven't noticed I have a thing for you too, baby doll.*

"Okay. But I get to sit on your pelvis."

He grinned. "Deal."

Cord actually felt his mouth water when AJ stripped off her bright pink tank top and unhooked the plain white cotton bra. He longed to touch those tempting points. To lick. To suck. To bury his face in those pillowy mounds.

She leaned over to grab the oil and his tongue shot out to swipe across a ripe tip.

"No licking."

"If I started I doubt you'd make me stop."

"That's why you're not gonna start, Cord McKay. Now hold still."

"Bossy. You don't have to do the same on my account. The bouncier the better."

Although she straddled his pelvis, she didn't writhe on his groin as she concentrated on massaging his pecs and lats. She spent a long time rubbing the area around his nipples.

Conversation was at a standstill. His breathing changed. Her breathing changed. They didn't look at each other; they just focused on body parts.

After AJ dug her fingertips into his hips, she nonverbally urged him to spread his legs wider. Without commenting on his raging hard-on, she continued to work his quads. Her breasts swayed so provocatively he clenched his hands into fists to keep from reaching for them.

A soft whip of hair lashed across his distended cock. Cord's eyes flew open a second before the warm, wet heat of AJ's mouth enclosed him.

"Christ. What the hell are you doin', AJ?"

"I must be doing it wrong if you don't know." She sucked him deep. And dragged her bottom teeth up the vein before she released him from that velvet warmth.

"But I wasn't expectin'—"

"I know. That's why I want to do it. Let me bring you. I want you to come in my mouth. I wanna know what you taste like."

"Ah. Okay." Right. Like he could say *no* to that.

AJ licked and lapped his cock, suckling his engorged cockhead, bringing him higher with every sweeping breath and delicate lick. Her single-minded intentions roused him to a whole different level of pleasure. When she brought her magic hands into play, rolling his balls and stroking the base of his shaft, holding back was a joke. He groaned as his cock emptied on her tongue in short, intense bursts and she swallowed every hot drop.

While he drifted down from her sweet, unselfish loving, she finished his massage and wiped the oil from his body.

Finally, he opened his eyes.

AJ offered him a shy smile.

"C'mere."

She scooted up and placed her head on his chest.

He skimmed his fingertips up and down her naked spine. "That was the best massage I ever had."

"That was the first massage you've ever had."

"True. But that wasn't the first blowjob I've ever gotten and that one was the best too."

"Really?"

"I wouldn't lie to you, baby doll. It was fuckin' amazin'. Come up here and kiss me."

The tentative movement of her lips and tongue against his as she tried to hold back amused him. Cord knew she liked it when he controlled her mouth, when he urged them a little toward desperation. But the desperation he felt tonight owed nothing to sexual heat.

AJ sensed his mood and placed gentle kisses on every mark Colt left on his face. His stomach churned when he thought back to Colt's words and actions and the realization his brother was sick and there wasn't a damn thing he could do about it. No way he could fix Colt like he'd fix fence. He'd try like hell, but Colt wouldn't beat this if he couldn't admit he had a problem. He sighed.

"You thinking about Colt?"

"Yeah."

A pause. "It's late. I should go."

"Stay. I can put it aside when you're here. Besides. I haven't kissed you proper. I need a taste of them sweet, sweet lips."

She smiled against his throat, nibbled his neck up to his mouth. "Show me a proper kiss, McKay."

"I wasn't talkin' about your mouth, baby doll."

Her gray eyes widened.

Cord grinned. "Take off them panties and crawl up here."

"But—"

"You wanna get your butt slapped?"

"No."

"Then slide off those bikinis and pull up your skirt."

Rather than take off just her panties, AJ stripped off everything. "I didn't come here for this, Cord."

"I know. But I'm dyin' to put my mouth on you because, sweets, I love to watch you come. It's like you're getting an unexpected present every damn time."

AJ blushed.

Cord shifted down on the mattress. "Straddle me. Up on your knees. Grab the headboard." When she hesitated he urged her closer so he could suck a nipple. "Don't act all shy on me. I'm gonna make you feel good. You know I can. You know you want it."

She moved into position. So did Cord. He slid his head between her knees.

"It's like I'm sitting on your face."

"And thank God for that. They used to call them mustache rides."

"Cord!"

He laughed. "Angle yourself a little farther back. Hold tight."

Before his tongue lapped the shiny wetness, before his hands spread her wide for the invasion of his fingers, he simply inhaled her. The sweet scent of AJ's arousal—like sunshine and cotton. Like home.

He delved his tongue into her tight channel, long strokes as deep as it could reach, as his thumb flicked her clit in the same cadence.

AJ began to whimper immediately.

Cord sensed her orgasm gathering steam and her pussy muscles clenched around his tongue as she went over the edge. He figured the first one would be fast. Kissing a path down the inside of her thigh, he rotated his hands to clutch her ass.

"Cord."

"Again, baby doll. You can go again."

"But—"

He smacked her butt hard and she yelped. Leisurely, he licked every spot in her engorged pussy but her clit and blew a cool stream of air across the wetness. Petted the curve of her mound with his chin and cheek, intrigued by the contrast between her pale blondness and the darker tones of his hands on her skin.

When she could take direct contact, he fastened his mouth to her clit and sucked relentlessly, refusing to release that sensitive nub until he felt blood beat against his lips and she cried out his name.

Then she wailed, "Oh-man-oh-man-oh-man. Stop."

"No. One more. This one will take longer, but it'll be worth it, I promise. Come on, let me bring you off once more."

"But—"

Another spank. "Every time I hear a but, I'm whackin' yours."

"But. Crap. That one didn't count."

"Yes, it did." *Whack.* "I think maybe you like a little ass play." Cord smoothed his hands over the curvy, hot cheeks. Then he traced the seam of her ass down to her tailbone. "You know I'm gonna want in this ass, AJ."

She looked down at him. "In. Meaning—what in?"

"My fingers. My tongue. But mostly I wanna grind my cock in there. I've been the only man in your pussy, the only man in your mouth. The way I see it, that last bit of virginity belongs strictly to me."

"But—"

Another crack across her tush. Both sides this time. "I can

see the interest in your eyes, so don't lie to me. You wanna know what that feels like, but you think you shouldn't wanna know stuff like that. Feels dirty, right?"

She nodded.

"If thinkin' about me doin' that to you turns you on? Nothin' wrong with that. Nothin' that happens between us is wrong unless it ain't consensual. If you say no, I'll respect it. But sweet baby Jesus I'd be lyin' if I didn't say I'm hopin' for a big yes at some point. Soon."

He flattened his tongue and licked her from her bottom hole to the top of her sex. "Hang on."

Cord nuzzled the seam of her thighs. He dragged the wetness from her pussy down the crack of her ass to her tight hole, which was as pretty and pink as the rest of her.

She immediately tensed up.

"Not doin' anything. Just givin' you an idea on how this'll feel." He circled the tip around those blood-rich nerve endings, suckling her clit in time to his finger until she began to bump her hips.

"Cord. Please. Make me come. No more teasing."

What AJ didn't know was he wasn't teasing her. After two fairly quick orgasms she'd need time to recover, just like a man would.

Evidently *Cosmo* hadn't mentioned that factoid.

He built her again, circumventing her clit entirely. When he knew she was close, he twisted two fingers inside and stroked her G-spot. He held her clit between his teeth and flicked it with the very tip of his tongue, keeping his lips suctioned around it.

AJ went wild. Her legs shook. She alternately whimpered and begged. It was so unbelievably hot having her riding his face, that after her intense orgasm left her hoarse and gasping, Cord dropped his hand to his cock and jacked off like a randy teenager, letting come spray across his belly and losing his mind in AJ's willingness to try anything.

Finally, her sex quit pulsing and AJ flopped to the mattress. He retreated to the bathroom to clean up.

She murmured a protest at the sensation of the warm cloth, but ultimately let her legs fall open to him. He swiped the area between thighs sticky with her juices and his saliva, with a few red marks from his beard.

He looked at the clock. Two a.m. Then he glanced at her. AJ looked so comfortable, so cuddly, so perfect in his bed he didn't have the heart to make her get dressed.

Cord tossed a few pillows at the headboard and nestled her against his chest.

"I'm tired. I know I have to go home."

"Just rest, baby doll."

"Mmm. I like this. Your body is so hard. And warm. Like snuggling up to a sun-warmed rock."

A much better description than Colt's accusation of him being a cold bastard.

"You'll wake me up?"

"Early in the morning so you can sneak in bed before anyone knows you were out all night." Selfish of him, but he didn't want her to leave.

"Good plan. Which means that's another virginity you can claim."

"What's that?"

"I've never slept in the same bed with a man. Ever. Not for an hour, especially not all night. I'm glad it's with you."

"Me too."

Chapter Eighteen

AJ woke with a start. Where was she? And why was she...naked? A snore behind her made her jump. She turned slightly and saw Cord sprawled face down on the mattress beside her. Just as naked as she.

She was in Cord's bed? Her gaze flew to the clock. Five a.m.

Damn. She'd been out all night.

So? You're an adult. You're entitled to cut loose once in a while.

True. But neither her mom nor sister needed the extra worry in their lives.

AJ slid off the bed and kept an eagle eye on her lover as she dressed. Part of her wanted to wake him; part of her wanted to sneak out and deal with him later. She withheld a snort. How very Bridget Jones. She never thought this situation would happen to her. She and Cord hadn't had sex—well, technically not penetration sex, but oral sex counted as real sex, right?

Stop with the dissection and move your behind.

She retrieved her purse from the kitchen counter and checked her cell phone as she tiptoed out the front door. No missed calls, no new voice mail messages.

Whew. Dodged a bullet this time.

She climbed into her Jeep. The sun was a salmon-colored speck, lightening the sky to a myriad of pinks and orange. When she hit the gravel road running in front of Cord's place, she stopped.

Even after twenty-two years, the magnificence of this land flat out stunned her. This early in the morning the hills were still hidden in darkness, but the promise of dawn burned across the fields and valleys in a splash of pastel colors. The only part AJ had loved about getting up at the crack of nothing to do chores was the sense of accomplishment that she'd managed to help them hold on to the ranch—the place she'd called home—for another day.

Home. She'd never bought into that old saying, "home is where the heart is", mostly because it'd never applied to her.

It wouldn't be easy for her mother to move. Florence Foster had spent more years living on the ranch than her daughter. And AJ felt childish wishing for childish things—for things not to change.

Oddly enough, she accepted things wouldn't change with Cord. His serious nature and need for control never scared her, mostly because she'd experienced the same weight of responsibilities that still hung on his shoulders. He'd always been curtly polite with her, never teasing her mercilessly like Keely's other brothers, so discovering Cord's sense of humor was an unexpected bonus.

Wouldn't do her any good to dwell on all the things she liked about him because that could eat up her entire day.

Since she was already up, she fed Lucy and the other horses and cleaned stalls.

Three hours later Jenn and the kids waved as they left for the day. She and Jenn had debated on keeping the kids at the ranch with Aunt Amy Jo instead of sending them to the summer day camp. But Jenn wanted one normal thing in her children's lives in light of the divorce and their impending move.

AJ dragged into the house. She started a pot of coffee and ran upstairs to shower. As she dressed, she looked longingly at her pristinely made bed, but there'd be no rest for the wicked today.

Three cups of coffee lifted the mental cobwebs and she heard her mother stirring in the front room. "Ma? You ready for breakfast?"

"Just coffee this morning, sweetheart."

AJ set the cup on the tray and perched on the chair by the bed. "A couple of things I need to know before I get started. All the farm equipment is property included in the deed? We don't have to worry about holding an auction or cleaning out the machine shed?"

"No. Carson said they'll deal with it."

"Everything in the attic is boxed. Where should I start next? The cellar?"

Florence shook her head. "Jenn tossed most of that old junk when the propane guy came."

"When was that?"

"Couple months back when I was having problems with the heater again."

"Has the temperature been better in this room? I know you said it was too cold."

"It fluctuates, as usual. The heating problems are one thing I won't miss about this old house." She sighed. "You should start by throwing away a bunch of stuff like the magazines in the middle room upstairs. Your daddy loved 'em but there's no point in keeping 'em."

"Good. Which leads me to my next question. We haven't talked about what to do with the horses. I want to keep Lucy. As far as the rest? I know Macie's dad, Cash Big Crow, is looking for stock. He'd treat them well."

"Tell you what, you take care of that part of this ranch sale business and I'll let you keep the money from the sale."

That was an unexpected surprise. "You sure?"

"Positive." She drained her coffee and AJ brought the pot over for refills. "Thanks. Sorry to be such a pain."

"Mama. You're not a pain."

"Well, I am sorry you're doing all the packing up. I won't be any help and Jenn has packing of her own to do."

"That just means I get first dibs on the cool stuff for my apartment." AJ scrutinized her mother head to toe. "What do you need me to do for you before I get to work? Are you ready for your massage?"

"Later. I'll probably watch some TV." She stared into her cup. "Maybe you should rest since you were out all night."

AJ hated the guilty heat burning her cheeks. "Were you worried?"

"No. I probably wouldn't have known if I hadn't gotten up to use the bathroom and saw your car pulling in at a quarter after five this morning." Florence sighed. "No lecture. You're an adult. Can I ask if you were with a man last night?"

She debated on lying, but she saw no reason to. "Yes, I was."

"Do I know him?"

"Ma!"

"Just curious." Her mom winked. "I'm gonna say *be careful* and let you escape before your face turns any redder, sweetheart."

"I'll be upstairs. If you need anything, just holler."

Later, she hauled a bunch of full garbage bags downstairs. By the third trip she took a breather on the porch steps. It'd be another hot one today—the thermometer read ninety at ten o'clock. She'd finished her second glass of iced tea when her cell phone rang. Caller ID said *MM*.

"Macie McKay, what's up?"

"My breakfast," she grumbled. "Anyway, how are you?"

"Tired."

"Know the feeling. I remember how much work it was being a caretaker and I feel for ya."

AJ couldn't confess the real reason for her tiredness—playing grab ass with Cord till the wee hours. Macie would blab to her husband, Carter, and then all the McKays would know about her and Cord. "So didja call me to lend your support?"

"No. I called because I'm coming to Sundance tomorrow."

"Really? Cool. What time, how long, and all that?"

"Early, we'll be there overnight."

"We, meaning you and Carter?"

"No. Me, Gemma and the twins."

AJ squealed. "Not that it's not awesome you're coming, Mace, but I love love love those darling babies."

"You and everyone else. Channing hasn't been feeling well enough to travel, so she's dying to see Gemma and the babies again. Gemma's a little stir crazy stuck in the house breastfeeding twins every two hours, and I have a building I need to check out."

"A building? For what?"

"Tell you when I get there. In fact, is there any way you can get tomorrow afternoon and tomorrow night off from your caretaking duties? After the business deal, Channing wants a girls' night with the four of us. I guess she's kicking Colby out too."

"Cash isn't coming?"

"No, it's haying season and he'll be working until dark. It'll drive Dad bonkers to be away from his twins for even a day, but between us, I think Gemma's looking for a break from him too."

AJ grinned. Cash Big Crow was all gooey-eyed and awestruck over the newest additions to his family. To hear Macie tell it, because Cash hadn't been around at all during Macie's early years, he was determined to do and learn everything this go around and be a very hands-on daddy.

"I'll talk to my sister and see if I can work something out. If nothing else, maybe one of Mama's friends would like to come over, especially since we're moving and it might be a last chance."

Macie was quiet. "You okay with the McKays buying the Foster ranch, AJ?"

"I don't really have a choice but to slap on a happy face. I won't lie; it's gonna be hard."

"I know, sweets. We'll talk more tomorrow."

Over margaritas, AJ hoped. "Where are you staying?"

"You think Channing would let Gemma stay anywhere besides with her?" Macie laughed. "I'd planned on staying there too, but Carter wants me bunking at Carolyn and Carson's."

"They'll be glad to have you."

"I'll call from Channing's and let you know what time I'll swing by to get you. I'd like to see how your mom is doing before we head out."

Might be ridiculous, but AJ was touched. Macie's thoughtfulness and feisty sweetness were just a couple of reasons why they'd become close friends in the last year. "I'd like that. Mama would too."

"Good. Then when we're alone we can gossip about Keely's latest cowboy on a string and you can tell me exactly how my sexy, gruff brother-in-law deflowered you."

"Macie! How'd you know?"

"I didn't until you just told me." She laughed again. "You're so easy to tease. Oops, Carter's bellering at me, gotta go."

The rest of the morning zipped by. AJ fixed lunch, and settled her mother down for her afternoon nap and a massage. She packed more boxes, pleased by how much she'd accomplished. She'd gone into the garage to find a crowbar, when she heard a vehicle pull up. After stepping outside, she blocked the bright sunlight with her hand and squinted at Cord's 350 diesel.

He climbed out and the truck door slammed.

"Cord? What're you doing here?"

"AJ. My dad asked me to stop by and give Flo some papers."

Disappointment made her shoulders sag. He wasn't here just to see her. "She's sleeping. Since she hasn't been sleeping well, I don't want to wake her."

"I understand."

"You want to leave the papers with a note?"

"How long before she wakes up?"

"Probably an hour."

He frowned. "Huh. Is Jenn around?"

"No. She and the kids are in town. Why?"

"So you're all alone?"

"Yeah. Why does that—"

Cord crushed his mouth to hers and pushed her into the barn.

This was what she wanted. Darkness, heat, need. Cord devouring her. Kissing her like she was everything. His rough hands racing all over her body as if he couldn't decide which part he wanted to touch first.

He ate at her mouth and trailed his teeth down her throat. "Drove me insane when you weren't there this mornin'. Why didn't you wake me?"

"Was I supposed to? I don't know anything about morning after stuff like that. I saw the clock and panicked. You said no overnights and no one knew where I was."

"I wanted you. I woke up wantin' you. Seein' the imprint of your head on the pillow. The room smelled like you. Sunshine. Sex. The scent of your sweet juices was still in my beard. Made me instantly hard, rememberin' tastin' you. Feelin' your hands on me. That naughty mouth suckin' me dry. I've spent all goddamn day hard as a posthole digger."

"Cord—"

"Right now, AJ. I wanna pin you against the wall and fuck you hard enough to rattle the stalls. Then I want to bend you over the railin' and take you from behind, sinkin' my teeth into that spot at the base of your neck that makes you scream my name."

AJ swallowed. "Um. Let's start with just one and work our way down the wish list, okay?"

Cord slanted his mouth over hers. Somehow he lifted her and wrapped her legs around his waist, all while kissing her, all while walking backward.

She opened her eyes. They stopped outside the tack room.

After setting her on her feet, he grabbed her wrists and held them above her head. "I'm tyin' your hands. I can do whatever I want and you hafta hang there and take it like a good girl."

"But—" *Crap.*

His dark blue eyes narrowed. "That's one." He looped her wrists with baling twine and fastened it through a rope pulley above her head, which was used for loading bales.

Cord's show of domination made the inside of her thighs moist, her sex ached for the attention of his fingers or his mouth or his cock.

He ripped open her blouse and unhooked her bra. Stripped off her shorts and underwear. He leisurely traced the contours of her body from the valley of her breasts straight down to her slit. Although his mouth never touched her, his hot breath drifted against her damp skin. "You like this. My sweet angel has a devilish streak, huh?"

"Yeah."

"Good to know. 'Cause you're dealin' with the devil himself right now, baby doll."

Cord unbuckled his belt. "Such a pretty picture you make." He released the zipper on his jeans a tine at a time.

The sound of his buckle jingling as he worked his jeans down his thighs drove her wild. No other noises existed. Nothing existed but this man and her burning need for him. Her nipples were hard as cherry pits and her whole body quaked. "Please."

"Please what?"

"Please touch me."

"No."

"But—" Double crap.

"That's two. And trust me, I am keepin' track." Cord fisted his hand around his cock and stroked himself with more force than she'd dared try.

She rubbed her thighs together, searching for any kind of friction. "It doesn't hurt when you pull hard like that?"

He grinned. "Nope. You are such a curious little kitty-cat. Have you thought about jackin' me off?"

Yes. "No."

"Liar. I jacked off last night while I was havin' you as my midnight snack."

"You did?"

"Yep. You weren't next to me this mornin' when I woke up with a dick hard enough to break concrete, so I had to whack off right there on the sheets that smelled like you."

Something shifted between them—maybe the balance of power, maybe a sense of inevitability.

AJ locked her eyes to his. "Enough teasing. Either get over here and fuck me or let me go."

"Mmm. This kitty-cat has claws?"

"This *pussy* has an itch and if you ain't up for scratching it right now, Cord McKay—"

He lifted her, pressed her knees wide against the partition, and slid into her in one fast stroke.

"Yes. Oh *yes.*"

Cord buried his face in her neck, withdrew and plunged in again. And again. He changed the angle by bending his knees, and clamped his fingers on her butt, pistoning his hips fast as a jackhammer.

AJ twisted her body, trying to grind into his pelvis, wishing she had the use of her hands.

"Hold still," he growled.

"But I need—"

"That's three. What you need is to not get slivers in this sassy ass. We are doin' this the way *I* want, AJ."

"Please."

He never moved his head, never missed a stroke when he said, "No."

She circled her legs around his waist and jerked him closer. Sweat trickled between her breasts. The hair on the back of her neck lifted. Every inch of her skin tingled. All that energy shot straight to her core and the orgasm blindsided her.

"Oh-man-oh-man-oh-man."

Colt whispered against her throat, "Harder, baby doll, bear down on me harder. That's good." His climax burst with enough force she felt her insides bathed with his heat.

Her womb kept contracting to keep all that seed inside. Each throb and pulse was longer than the last and she whimpered.

"Ssh." His mouth found hers. A gentle brush of his lips as he looked into her eyes. While he kissed her, his hips kept bumping in tiny increments. Not fast or slow. Steady until the spasms ended. With the last movement he withdrew from her completely and set her on her feet.

Wetness gushed out. She wondered if the twine wasn't holding her up if she'd even be able to stand.

Cord stepped back and yanked up his jeans. "Like I said earlier. I was needin' you bad, AJ."

Not missing her, needing her. "Untie me. I have to get cleaned up before I go in the house."

Zipped and buckled, he ignored her request and demanded, "There any baby wipes in here?"

She frowned. "Why would we have those?"

"Most places have them around for one reason or another."

"I don't know. Might be some in the tack room. Can't you let me loose before you go looking?"

Cord's gaze traveled the length of the rope. "Your arms hurt?"

"Not bad."

"Then you can wait until I find somethin' to clean you up."

"But—"

"That's four."

Feeling surly, she snapped, "Why don't we get it up to an even ten? *But but but but but but.*"

"Smarty. Lord. I am gonna enjoy the feel of my hand on those soft cheeks. In case you were curious, kitty-cat, that means ten *each side*, not ten total."

She averted her eyes to the hay-strewn ground.

"What's wrong? Does that scare you?"

"Never had a spanking. Not as a kid, definitely not as an adult."

"Never was a bad girl?"

"No. I followed the rules and did what I was told."

"Just like me."

She snorted. "You were the bad boy of the county, or so I heard."

"Maybe you heard wrong. Anyway, we're just gettin' into all sortsa new things, ain't we?" Cord grinned cheekily. "Sit tight. Or stand tight. I'll be right back."

"Ha ha, McKay. I'd like to see how you'd react if the tables were turned."

He poked his head back around. "You'd like to tie me up? Or just whup my ass?"

"Both. Let me down."

"After you threatened me? No way." He cracked open the pop-top on a plastic cylinder and pulled out a couple of sheets. "These'll work." Cord gently wiped the inside of her thighs.

AJ gasped, "That's cold."

"Almost done." Cord shook the hay from her panties and

shorts, helping her get redressed. Then he released the pulley, loosening the rope and freed her hands from the twine. Before he allowed her to rub her wrists, he checked them. "Does it hurt?"

"Not much."

"Good." He gave each ligature mark a quick kiss. "I'll get the papers and you can pass 'em to Flo when she wakes up."

"You aren't gonna wait around?"

A sheepish look crossed his face and she knew he'd used the papers as an excuse to see her. She was absurdly pleased.

"Nah." He brushed the dust off his hat and put it back on before he headed outside. She followed.

After she had the manila envelope in her hand, he said, "Don't be late tonight. Seventeen penalties is plenty to get me started," before his rig took off in a cloud of dust.

Chapter Nineteen

AJ arrived at Cord's house early evening to find a note taped to the door.

Strip. Lock the door. Sit by the fireplace, put on the blindfold and wait. No talking.

Oh man. What did he have in store for her?

She'd anticipated he'd want her naked as soon as possible, so she'd worn a summer sun dress—easy on, easy off, no bra, no panties. After she was naked, she paraded into the living room. The coffee table had been shoved against the far wall, leaving the big area rug empty.

The sitting area directly in front of the fireplace grate was constructed of slabs of slate. Despite the hot day, that dark rock never heated, so she knew it'd be like sitting on a block of ice on her bare ass. Still, she did it and slipped the neckerchief over her eyes.

While AJ waited in absolute silence, she listened to the sounds of the house. The chimes on the porch. The wind rattling the rafters. The whir of the ceiling fan. The hum of the refrigerator. In the distance she heard the horses neighing and the answering low moos of the cattle.

She inhaled slowly and deeply to counteract her racing heart. AJ smelled bacon and laundry soap and Windex and sage. And Cord.

Then she heard his bare feet shuffling across the wood floor. Muffled by the rug. Closer. Closer. She swallowed hard when the footsteps stopped.

"Your penalties for tonight include no talkin' unless I say so. Which also means you don't get to argue with me. So let's get started right away. Hold out your right hand."

She did. A drop of something landed on her finger.

"Rub your fingertips together."

She smeared the slickness, like oil or K-Y, around the pad of her thumb and index finger.

"Kick your heels out but make sure you're still balanced on the hearth. I wanna see your pussy."

A strange feeling unfurled as she did as instructed, even as her cheeks burned: one set with cold, one with heat.

"Touch yourself. Show me how you make yourself come."

Her mouth opened to protest and she remembered the no talking rule.

"You're learnin'. Move them fingers down to that juicy pink pussy."

AJ tentatively stroked from her clit down a few times, worried what would happen if she couldn't come on his command.

"Just you and me here, baby doll. Don't be embarrassed. Tease me. Make me wish it was my fingers gettin' you off. Give me a show that'll make my dick harder."

With his encouragement, she lost some of her fear and pushed her middle finger into her pussy. She pumped that long digit in and out, getting it good and wet, using the bony section of her thumb to grind into her clit. When her finger was slick enough, she slid it up to her clit and rubbed. Lord that felt good, even when she did it to herself.

"So sexy. Keep goin'."

Knowing he watched her was a complete turn on. She rubbed directly on that little nub and thought of Cord stroking his cock at the same time. Not allowing himself to come until she did. AJ bit her lip. So close. She tweaked her nipple hard with her free hand while she rubbed short strokes on her clit and that did it. She came with a low moan.

Soon as the orgasm ended, she felt Cord in front of her. He plucked up her right hand to suck the juices from her fingers and her belly swooped.

"Jesus, that was hot as hell, my porn-star rodeo queen." He helped her to her feet and carefully led her to the rug, urging her to lay on her back. "My turn." Cold oil dripped between her breasts.

She gasped.

"Been wantin' to do this since the first time I got my hands on these." Cord straddled her waist and held the mounds together with his hands as he slid his warm cock in the deep valley of her cleavage. He hissed and began to thrust. "Between how goddamn good this feels and watchin' you touch yourself, I ain't gonna last long at all."

AJ wished she wasn't blindfolded so she could see his face. Yet she already knew the rhythm of his body. He was frantic, about to blow. When he gave four short thrusts, she felt his balls draw up off her belly.

Cord groaned and squeezed her breasts tightly as liquid warmth seeped out the end of his cock onto her chest.

She didn't realize she'd been holding her breath until he wasn't sitting on her ribcage. AJ expelled a quiet sigh.

He used a soft cloth to wipe her down. His rough-skinned hands sweetly caressed her arms and legs. Callused fingertips traced the line of her jaw and throat, then her collarbones.

Just his hands, not his mouth. Why hadn't he kissed her yet?

"I'm bettin' that wasn't your favorite position."

She shook her head.

"I've got a couple of other ideas for tonight. You need to be on the fireplace for the next one." He helped her up and her butt met cold stone again. "Hang tight."

And she was tired of not talking. "For what?"

Immediately Cord's breath burned her ear. "You don't get to ask questions. And that one just earned you another penalty, baby doll. Stay put and stay quiet."

As his footsteps faded she debated on taking off the blindfold when a thought occurred to her. Maybe withholding kisses was her penalty. If that was the case, she'd sit here like a lump all night because she absolutely craved the man's kisses.

Her heart thudded when she heard him return.

"Arrange yourself like you were before."

AJ put her hands behind her and spread her legs open.

"Good. Stay like that. No touchin' me unless I say so."

Cord's lips brushed hers so softly she whimpered. He teased her for an eternity with his mouth and breath and little bites and flicks of his tongue until she was wet and lightheaded from the sensual onslaught.

"Open your mouth."

Something long, cold, sweet and decidedly phallic brushed her top and bottom lip and tongue before Cord's mouth devoured hers in a kiss so hot her body went up in flames.

Which would explain why the Popsicle melted so quickly when he placed it on her nipples.

He swallowed her scream as he circled the icy tip around and around those rigid twin peaks. Then his mouth was licking the sticky sweetness from her left breast as he traced the frozen treat down the center of her body. Past her belly button, down her pubic bone, making a couple of tiny circles over her clit—surely he wasn't planning on—and he pushed the icy pop inside.

"Omigod!"

"That's another one, AJ." Cord switched to her right nipple and suckled while twirling the ice pop inside her clenching sex.

Her pussy was on fire. It quickly became numb as Cord fucked her with the Popsicle. She heard drips—a combination of her flowing juices and the melting ice splatting on the floor beneath her, and she moaned at the eroticism bombarding her from every angle.

Darkness. His warm tongue bathing the very tips of her nipples. The sucking noise of the Popsicle and the sweet orange scent. The hard stone digging into her butt. The ache in her arms from keeping herself upright. The sound of Cord's broken breaths and the feel of his goatee gliding across her tingling skin.

The Popsicle disappeared and was replaced with Cord's mouth. His hot tongue burrowed into her cold pussy and she screamed.

He slurped and sucked, eating at her with finesse, then gluttony. His mouth covered her mound completely as his teeth and tongue and lips demanded her total surrender.

She gave it.

AJ wailed as the orgasm thundered through her, every pulse point in her body was synchronized to the flicking of his tongue. Before she could catch her breath, Cord lifted her and reversed their positions. He sat on the hearth and stretched her over his lap.

"Now that you've been rewarded, you will take your punishment like a good girl." *Smack smack*—he landed a firm blow on each cheek.

She yelped at the sting of pain, which felt unbearably hot against the coldness of her butt cheeks.

"That's one. Not a sound, AJ. Each sound earns another penalty."

Whack whack.

"But—"

Two more spanks, harder than the first ones. "That's another. I ain't kiddin'. Hold still."

Whack whack.

AJ bit her lip and braced herself. She hung upside down, naked, across a man's lap as he peppered her ass with swats. Why wasn't she humiliated? Why wasn't she running away?

Because she knew it turned Cord on to epic levels. He was strung tight with exhilaration and heady with sexual power. He never hit her hard enough to hurt, just enough so there was no doubt who was in charge.

God. Was Cord McKay *ever* in charge.

Whack whack.

At some point around spank nineteen, AJ wasn't dreading that connection of his big hand to her ass; she anticipated it. She craved it. So much to the point she moaned. Loudly. Twice.

"That earned you two more, baby doll."

Whack whack.

"This ass is beautiful, all pink and white." *Whack whack.* "Warmed up from bein' on that cold hearth."

"Warm. It feels hot and—"

Whack whack whack whack. He hissed, "I can keep goin' all night. I'm findin' I like this way more than I ever imagined. *Way* more."

Whack whack. His hands smoothed over the heated mounds, down between her legs. He wormed two fingers inside her pussy.

"You're soppin' wet. This little spankin' stopped bein' a punishment, didn't it?"

She didn't answer.

Whack whack. "Answer me."

"Yes! I thought about talking the whole time just so you'd keep doing it—"

"Enough!" Cord snarled and rolled her so she was in his arms. Holding her like a baby, he walked them to the rug. He set her on her feet, keeping her back to his chest. His heavy, harsh breathing stirred her hair. "On your hands and knees. Now."

AJ dropped to the rug, once again that slight edge of fear—that feeling of the unknown heightened her excitement.

Cord said, "Move your knees out wider."

She felt the rug scraping her kneecaps as she followed his command and he knelt behind her.

Then his tongue bathed the burning marks on each cheek. She whimpered when that wicked tongue traced the crack of her ass down to her tailbone and back up.

The blunt head of his cock connected with her pussy briefly before Cord impaled it in one hard stroke.

"Cord—"

He smacked her ass twice. He didn't speak. He just gripped her hips and methodically fucked her. Each stroke equal. No variation. Slow and shallow.

Sweat poured from her. From him. Her body shook. His body shook. She couldn't stand it because it felt so damn good, he was purposely holding them both off from orgasm as long as possible. AJ knew if he deepened or lengthened the thrusts it'd send them both soaring.

Finally he said gruffly, "I'm too far gone to be gentle, baby doll."

Cord increased his pace to that of a runaway jackhammer, she splintered into a thousand shards. So did he.

When he removed the blindfold would she see the crown of her head lying on the rug? The man had positively blown her top.

Cord grunted. He stretched his chest to her sweaty back, caging her in his arms. He sank his teeth into her nape, sending goose bumps in a wave across her skin.

She sighed in complete contentment.

"Enough? Or do you wanna go for a couple more and see if you end up in the penalty box?"

"What's the penalty box?"

He whispered, "The hot tub."

Ooh. That could be interesting. "But—"

"That's one," he warned.

"I really don't think it's fair you get to—"

"That's ten, wanna keep goin'?"

AJ stayed quiet.

Then Cord helped her to her feet. He removed the blindfold and kissed her with exquisite tenderness.

"Are we done playing games?"

"I figured we were, why?"

AJ casually murmured, "Have I ever told you how long I can hold my breath under water?"

Stunned silence.

"But if we're done..." She shrugged and spun on her heel.

Cord scooped her up and headed for the hot tub on the deck. "Oh we ain't done, baby doll, not by half." He bit her earlobe. "And that's another five."

Chapter Twenty

The next afternoon they were on the road headed toward Sundance in Macie McKay's car, when Macie commented, "Your mom looks good, AJ. Better than I expected."

"Thanks, Macie. It was sweet of you to make her lunch. Fancier than she gets from me, that's for sure."

Macie waved her off. "All ingredients you had on hand, no biggie. How long's it take to get to town again?"

"Thirty minutes. So, what's the big secret? What are you looking at in Sundance?"

"Dewey's Delish Dish in the Sandstone building."

AJ turned slightly to look at Macie. "You quitting the Last Chance Diner?"

"God no. I swear Velma would hunt me down and kill me. We're expanding. Velma's interested in taking over Dewey's place. He's getting ready to retire, he's got no one to pass it down to, but he doesn't want to leave Sundance without a family style restaurant. I'm here to check it out and see how much remodeling we'd have to do before we make a commitment or whether we'd be better off looking for a different location."

"Those other storefronts are empty, which is sad because it is a cool building right in the middle of everything in town."

"That's why I hope we can salvage Dewey's place."

AJ focused her attention on the landscape outside her car window. How many more times would she make this familiar trek from her house into town? Twenty? Thirty?

"AJ? You okay?"

"I don't know. I'm trying to be mature about the ranch sale, because I understand I can't run the place from Denver."

"But?"

That single word made her think of Cord and the wicked penalties she'd earned last night. A shiver worked down her spine despite the unrelenting heat. "Part of me wants to throw a weeping tantrum about losing my home." AJ sighed. "Do I sound like I'm about four?"

"Not at all. I never had a home up until the last year, so I have nothing to judge it by."

"Is it a home because of Carter?"

"Yeah, that 'home is where the heart is' saying is true, but Gemma and Dad's ranch feels like my physical home now."

"Does Carter feel the same? Isn't he missing the McKay place?"

Macie was quiet for a little too long.

"What?"

"If I tell you something, you have to swear not to tell anyone, AJ." Macie shot her a glance. "Especially not Keely."

"I swear."

"I'm pregnant."

AJ's jaw dropped. "Get out. You guys haven't even been married a year."

"It wasn't planned, but it wasn't unplanned."

"That's cryptic."

"After Dad and Gemma had the babies, Carter and I realized we wanted to have our kids while we were young. Plus, we want them to be raised around family—his and mine. Ky's already four. Channing is pregnant, so our baby will have instant cousins and playmates. I didn't have family growing up. Carter did. He says the best part of his life is that connection. Dad and I are figuring that out." She smiled. "We are really excited about having a baby, but I promised Carter to let *him* tell his family the news."

"Can I squeal now?"

Macie nodded.

After AJ did a happy dance in her seat, she demanded,

"How far along are you?"

"Barely. Like three weeks. Carter insisted on one of those early pregnancy tests, so we've known since I was five days pregnant. One of the other reasons we wanted to wait to tell anyone was because Channing just announced her pregnancy."

"Yeah, but she's almost four months along."

"Timing is everything in the McKay family."

"Why would you be adding more work to your schedule with a baby coming?"

"I would oversee the one in Sundance, not run it. Remember my roommate Kat? She'd run it fulltime."

"If you're not quitting the diner that means you'll be traveling. Won't Carter demand to be with you all the time now that you're preggers?" AJ whirled in her seat. "That's it, isn't it? Are you guys moving back here?"

"Yes...and no. We'll be living here half the time and half the time at the Bar 9. Carter misses the McKay ranch and his brothers. And with all that's going on with Colt, I know Colby and Cord would appreciate his help."

"Where would you live? Someplace on the ranch?"

Macie squirmed.

Then AJ knew. "You'll be living in my house, won't you?"

"Yeah. Are you upset?"

During the moments she'd allowed herself to think about it, she'd wondered what'd happen to their home. Colby and Channing owned a gorgeous place a couple of miles from Carson and Carolyn's homeplace. Cord didn't need a house. Cam was in Iraq, Keely in Denver, Colt shared the old Andrews place with his McKay cousins. Her biggest fear had been the house she'd loved and grown up in would be turned into a den of iniquity like the infamous Boars Nest.

"AJ? Say something."

"I don't know what to say. When was this decided?"

"Colby and Carter had been kicking around an idea of putting a trailer up the road from your place, when Carson told us about them buying the Foster ranch. Cord suggested it'd be perfect for us with the extra large barn Carter can use as a permanent studio. And it's close enough to Cord's place that he could check on it when we were at the Bar 9.

"In fact, when Cord called us to tell us about Colt, he asked me to talk to you about it first, since we're friends." Macie's hazel eyes were filled with concern. "We'll still be friends, right, AJ? I can't stand the thought that this would hurt you."

"Hurting me is inevitable, you heard my mixed feelings about moving."

AJ stared out the window and Macie let her.

"Nothing would make Mama happier than knowing the house was filled with a happy family. Why didn't Cord tell me?"

"I honestly don't know."

Her cynical side thought Cord worried the news would lessen his chances of getting laid. But Cord probably believed hearing the news from Macie would be easier. She might've been resentful to the whole McKay family if it'd come from any of them—even Keely. Cord's intuitive side surprised her. Lots of things about him surprised her.

The car stopped in front of the Sandstone Building. "We're here."

"So tell me the truth, Macie McKay, were you mentally redecorating my house while we were eating lunch?"

"No." Macie reached over and whapped her on the knee. "Being around my sis-in-law has made you a real smartypants, Amy Jo Foster."

AJ laughed and it didn't feel as forced as she'd imagined.

The lunch rush at Dewey's was over. AJ trailed behind Macie as Dewey gave her the nickel tour. As many times as she'd been in, she hadn't noticed the details that made the interior unique until Dewey pointed them out to Macie.

When they started discussing ventilation systems in the kitchen, AJ excused herself and loitered outside the empty storefront next to the diner.

A woman riding a motorcycle parked next to Macie's Escape. A tattooed and pierced woman with short, jet black hair, the ends of which were dyed bright pink. She bounded up the steps, the jangling of the keys in her hand rivaled the jangling of the rings in her nose, ears, lip and eyebrow. She stopped when she caught sight of AJ lurking by the door and looked up.

Double whoa. The woman was absolutely stunning. Her face was sharp angles—razor blade cheekbones, a square jawline. Her features were softened by pouty lips the envy of Angelina Jolie.

The woman didn't smile. "Can I get you to move please? That door opens out, which is the first thing I'm going to change."

AJ's ears perked up and she shuffled aside. "Change?"

"My sister and I are opening up a shop here once we can get the changes approved from the landlord."

"Landlord? Doesn't Dewey own this building?"

"It'd be easier if he did. He sold it last year. Any changes have to get approval from this mysterious owner." The woman's vivid blue gaze narrowed. "Why?"

"Because Dewey neglected to tell my friend that. She's talking to him about taking over his restaurant."

Blue eyes finally smiled. "Dewey is a miscreant. Let's crash their meeting and see how old Dewey reacts."

AJ led the way. Dewey blinked rapidly when he saw the woman behind her.

"Now, Dewey, please tell me you aren't misleading this lady? She does know you don't actually own this building anymore?"

Silence.

Macie said, "Dewey, Velma is gonna be majorly pissed if that's true. And you know what she's like when she gets a burr under her saddle."

"B-b-but it's not what you think. The owner gave me full authority to turn over the restaurant to you, Mrs. McKay. You still have to submit your remodeling plans, but he already gave the go-ahead to proceed, if you're interested."

"Who the hell owns this building?"

"I'd say that I can't say, but the truth is I doan know. All our communication is done through email. I send my rent checks to a P.O. Box in Denver." Dewey swallowed nervously. "Never talked to a live person, it's some sort of architectural firm specializin' in historic Western preservation."

The blue-eyed woman demanded, "I still haven't received approval on my proposed changes and I signed the goddamn lease a month ago."

"Maybe because you're puttin' in a tattoo parlor, Ms. Ellison? Not the same as upgradin' a restaurant."

AJ whirled around. "A tattoo parlor? In Sundance? That is so cool!"

"Yeah," Macie chimed in, "I'd like to hear what you've planned for the space, since it appears we'll be neighbors." Macie thrust out her hand. "Macie McKay. This is AJ Foster."

"India Ellison. Come on over and take a walk on the wild side." India winked. "I'm prepared to be the new resident bad girl who leads this sleepy Wyoming town into the temptations of body art."

Macie filled India in on her tentative plans for the restaurant while AJ explored the space, which'd been a hair salon in a former life. A couple other eclectic businesses had tried to make a go of it, but none succeeded.

"Only half is for tattoos and piercing. We'll use the front half as a salesroom for the products my sister manufactures."

"What's she make?"

"Natural skin and hair care products made in Weston County. Ever heard of Sky Blue?"

"I have," AJ said. "But you can't find it here. You have to drive to DeWitt's Pharmacy in Moorcroft to get it."

"Which is why Sky wants to expand to Sundance. We both fell in love with this building, plus the third floor spans the entire length. I'm waiting for approval on changes to make it an apartment for when I move here permanently."

"Where do you live now?"

"Denver." India sighed. "So, help me out, guys. I'm looking for a reputable construction company to do all the remodel work if I ever get approval. You're local. You won't bullshit me."

Macie said, "West Construction. My husband's cousins Remy and Chet own it. Not to be biased, but they do outstanding work. We'd planned on using them for the diner remodel and ah...a house remodel."

AJ ignored the house remodel portion of the comment and

added, “They built a couple of beautiful homes for the McKays. I’m not related to them, so I can honestly say they’re the best around.”

“Cool. Do you have their number?”

While Macie and India chatted, AJ wandered over to another door. “Hey, India, mind if I look in here?”

“Go ahead.”

“Will this be part of India’s Ink and Sky Blue?”

“No. That’s a connecting hallway to the other store and the access to the upstairs.”

AJ brushed aside cobwebs and stopped in front of another door. She pushed it open and ventured inside. Dusty, dirty and the windows were covered with soapy grime that filtered out most light. The space was identical in size to India’s place, a long narrow single room with high ceilings, accented with crown molding at the top and parquet floor beneath her feet. With a little elbow grease and a couple of well-placed walls, this would make a perfect massage studio. And it was close to home.

Her excitement lasted about ten seconds. She realized when she finished school she wouldn’t have a home around here. Not an insurmountable problem if Keely had planned to come back. They could rent a trailer, split the rent and the workload.

But AJ was realistic. Massages would be a hard sell in Crook County. It’d take a few months to build up a clientele and a couple years to make enough money to earn a living. Whereas in a bigger city she’d start making money immediately. After one last regretful look, she returned to Macie and India.

“This is karma or something,” Macie said. “Did you know my middle name is Blue? And my mother considered naming me India?”

“Seriously?”

Macie nodded. “India the Indian. My mom was slightly nuts.”

India whirled on AJ. “If you tell me you have a monarch butterfly tattooed above your butt crack, I’ll freak out.”

“Nope. Sorry. No tattoos.”

India smiled slyly. “We’ll see about changing that tattoo

virgin status sometime soon."

Macie's grin rivaled India's. "Losing one's virginity is always a good thing. Nice meeting you, India. Keep in touch. If all goes according to plan, we'll start the remodel in about four weeks."

On the way back, AJ managed to keep Macie talking about Carter's upcoming art show, the horses Cash expressed an interest in, and not the situation between her and Cord McKay.

"Do you mind if we stop at Carolyn and Carson's house first before I take you home? I'm feeling a little woozy all of a sudden."

"No problem." It drove home the point how intertwined her life was with the McKays' when she noticed Cord's truck parked out front at his folks' house.

Her stomach pitched. Be hard to act normal around him after last night.

Carolyn McKay was in her usual spot in the kitchen. She beamed at Macie. "Hey, sweetie, how'd it go?"

"Great. But I actually feel nauseous from the excitement. Do you mind if I lay down before supper?"

"No, go ahead. Can I get you anything?"

Macie shook her head and made a mad dash for the bathroom.

Carolyn's worry lines faded when she saw AJ. "How are you?"

"Good. Any problems with the lawyer today?"

"Nope. Once the money is squared away and Florence pens her signature to the deed, you and your mother are officially squatters on McKay land."

AJ's face fell.

"Oh, honey. I was kidding."

"Nice goin', Ma," Cord said dryly. "Got salt in your hand, wanna throw that in her eye too?"

"I need to get going." AJ purposely avoided the word "home". She frowned. "Shoot. I don't have a car."

"I'll take you. I'm headed that way." Cord pecked his mother's forehead. "Behave. No pesterin' Macie about you-know-what."

"Like I have a choice. Carter made me promise." Carolyn winked at her. "Have fun at your girls' night. Call if you need a designated driver, but I believe you'll be the only one drinkin'."

She and Cord didn't speak at all until they were in the truck and a mile down the road. "Macie told me she and Carter will be living in my old house."

"You okay with that?"

No. "I guess. Thanks for suggesting Macie tell me." She looked out the window. "So are the McKays officially land barons? Buying up everything in Crook and Weston County?"

Cord didn't answer.

"Sorry. It's just hard."

He slowed down at the next pullout and parked. "C'mere."

AJ buried her face against his chest. He didn't say a word; he just held her.

After a while, he said, "I wanna be with you like this, dust devils swirlin' around us in the late afternoon heat. Just us, sneakin' some alone time. What do you say?"

She nodded.

Cord slipped out and climbed back in the passenger's side, pulling her on his lap. "Let me love you up. You look a little lost."

I am. Oh, she'd like it if he loved her, but she accepted the only type of love Cord could offer her was physical.

He kissed her softly, sweetly, running his rough hands up her spine beneath her damp shirt. The languorous kiss seemed endless. Cord seemed equally content just to touch her. He eased away from her mouth and whispered, "Lord, I'm gettin' addicted to your kisses, AJ. I feel plain, damn drugged when you're kissin' me. I feel plain, damn lost myself when you ain't around." Then he dove in for another thorough taste of her mouth.

When his erection twitched, she fumbled for his belt. "Pants off, cowboy."

"Hang on." He lowered the bench seat back. "Scoot to the middle for a sec." He shimmied his jeans down his legs. "Now you. Take them britches completely off."

AJ kicked her sandals to the floorboard.

"And the shirt and bra."

"If my shirt comes off, then so does yours."

He grabbed the hem and yanked. "Now come here, cowgirl up and show me how good you can ride."

Bracing her hands on the sculpted muscle and hardness of his chest, she straddled his pelvis and began to lower down.

His hand curled around her hips. "Slow. I wanna see your body takin' me in. Oh yeah, that's so goddamn sexy. Bring those pretty, tasty nipples to my mouth." Immediately Cord expelled a groan and began to lick and suck, not in his usual, forceful way, but with as much languor as he'd kissed her mouth.

Witnessing the sheer joy on his face as he suckled, feeling him gliding deep—touched something inside her. Every rapid inhalation of the air in the cab filled her lungs with the scent of him. Of them. Of dust, hot sage, wool seat covers, sunshine and home. A bead of moisture zigzagged down her chest and Cord lapped at it, following the wet line back to the source behind her ear.

He whispered, "Need it faster, baby doll. Let's move from a canter to a trot."

She rocked her hips more briskly, gripping the headrest above Cord's head. Each downstroke ground her clit against his pelvic bone and she moaned in complete abandon.

"Such sexy noises. Arch back. I wanna watch your face as I make you come."

Cord cupped her breasts and squeezed, latching on to the right tip as his thumb scraped across the left.

The swirling sensation in her groin gathered momentum and the next wave catapulted AJ over the edge. She closed her eyes, losing her sanity as the pulses in her nipples synchronized to the deep pulses inside her.

He rolled his pelvis, his hands clamped her ass and he thrust hard three times. Cord hid his face in her hair, his groan a husky rasp of pleasure.

They stayed plastered together until their breathing evened out. "You fit me so damn good. Maybe we could just nap like this for a while."

"Last time we napped together, I woke up at five a.m. I don't particularly want old Sheriff Comas finding us naked. Old guy might have a heart attack."

"True. And I do have chores to finish." His mouth grazed the inside of her arm. "I'm gonna miss you tonight."

She peeled her body from his. "Is that what this was about? Needed a little nookie to get through the lonely night, Cord?"

"No. That *nookie* wasn't because I needed TLC, AJ, it was because you needed it."

Her eyes swam with tears.

"Hey now. None of that." Cord soothed her, raining soft kisses on her face and gentle caresses on her body.

Finally he lifted her off his softened cock. He yanked his jeans back up, zipped and buckled.

While he left the cab to climb back into the driver's seat, AJ grabbed her capris, bra and shirt and dressed.

How had Cord known her mood? Known exactly that she'd needed tenderness and understanding?

"Baby doll, you okay?"

"Yeah. Have you heard from Colt?"

"Dad has him workin' someplace else. Don't know where. I do know what Ma and Aunt Kimi found at the Boars Nest made 'em madder than wet hens: excessive empty condom wrappers and liquor bottles. They said it would've been easier to set fire to the house than to clean it."

Cord turned into the driveway leading to her home. "First Ma sent Dag back to Uncle Harland's. Then she left an angry message on Colt's cell. Colt blew a gasket, railin' about invasion of privacy and so forth. It was another ugly scene and now Dad's pissed 'cause Colt made Ma cry. Probably a good thing Carter didn't come with Macie."

"Why, because you think Carter's a Mama's boy and her crying would piss him off?"

"No. Carter would try to reason with Colt first. Then he'd use his fists. When Colby catches wind that Colt beat on another brother, hurt Ma and pissed Dad off, well, I ain't sure Colby wouldn't kill Colt outright."

"I'm sorry. It's a bad situation."

"I have a feelin' it'll get worse before it gets better."

AJ did too. She opened the cab door. "Thanks for the ride."

"What? No goodbye kiss?"

"We're in public, remember?"

Cord scowled. "Yeah. Be careful tonight."

"Of what? The thing I'm most in danger from is being barfed on either by the babies or the mothers-to-be."

"She told you?"

She blinked innocently. "Who told me what?"

"Macie. She told you she's pregnant?"

AJ gaped at him. "You know?"

"Carter can't keep his mouth shut to save his life. Macie should've made him the last person to know."

"Hard to do when he's the father."

"I imagine that boy is struttin' around like a damn peacock." He smiled wistfully. "I remember I did."

"I'm excited for them. I can't wait until I get the all clear to tell Mama. She'll be happy to hear this house will be filled with kids again."

"Listen, AJ about that—"

"Have a good night."

AJ bounded up the steps without looking back.

Chapter Twenty-one

"I still can't believe you had a baby before I did," Channing said.

"Two babies." Gemma pointed at Channing's belly. "And unless you're growing a pair, you'll have to go through the whole pregnancy thing again to catch me."

"I can't wait. Look at this sweet little face. What wondrous things babies are." Channing cuddled Ryder close and smiled at him. "He is beautiful. Perfect everything. So much hair. Such a mellow disposition. Definitely takes after Cash, not you, Gem."

Just then Ella wailed.

Macie grinned and handed Ella to Gemma. "That's Mama's rowdy girl. Feeding time for my loud sis."

"Chan, bring Ryder after I get Ella settled, willya? He'll smell food the second my milk lets down."

"Do I have to? He looks so comfy. I think he's fine," she cooed, kissing his forehead, "aren't you darlin' boy?"

"You'll see."

AJ watched the scene unfold with complete fascination. Her sister had opted not to breastfeed, so this whole "letting it all hang out" philosophy with bare breasts, well—bared and literally hanging out—had thrown her for a loop.

Gemma clutched Ella like a football on her left side, propping Ella on a pillow and lifting her shirt. Ella's dark head swiveled toward the direction of the scent of milk. Gemma brought Ella closer so that rosebud mouth could latch onto the nipple. Gemma stroked Ella's hair and murmured, "You'd think you hadn't eaten in hours, baby girl."

Ryder began to fuss. Channing sighed. “I tried to give you a break. But this little guy knows what he wants.” Channing nestled Ryder on Gemma’s right side and he started sucking with happy baby grunts.

“I need a drink,” AJ muttered.

“Oh, sorry, I’ll get you a beer.”

“Sit, Channing. I’ll grab one.”

AJ sipped and studied the front of Colby and Channing’s refrigerator, covered in family pictures and Ky’s artwork. Ky had drawn a picture of the entire McKay clan on a long sheet of white paper. Grandma and Grandpa were prominent on the right side. Colby and Channing were at the top with their arms around each other. Colt was lying down in the lower right corner. A tiny image of Cameron holding a rifle was crayoned below Colt, meant to show that Uncle Cam was far away in Iraq. Keely cracking a bullwhip, wearing a sparkly belt and a big grin. The smaller mirror images of Kane and Kade were below her. Carter and Macie holding hands at the bottom of the page on the left. And dead center was Cord McKay, his visage bigger than all the others.

On Cord’s right side, a smaller identical likeness of him, aka Ky, beaming up at his dad. She squinted. Yep. A crude red cape fluttered behind the dynamic duo. The boy had a serious case of hero worship.

She knew the feeling.

AJ drank half the beer before returning to the living room.

Ten minutes of baby chatter continued.

Macie said, “Much as I love talking about my new brother and sister, and the impending new McKay boy baby, let’s talk about something else. I’m pretty sure AJ is bored to tears.”

“Let’s talk about sex.” Channing addressed the comment to Gemma. “When will we get back to our normal sex life? Because it’s been so hit and miss for us for the last two months.”

AJ shot a quick glance at Macie, who suddenly had a panicked look on her face.

“In another couple of weeks, things should be back to normal. At least until the last month. I didn’t want Cash to touch me at all. I was big as a house, I wasn’t sleeping and I had to pee every five minutes. I felt about as sexy as an old cow."

"So the six week ban on sex after the birth? How on earth did you make it through that?"

"I went to the doctor two weeks ago and she gave us the go ahead. I adore my husband. I especially adore sex with my husband. I can't wait to make it up to him when we have more than five minutes before one of the babies needs something. But right now if I had the choice between sex and sleep? Sleep wins."

Channing gasped, "No."

"Yes."

Macie looked positively ill.

AJ changed the subject. "Guess who I saw dirty dancing together at the Golden Boot two weeks ago? Your husbands' cousin Chassie West and Trevor Glanzer."

"Really?" Channing and Gemma exchanged a look, which was lost on Macie and AJ.

"Yep. Rumor is they've been seeing a lot of each other."

"How long has this been going on?" Gemma asked.

"A few months. I've heard from a couple of sources that they're serious."

"Wow. Surprised that hasn't made it into the McKay gossip channel."

"Like the situation with Colt did?"

All eyes zoomed to AJ.

"What?"

"You were there. What really happened?"

AJ retold the story with as much detail as she'd remembered.

Channing took Ella to burp her. "Do you know what Colt said to Cord that'd make Cord act like that? Because Cord never acts impulsive."

He'd acted pretty damn impulsive earlier when he'd had her naked in his truck. "No one knows."

Macie, Gemma and Channing gossiped about other members of the McKay family. AJ already knew most of it, since she'd lived in the county her whole life. Since she'd known the

McKays her whole life.

So why did she still feel like the outsider?

The conversation swam back into focus.

"Dag and Chassie are brother and sister?" Macie asked Gemma. "Didn't Dad team rope with Dag on the circuit a couple of times?"

"Yep. Dag roped with Trevor after Edgard went back to Brazil."

Channing said, "I overheard Carolyn and her sister discussing Dag. Since he quit the circuit he's been drinking. A lot. Even more than Colt.

"That's why Harland West hired Trevor, to keep an eye on Dag. So it makes sense that's how Trev and Chassie hooked up. I can't believe Colby didn't tell me that part." Channing kissed the top of Ella's head. "She's asleep. Want me to put her down?"

"Yeah. Ryder's out too. I'll come with and tuck him in."

They left the room and AJ looked at Macie. "I think I'll head home."

"Why?"

Because I feel awkward and out of place. "I'm tired. I have a bunch of packing to do tomorrow."

Macie stood. "Would you give me a ride back to Carter's folks' house? My car is packed with baby stuff and I might as well leave it here rather than unpack it."

"Sure." AJ and Macie said a quick good-bye.

Once they were in AJ's Jeep, Macie sighed. "I'm sure they were glad to see me go."

"Why do you say that?"

"Don't get me wrong, Gemma and I get along great. She's more than just a stepmother; she's a good friend. But she still is sort of like my mother. Whereas she and Channing are great pals and they talk about everything. Gemma won't discuss her relationship with my father when I'm in the room, which is completely understandable. And Channing and I are still feeling our way around our relationship to each other and our places in the McKay family. Sometimes I wonder what it'd be like to already know all the ins and outs of this family." Macie grinned at AJ. "Someone like you."

"Doesn't make me a part of it."

"What's going on with you and Cord?"

"Sex."

"That's it?"

"Yep. Great sex, not that I have anything else to judge it by, but the man definitely knows what he's doing between the sheets."

"And in the barn, and in the pasture, and on a horse if he's anything like Carter."

"Haven't tried it on a horse." AJ grinned and turned onto the paved highway. "Yet."

"Does he know how you feel about him?"

"No. I'll bask in his sexual attention and expertise for as long as I can. But we both know it has a finite end—when Ky comes home."

"I worry about you, AJ, because I think you'll take whatever little Cord McKay offers you just to be with him."

"That might've been true if I hadn't moved away last year."

"But?"

"Even though this is my first sexual relationship, it's opened my eyes about a lot of other things. I believed the sex was good because I love him. But Cord doesn't love me and the sex is still good for him. Which shows me that I might have a skewed idea of what love is, now that I know sex and love aren't intertwined."

"That's a bit cynical, isn't it?"

"Maybe. Or maybe I stopped being naïve."

"So if he asked you to marry him—"

"He won't. His family comes first. His ranch second." She wasn't his family and he now owned her ranch.

A quiet pause hung in the tepid evening air.

Macie stared out the window across the moonlit fields. "It's so beautiful here. I can see why Carter wants to divide our time and have the best of both worlds."

At the McKay homestead, AJ said, "Drive safe tomorrow. Let me know when I can tell my mom your good news."

"Will do. I'll call you soon."

AJ watched Macie disappear into the house. Cord's truck was parked next to Colby's. When she remembered what'd happened in that truck a few short hours ago...her toes curled in her flip-flops. She left before she found a reason to track Cord down for a repeat performance.

Jenn was still awake and sipping a glass of Jim Beam. Straight up.

"Is Mama asleep?"

"Yep. The kids wore her out. Everything wears her out these days." Jenn shoved the bottle across the table. "Join me in a drink. I could use the company."

"Sure." AJ grabbed a juice glass, ice, and a Coke to mix with the whiskey. "What's got you drinking alone?"

"Alan and I met this morning. I wanted to talk about visitation rights, summer vacation and school breaks over the holidays, you know, normal stuff that most fathers should care about." She sipped her drink and didn't look up. "Not him. As I sat across from him, the man I'd been married to for the last twelve years, I realized I didn't know him at all.

"He doesn't care about me or the kids. It's embarrassing to admit I've been living a lie, trying to make something work that should've ended years ago. So as I sat there, sensing his impatience and his desire to 'be done with the whole goddamn thing' I knew how wrong I was to push for marriage with him in the first place."

"Why?"

"He didn't love me, Amy Jo. He liked me. The sex was really good. I believed I could work with that. I could make him love me. Or I could love him enough for both of us." Bitter tears spilled down her cheeks.

"Jenn—"

"I can deal with him discarding me. But how am I supposed to tell our children, *his* children, that their father is discarding them too? That they might not ever see him again and that is *his* choice? How do I look them in the eyes and break their hearts?"

"You don't. It's not your fault Alan is a selfish dickhead who's leaving you no option but to pick up the pieces. The only thing you can do is what you've been doing. Show Krista and

Mason and Ariel you love them. *We* love them. We are a family no matter what. No matter where we live."

Jenn made a sound between a gasp and a laugh.

"You are a great mother...and a great father too." AJ went to her broken sister. Jenn wrapped her arms around AJ's waist and sobbed in silent misery. AJ cried right along with her and felt like she'd aged ten years in the last ten hours.

After Jenn quieted down, AJ handed her a tissue.

"When did you get so grown up?"

"I've always been grown up. I didn't exactly have a choice."

"You did more things around the ranch after Daddy's heart attack than you ever let on, didn't you?"

"It had to be done. I didn't know any different."

"I wish I would've known. Makes me feel just as selfish as Alan." Jenn blew her nose. She gathered up the glasses and put the whiskey bottle back in the liquor cabinet.

"Anything else you need tonight before I go to bed?"

"No, but since you're dispensing advice, I'm gonna return the favor."

AJ looked up. "What?"

"I know you're seeing someone. I won't ask who. I'd like to think if it was a serious relationship you would've brought him around to meet your family. You have a lot of years ahead of you in the dating scene. Remember this, when you find that special someone, whatever you do, don't settle for less than a man who loves you completely."

"I won't."

"Good. I'll see you in the morning."

"Night."

Rather than heading upstairs, AJ snuck outside. She stood on the front porch staring at the stars, contemplating family dynamics and her place in the universe for a long time before she finally crawled into bed.

Chapter Twenty-two

"What do you mean you can't come over tonight?"

"Jenn stayed with Mom yesterday afternoon when I was helping Macie. She has things to do tonight when she gets off work."

"Christ, AJ, that's two nights in a row. You're supposed to be here every night. That was the deal."

The phone went silent.

"What?"

"You know, Cord, I think it might be time to renegotiate the deal. If you're gonna get pissy about me taking care of my *mother* because you aren't getting a piece of ass, then maybe I'm done dealing with you. Maybe you can continue to be a jackass on your own time." She hung up.

"Goddammit!" Cord was half-tempted to whip the cell phone at the wall. He snapped it shut and threw it on the coffee table. Great. He oughta go over there and set her straight. Right. How was he supposed to come to terms with the idea that he...missed her?

What the hell was he supposed to do with himself tonight?

Cord stared at the fan spinning lazily on the cathedral ceiling. Maybe he should take up a hobby. Bowling. League darts. Whittling.

He headed for the barn. The farrier was coming in the morning to shoe all the horses. He might as well clean up the tack room.

Ky had made a mess of the place. Put him in a time warp to think he hadn't been in here since Ky had left. Even more humbling was the knowledge he hadn't ridden his horses for a couple of weeks. He'd have to rectify that tomorrow after they wore new horseshoes.

Cord dragged in the garbage can and cleaned up. Finished with that chore, he rearranged the ropes according to type and length. He restacked the saddle blankets. Gathered the horse's grooming supplies for a thorough washing. Set all the saddles on the ground and checked for wear and tear he might've otherwise missed.

Took him ten minutes to find a clean rag. He kicked over a plastic pail and sat on it while he cleaned Ky's saddle. The kid needed to climb on a ladder to get on his pony, Plug. But he'd been determined to get on "the cowboy way" so he'd swung his short leg over like an experienced buckaroo the second time he attempted to mount. Cord had been absurdly proud.

After he'd finished wiping the grime off and coated the leather with leather conditioner, he picked up the next saddle. He'd bought this saddle for Marla right after they'd gotten married and she assured him she'd love being a rancher's wife.

What'd he been thinking, marrying her in the first place? So she'd been pretty. So she'd fawned over him like he was John Wayne reincarnated. She'd lacked a sense of humor, although that wasn't fair because most folks would say the same about him. She hadn't been adventurous in bed, nor had she understood his occasional appetite for domination and a bit of kink. Somehow she'd equated those scenarios as a threat to her female independence.

Marla hadn't been driven to success; she more or less floated along, flitting from one thing to the next. From the get-go she exhibited an aversion to working outdoors, and to working hard, so he didn't know why he'd ever believed she'd've been happy living in Wyoming.

Why *had* he fallen for her? Hell, why had he imagined himself madly in love with her? Why had it crushed him that she'd left? Because he hadn't the balls to admit he'd made a mistake and she'd made the first move to rectify it? Had his pride concocted a lie after the fact about his deep, abiding love for her just to keep him infallible in the eyes of his son? The responsible Cord McKay had loved once and would never make the same mistake twice?

That bit of truth sliced him to the bone.

Cord racked his brain to counter that thought. Seemed to be a blank spot where Marla existed in his memory. A bitter, dark hole. If he couldn't remember the good or the bad times, just a whole lot of nothing, why was he so bitter? Why had he sworn off all women? He'd always chalked up his reasoning to the old adage that one bad apple spoiled the whole barrel, but now he had to admit his line of thinking was seriously fucked up.

The outer door to the barn crashed open. "Cord? You in here?"

"In the tack room. Come on back."

Kade paused in the doorway holding a six-pack. "Wanna beer?"

"Yeah." Colt took one, twisted off the top and the metal cap pinged against the garbage can. He sucked down a mouthful. "Thanks."

"No problem." Kade flipped over another bucket and sat. "Whatcha doin'?"

"Cleanin' up. Haven't been in here since Ky's been gone. The boy left his mark."

They drank beer and talked about Ky's adventures in the big city. Kade adored Ky and his son considered Kade another one of his uncles. The three of them hung out at least once a week, watching "guy" movies, taking in a rodeo, riding horses or target shooting.

"I've never seen that saddle before. Whose is it?"

"It was Marla's."

Kade picked it up and scrutinized it. "No bullet holes in it so I know you ain't been usin' it for target practice."

"Har har. Forgot I even had the damn thing. Big waste of money. I think I coaxed her onto a horse maybe four times."

"I don't wanna be a nosy dick, but you still got it bad for her?"

Cord's gaze zoomed to Kade's. "No. Why'd you ask that?"

"Dunno. You ain't been lookin' for another woman since the divorce, at least not in this county."

"Maybe I'm concentratin' my efforts on the next county

over."

Kade's whole posture went rigid.

"What?"

"Nothin'."

"I ain't lookin' to get hitched again any time soon."

"That's odd, what with your brothers finally takin' the plunge. Least now any woman you brung home as a bride would have other female family around."

"Worried about me becomin' a grouchy ol' bachelor, cuz?"

"Worried about a lot of my kinfolk, but you'd be damn near the bottom of the list."

Cord swigged his beer. "Who's on the top?"

"Colt. Followed by Dag. Then Cam since he's gettin' shot at in Iraq. Kane."

"Why Kane?"

"He's been influenced by Colt. Neither of our mamas would be happy to learn how they've been treatin' women."

"That why you moved out?"

"Partially. Mostly because I found myself skatin' toward that callous attitude. It ain't right. I don't wanna go through life with that sense of entitlement. Any woman oughta open her legs for me just 'cause I smiled at her or my last name is McKay. Leads to a bad outlook on all women."

Cord wondered if that last comment was a shot at him. "When you find a woman you wanna date, I'm sure she'll appreciate you not bein' a bitter dickhead only lookin' for a piece of tail."

"I am datin' someone now."

"Yeah?" Cord didn't hide his surprise. "How come I haven't heard about it?"

"Keepin' a low profile. Don't wanna mess it up and introduce her to our crazy family before I have to. And I definitely didn't want her knowin' what was goin' on at the Boars Nest."

"Do I know her?"

Kade shook his head. "She's from out of state. She and her sister inherited a small family place and she relocated."

"You ain't gonna tell me her name?"

"Nope. But I will tell you I ain't never met anyone like her. Makes me sound totally fuckin' moon-eyed, but she's funny and smart, sexy as shit, and she don't take no shit, neither. There's somethin' there worth stickin' around for."

"I assume you're bangin' her anyway despite your respectin' women spiel?"

A hangdog look crossed Kade's face. "No. Ironic, huh? The guy who weeks ago couldn't talk about nothin' but gettin' laid is...not gettin' any at all. And I'm good with that. What about you?"

Cord thought of hedging, but as long as Kade hadn't named names, he wouldn't either. "Actually, I am seein' someone."

Kade's eyes widened like Cord smacked him upside the head with a 2x4. "Get the fuck out. Seriously?"

"No, it ain't serious. It's casual," he lied, mostly to himself. "Probably last until Ky gets back home."

"I assume you're bangin' her?"

Cord grinned. "Every chance I can get."

Kade chinked his bottle to Cord's. "'Bout time."

Another beer loosened Cord's tongue. "I wanna run somethin' by you that Dad and I'd been talkin' about before all this shit happened with Colt."

"You seen Colt?"

"Nah. Dad's keepin' him away from me. You seen him?"

"Nope. Kane and I are doin' the shit hayin' along the ditches in the public thoroughfare on either side of the county line so I ain't seen much of my brother either. What've you and Uncle C been talkin' about?"

"Keepin' the part of the herd that's up on the western edge on summer grazin' over the winter and through calvin' season."

"Why?"

"There's plenty of feed and water. We need to rest the grazin' where we'd keep 'em here anyway. I'm sick of drivin' cattle a hunnerd miles, and back and forth twice a year. If we don't lose too many head, we might expand up there with a fulltime operation. If we do have losses, chalk it up to a failed experiment and we know for sure it can only be used as summer grazin'."

"That's damn isolated country out there, Cord. No town for sixty miles." Kade's eyes registered recognition. "You're thinkin' of sendin' Colt out into the boondocks? As a way to get him to dry out?"

"We're considerin' it. Don't know if he'll go for it. We can't force him. Even out in the middle of nowhere he could invite some of his boozin' friends. Then our experiment wouldn't matter—either for him or the cattle, 'cause I've no doubt the cows wouldn't do well under his half-assed drunken care." Cord sighed. "Like I said, nothin's decided, somethin' we're kickin' around."

"Keep me in the loop." Kade eased to his feet.

"Don't say nothin' to nobody."

Kade snorted. "I'm a little short on roommates these days. Do most my talkin' to the tractor or the cattle."

"I hear ya there." Cord followed Kade out to his pickup.

"This sucks sometimes, don't it?"

"What?"

"Bein' the oldest next generation McKay son. You. Me. Quinn. Knowin' that keepin' the McKay ranch goin' is on our shoulders. Feelin' responsible for every damn thing that happens on our place. Bein' stewards to the land and the cattle and feedin' the mouths of our family. Makin' sure everyone and everything is properly tended. Can be a heavy weight, cuz. Can be damn lonely."

Cord didn't respond. Kade wasn't much for philosophizing, but when he did, he was always dead on. Cord was smart enough to keep his mouth shut and listen.

"Least you got an heir. I thought I'd be married by now. Have a couple of kids. It ain't really bothered me until recently. I figured there was time. Now that I've been livin' with my folks, might sound sappy as shit, but I want what they have. I'm afraid I'm gonna wake up in ten years and be a grumpy forty-year-old man and be in the same damn place I am now."

Was Cord an example to his cousin of the kind of man Kade did *not* want to become? Why'd that sting so bad? He wasn't so set in his ways he couldn't change, could he?

"Maybe things are gonna change."

"Whenever you say that, it's usually for the worse," Kade said wryly.

"Lemme know when you're ready to introduce your lady friend."

"Like hell. She'll dump me and go for you—the broodin' cowboy with the wounded soul and the cute-as-a-button motherless son. Plus, you've got a bigger"—he grinned—"section of the ranch than me. She'll drop me like a cow pie." Kade added slyly, "That is, if you ain't already spoken for by *your* lady friend by the time I get up the gumption to bring her around."

Right. His lady friend would be living in Colorado in a few short weeks.

Kade drove off and Cord trudged up the steps and into his house.

He wandered from room to room. Watched TV. Felt loneliness beating on him from all sides before he finally went to bed.

Chapter Twenty-three

Later the next morning, AJ's mother said, "You're gonna wear yourself out."

"Probably. But I'm used to working hard around here and it has to be done. I'm about finished with the bedrooms."

"What's in those boxes?"

"The clothes going to the mission on the reservation." AJ dropped the box and dust shot up, making her cough. "Three more and I'll take a break."

Ten minutes later she carried two glasses of iced tea into the front room. "I might curl up beside you and take a nap this afternoon."

"I'd welcome it. I used to love that you were such a cuddler when you were a little girl. Jenn never was. You would crawl right up on my lap." Her mom fussed with the straw in the glass. "That was about the only time you were allowed to be a kid. I'm sorry we relied on you so much later on. Neither your daddy nor I wanted to admit his health was failing. For him to go from being so robust, to so frail."

Mostly for him to spend years pretending not to be either.

AJ loved her dad, but like most tough Wyoming men, his pride overrode his common sense. From her thirteenth birthday until her father died when she was eighteen, she—in essence—had been their hired man. She'd done the chores in all seasons, except for haying, which they'd always hired out. She, her mom, and dad managed to muddle through that first calving season of her dad's weakened state. At least he'd realized she couldn't handle the livestock, so they'd quietly sold off all their cattle a few cow/calf pairs at a time and began renting sections to the McKays for grazing.

Yes, Floyd Foster's reputation as a keen rancher had remained intact until the day he'd died.

Amy Jo Foster's reputation in those years was nonexistent. She stopped participating in school activities, as she went home directly after classes ended to do chores. She'd morphed from an outgoing girl to a withdrawn young woman with more responsibilities than what clothes to wear to the next rodeo dance. Her classmates—including Keely McKay—believed she'd become a goody-goody, when in truth, AJ'd been too tired to *be* anything. She worked like a dog and she'd had few friends besides her horses.

She didn't complain. It was tough on her mother taking care of her ailing father and the household, plus keeping a false face to the community. Jenn was too busy raising three kids by herself to help.

But Jenn had no problem demanding you drop out of school and come back here to help her.

AJ knew Jenn felt guilty about asking AJ to temporarily withdrawal from school, but the bottom line was AJ was here right away after her mother's injury. Once again she was a daughter who did the right thing out of love. For her family. As she'd continue to do.

"You're awful quiet. Is everything all right?"

"Just thinking, which always gets me into trouble. Can I get you more tea?"

"No." Florence kept fiddling with the straw. "Since you were home last night, will you be out whoopin' it up tonight during happy hour at the Golden Boot?"

"Maybe. We'll see. I'm supposed to be helping Liza with her bachelorette party so I might head to her place to see what's up."

You're going to Cord's to see what pops up on him.

He'd be a little anxious after not seeing her for a couple of nights.

On second thought... "A nap might not be a bad idea."

A few hours later, after she'd packed the ranch truck with

boxes for donations, her cell phone rang. Caller ID said *Cord.*

"Hey, AJ. How are ya?"

"Good. You?"

"Lonely and lookin' forward to tonight." Pause. "You are comin' over later, right?"

Cord sounded...anxious. She smiled. "Far as I know. Why?"

"Just wanted to make sure you wear boots and long pants. No, baby doll, you don't get to ask why."

She paused.

"I'm sure hopin' I hear a 'but' in your response someplace."

"Don't you think I learned my lesson last time?"

"I sure as hell hope not."

Her belly fluttered. "Anything else?"

"No. Except to apologize for bein' a jackass last night when you called."

"Apology accepted."

"Good enough. See you at six. Got somethin' special planned."

Lord. She hoped it wasn't another one of his penalties.

Yes, you do.

ɞ

Soon as AJ pulled into the yard, Cord didn't cool his bootheels in the house like usual; he bounded out like an eager pup. He bent down and kissed her soundly, a mixture of sweetness, heat and gratitude.

He tugged her to the corral. "Come on. We're goin' ridin'. Mick put new shoes on the horses today. I haven't been as vigilant about exercising them as I usually am." His hot gaze flicked from her red ropers to her pink face. "Had more important things on my mind lately."

"I haven't put Lucy through her paces since that day—" She looked up at him.

"Say it." He scooted closer and stared at her lustful mouth. "The day I...?"

"Tied me up in the barn and screwed me silly."

"Complainin'?"

"God no. The way you make me feel, Cord, hot and needed—" She hastily added, "Sexually speaking, of course."

Cord wondered why she felt the need to qualify that?

Because this is a sexual relationship, dumbass. You shouldn't be taking her riding. You should be riding her.

"Come on, let's get saddled up."

"Did you pick a horse for me?"

"Nah. You had a chance to ride them all when you watched Ky, so you know which one you like better than I would."

AJ picked Nickel, a quarter horse retired from barrel racing. Which just proved he'd been right in letting her choose her mount because he would've saddled up Borneo, a much older and gentler horse than Nickel.

"Whose saddle is this?" She walked behind Nickel to his right side and reached under his belly to fasten the cinch.

"I bought it for Marla right after we moved back here."

"That's why it still looks new?"

Cord grinned. "Uh-huh. Might be a little stiff."

"I like stiff. I can work with stiff."

Surely she hadn't meant...he glanced over at her to see a big ol' smile on her not-so-innocent face. "And I used to think you were so sweet."

"*Used* to think?"

"Now I know under that sweetness is a wickedly naughty streak."

"Complainin'?" she mimicked.

"God no."

She returned to Nickel's left side, unhooked the halter and let it dangle while she slipped on the bridle. Damndest thing. Nickel, who didn't allow just anyone to slip a bit in his mouth, opened right up. She talked to him, slipped the bridle over his ears, undid the quick release knot on the leadrope and draped both over the hook on the fence.

"You gonna get the gate?"

He'd been so engrossed with her horsewomanship that he hadn't readied his own mount. Cord followed AJ into the pasture. She'd climbed on while he'd closed the gate. Damn. He'd wanted to see that very fine ass of hers in the air as she threw her long leg over the saddle.

Cord mounted up. "I thought we'd ride to the butte."

"Okay. Fast or slow?"

Soon as *fast* made it out of his mouth, AJ took off. She handled Nickel like a pro, giving him his head but staying in total control.

He caught her, but he suspected she'd let him catch her.

AJ faced him and her smile rivaled the radiance of the sun. "These horseshoes seem to be fine."

"Smarty."

They ambled along through the sagebrush and rocks. Letting the horses lead them around scrub cedar and stunted pines.

She sighed. "I love how every time I ride through the fields some new wildflower has popped up." She pointed. "See? That one wasn't out two weeks ago."

"Guess I hadn't noticed."

She reined her horse to a stop.

"What?"

"Cord McKay. How can you be out here all the time and not notice the flowers? Can't you see the daisies? The wild roses? The tiny purple starflowers? The yarrow? The lavender heads on the milkweed?"

"I see weeds. You see all that?"

She nodded. "Nothing on earth is as pretty as Wyoming wildflowers."

"Oh, I'd beg to disagree, baby doll."

AJ looked up and saw him staring at her. "You know what I meant."

"And you know what *I* meant. You're beautiful, AJ. Wild and free on the back of that horse. The wind in your hair, the sun glowin' on your face, miles of blue sky behind you. Wish I had a camera." To show her how stunning she looked because he didn't need tangible proof. The image of her would be burned into his brain forever.

Those sharp gray eyes narrowed. "Did you hit your head in the last couple days?"

"What do ya mean?"

"First an apology? Then a horseback ride? Now you're tossing me compliments like poetry? You gonna whip out a guitar and serenade me with cowboy love songs next?"

"No. Next, I'm gonna..." He spurred Jester in the sides and yelled over his shoulder, "Race you to the butte."

He heard her laughing and knew his playful side surprised her, hell it surprised him too, but he didn't let the reckless feeling deter him from winning for a change.

"I deserved that." She urged Nickel to the left to skirt the base of the butte as she shaded her eyes and looked up. "You ever climbed to the top of this?"

"Long time ago. Why?"

"How far can you see?"

"Pretty far. Not like on that plateau by Devil's Tower where everything is spread out for two hundred miles."

"There's a butte on our place—well, your place now—that I used to climb. Never imagined when I climbed it two years ago it'd be the last time."

They rode in silence until Cord realized it was an unnatural silence.

"I'm really gonna miss all this like crazy."

I'm really gonna miss you like crazy.

Cord checked his watch. "We should be gettin' back. I've gotta call Ky pretty soon."

"He ready to come home yet?"

"I have a sneakin' suspicion he ain't completely unpacked."

AJ smiled. "Last year when I watched him he showed me his ring bearer outfit for Macie and Carter's wedding, complete with 'packin' leather shoes. At first I didn't know what he was saying. When I figured out *patent* leather, I'll admit I asked him to repeat it a couple of times because it was so damn funny. I didn't laugh at him, but that kid cracks me up."

He grinned. "Me too."

"Channing said she wasn't picking out girl's names because she knows she'll have a boy."

"Sometimes I wonder how many brothers I'd have after Carter if Ma hadn't broken the hunnerd-year drought and birthed a girl McKay."

"Lots of girls in my mother's family. When I loaded up boxes today I found a whole bunch of pictures and letters. Was weird to think of them as relatives. Even weirder to think there's a whole bunch of family history I wasn't aware of. It's gonna be fun going through that stuff later, but packing has been a lot harder than I thought."

"Physically?"

"No. Emotionally."

They'd reached the backside of the fence. Cord dismounted and led Jester to the side closest to the barn. He didn't offer to help AJ; she knew her way around.

After she'd hung up her borrowed tack in the barn, she carried out two buckets of oats as he brushed the horses down. Once Nickel finished his portion, she gave Jester his bucket. She rested her butt on the fence and gazed across the horizon.

Cord wrapped his arms around her from behind and set his chin on her shoulder.

AJ snuggled into him. "Mmm."

"Whatcha lookin' at?"

"The sunset."

"Gonna be a pretty one tonight."

"It's pretty every night. I love the sky as it starts to fade from light blue to indigo to purple to black. You'd think I'd get tired of it, but I never do."

How many times had he sat out here, content to watch the sunset? He never tired of it either.

Tonight he'd forego Mother Nature's display because he wanted, *needed* to be with her.

"AJ. Come inside. I'm dyin' to put my hands on you."

"Don't you have to call Ky?"

"Yeah. It can wait a bit." Cord buried his lips in the slope of her shoulder. "Please."

"Well...since you asked so nice."

He hopped over the fence. They kissed all the way into the house. All the way up the stairs. All the way down the hall to his bedroom. Sneaking kisses as they undressed each other. Cord laid her on the comforter and lowered his body over hers.

"Baby doll, what's wrong? You're trembling."

"You always make me tremble." AJ's eyes were bright with something resembling...lust. Had to be lust because he couldn't fathom what that look on her face really meant.

Rather than dwell on it, he focused on mutual slaking of need. He groaned softly when the head of his cock brushed the wetness coating her sex. Sometimes he forgot she wasn't as experienced as her body indicated. Cord eased into her on a slow glide. Once he was fully seated he looked at her.

"Go slow like that again."

He'd never shown her the sweeter, slower side of making love after the first time?

Not really.

What a selfish prick. He'd make it up to her starting now.

"As slow as you want." He kissed her mouth. That sassy mole. The curve of her cheek. Her temple and her eyelids. Her mouth again. All while leisurely rocking in and out of her body.

Her strong hands drifted up and down his back to his ass in a teasing caress.

Cord nibbled the line of her jaw. Her delicate earlobes. The muscles straining along the side of her neck. His tongue flicked across the pulse point at the base of her throat before dipping into the hollow. It took effort, but he managed to hold off on his climax when her first one ripped through her like wildfire.

Still, he didn't speed up. He dragged his goatee across the tops of her breasts, offering the tip of each hardened nipple a swirling lick, then he returned to her mouth to toy with her well-kissed lips. Through half-closed lids he studied her face, lost in the pleasure he was bringing her.

He couldn't hold off forever—everything was too perfect, the tender way she touched him, the glove-tight feeling of her pussy sucking him to the root.

"Don't stop. I'm so close again."

"I'm right with you, baby doll," he panted against her throat, lost in the scent of her, the everything of her.

AJ canted her pelvis, curling her thighs around his hips to bring him deeper. "Cord."

"I'm here."

"Love me like this, slow and easy and for a long time. Make it last forever." AJ's fingers dug for purchase on his sweat-covered butt as her spine bowed off the bed.

"Been about as long as I can take." Cord sealed his mouth to hers as his balls drew up. The climax rolled over him, not a singular explosion, but in drawn out bursts, intensified by the rhythmic squeezing of her interior muscles around his cock.

He broke the kiss to press his lips to her temple, tasting sweat and sunshine and AJ.

When they'd recovered some, she nuzzled the side of his head. "Mmm. Slow is good."

Cord smiled. "Definitely."

She yawned. "Sorry."

"Why don't you crawl under the covers and rest while I call Ky?"

Once he'd gotten her settled she sighed. "Comfy as I am, don't let me fall asleep here for the whole night."

"Deal."

"That's assuming I can move. God. You're an exhausting lover, Cord McKay."

"I'm takin' that as a compliment."

"You should. I'm so glad I waited."

"Waited for what?"

No answer.

"AJ?"

"Waited for you to be ready for me."

Confused by her cryptic statement, Cord pecked her on the forehead, tucked the quilt under her chin and tried not to think about how natural it was to have her in his bed.

Chapter Twenty-four

"How many inches long you think his dick is?"

"Liza!" AJ nearly choked on her punch.

"Come on. Don't pretend you haven't been looking at him."

"Yeah, but I wasn't measuring him for condom sizes."

"Extra, extra large. Super magnum. That bad boy's gotta be at least ten inches."

AJ eyed the stripper, whose junk was peeping out of the top of a metallic snakeskin G-string. The man looked little more than a boy. With his hands fluffing his shaggy rock star hair and the seductive way his slender hips gyrated, she knew no mere boy could move like that.

Four women from Liza's church whooped, elbowing each other to line up first to shove money in the string circling the guy's tattooed pelvis. In the corner by the food, seventy-something Bebe was winning the deep-throat-a-bratwurst contest. Marijane Jackson Goodhue, the president of their graduating class and extremely pregnant, showed how well she could roll meatballs in her mouth.

Liza's wish had come true. This was one wild-assed party. Packed to the rafters with women from all over the county—including Cord's mother, Carolyn, and his Aunt Kimi. There were four six-foot-tall inflatable penises making the rounds. Any woman who played the bratwurst game won a headband decorated with bobbing light-up penises. AJ turned her head to the left and the spring on her headband caught in her hair again.

"Where's the bride-to-be?" someone shouted from the stage.

AJ lifted Liza's arm above her head and waved it madly. A horde of women descended on Liza, dragging her to a chair up front, which left AJ free to sneak to the punchbowl.

As she refilled her cup, Carolyn McKay sidled up. "Fancy meeting you here, Amy Jo."

"Likewise." AJ tried not to stare at the headpiece Cord's mom wore and wondered if Carolyn was trying not to stare at hers.

"Keely is gonna be so mad she missed this party. I think we oughta rub it in real good, don't you?"

AJ grinned and clinked her mug against Carolyn's. "I'll drink to that."

"How's Flo?"

"Better. She's anxious to get on with her life. We're going to Billings in a couple days to find a place for her to live."

"Why Billings?"

"The company Jenn works for had an opening. She can start in the next couple weeks, which will give the kids time to adjust before school starts."

Carolyn placed her hand on AJ's arm. "How are you adjusting, sweetheart?"

AJ shrugged. "We'll see. I haven't officially left here yet."

"I know you've probably heard it from Keely, but you are welcome at our home anytime."

"I appreciate that. And I know that Macie and Carter are looking forward to being around here more often. Exciting news about the baby, huh?"

"Very. Can you believe I'm gonna be a grandma again? Times three? I love my little Ky, but I'm beside myself about Channing and now Macie. Lord. Doesn't seem that long ago I was sittin' in a chair like that one, about to pledge my life to a wild McKay." A wistful look crossed her face.

"Lots of people told me not to bother trying to love a man like Carson McKay. I knew he was gruff from the get-go. He holds a grudge. He's set in his ways. Carson is a cowboy rancher to his very core. Not big on public displays of affection. But I never listened to what any of them said. In my heart I knew what kind of man he was and still is. It isn't the public displays that matter. The important affection in a relationship is given in private anyway."

Was that a hint that Carolyn knew the type of affection her son Cord was giving her in private?

"Good Lord *that's* not very private, is it?"

AJ's head swiveled to see what Carolyn was gawking at. Oh man. The stripper spread his legs wide and was doing the bump and grind—in Liza's face. His butt was completely exposed and seemed to be covered in a sheen of oil. To discourage women from grabbing onto him?

"Hang in there, sweetie, it's worth it in the long run," Carolyn said, the penises on her head bobbing merrily as she returned to her seat up near the action.

Was that a warning her son was a chip off the old block? Or an encouragement AJ should follow her instincts as far as Cord was concerned?

Problem was, AJ didn't trust her instincts anymore. She'd started the quest to win Cord's love weeks ago. Now she wasn't sure what she'd do with it if she ever got it.

Not that Cord gave off any signals he was falling in love with her. In lust? Definitely. They'd curl up to watch a movie or eat a meal together and rush to get naked together. Not that she was complaining—hello, world's hottest cowboy rancher had it bad for her—where was the downside in as much nasty, raunchy sex as she could take?

Near as she could figure, no downside. Except she still loved him. Not with the hero worship of a five-year-old girl, but with the eyes of a woman who knew a good man. With the eyes of a woman who knew she'd need years to capture the heart of Cord McKay...and she had two weeks.

Tonight was the third night in a row she hadn't been with him. Not to be churlish or to punish him. She spent her day fulfilling the needs of one person, only to race over to Cord's place to fulfill his needs. What about her needs? The ones that didn't have a blasted thing to do with family love or sexual gratification?

To cement the idea her personal needs and goals mattered, she'd driven by the Sandstone building in Sundance a couple of times. It was the perfect size for a start-up massage studio. Too bad she didn't have the capital to remodel—not even after the sale of seven horses. With her young age and no land ties to the community, she'd have a devil of a time convincing the local banker to give her a loan.

Now that she thought about it, she and Keely hadn't gone beyond the "wouldn't it be great to run a massage parlor in Sundance" pipe dream. No planning. Which allowed her to figure out a plan to make her dream happen on her own.

She needed a patron. Maybe the economic development department for the state of Wyoming had business incentives to keep natives in the area. It'd be worth looking into. The time had come for her to be assertive in all areas of her life.

As if on cue, her cell phone rang. Keely.

"What? No. I can't hear you. Who? No. Haven't seen him. But your mom is here. Look, K, I'll call you later with all the juicy details."

"Where are the bridesmaids?" Liza's sister Glenda barked in the microphone. Glenda scanned the room from the makeshift stage, grinning when she made eye contact with AJ. "There's one! Amy Jo Foster, come on down!"

Yippee. AJ wanted that skanky guy to rub his crotch in her face like she wanted to get gored by a bull.

She hopped up on the stage next to Liza, who didn't look the least bit humiliated. She was absolutely in her glory. AJ wouldn't do a damn thing to dim the gigantic grin on her friend's face—she'd play along and pretend she was having the best time in the world.

The only other bridesmaid besides Glenda was Darby Van Zandt and she was shier than AJ and Liza combined.

"Now, ladies. We're gonna have a little contest. Yes, there is a prize." Glenda waved a clear plastic purple phallus with pearl-looking things inside. "This vibrator, as seen on *Sex and the City,* is called the rabbit. It spins." She hit a switch and the vibrator started to make a buzzing noise as the tip circled.

The women in the crowd went nuts.

"It has three speeds, even reverse. It's waterproof. And this little do-hickey on the front? It vibrates in all the right places. I guarantee it won't move on you at the moment of truth. It stays exactly where you want it. For as long as you want it. This here is a girl's best friend because it can go all night without complaint...or until the batteries run out. And you don't *need* a man with this bad boy around."

Half the women cheered; half booed.

"Anyway, this fabulous prize will be awarded to one of these lucky ladies upon completion of a simple task." She paused for effect. "The most creative placement of a rolled-up twenty-dollar tip someplace in Mr. Angel's G-string with only her mouth. No hands allowed."

The room erupted in fits of laughter, clapping, wolf whistles and boot stomping.

"Who wants to go first? Our lovely bride?"

Amidst the cries of *Liza, Liza, Liza*, AJ heard the sound of glass breaking. Dear Lord, were these normally prim and proper ladies throwing...beer bottles? Or was that outside in the main part of the bar?

Glenda placed a rolled-up bill in Liza's mouth. Mr. Angel—what a stupid name—sashayed over and turned Liza's chair sideways so no one would miss out on the action.

Liza hammed it up. When she attempted to shove the money dead center in the pouch, it dropped to the floor. The stripper quickly picked it up.

A chorus of disappointed *aw's* arose...followed by the sound of shattering glass and heavy thumps that no one but AJ seemed to notice.

Darby scarcely raised her head when Glenda placed a fresh twenty between her tight lips. Mr. Angel did his bump and grind routine, taking extra time working the crowd since it didn't appear Darby was much of a sport.

Lord. Was this almost over?

Darby's half-hearted attempt to insert the money in his belly button fell short and the bill hit the ground. Mr. Angel scooped it up.

Where was he putting that cash? Wasn't like he had pockets.

A rowdier chorus of boos and whoops boomed. At the back table by the punchbowl, drinks were raised in a toast—then the members of the Ladies Guild of First Methodist Church...had a chugging contest.

Whoa. Getting out of hand in here.

AJ's focus returned to Glenda calling for order after a fistfight broke out. Carolyn McKay stepped in to stop it. No doubt she had plenty of experience breaking up fights with her brawling bunch.

"We're down to our final contestant." Glenda slipped a rolled bill between AJ's teeth. "Amy Jo, show 'em how it's done, girl."

Drunken bellows of encouragement floated from the church ladies' table.

Mr. Angel spun sideways and performed his cheesy lounge singer dance. When he gyrated in front of her, she said, "Turn around. We need to distract them before they riot." It finally clicked what she meant and he straddled her lap with his butt in her face instead of his bulge. She waited while he dry-humped the air in front of her.

Good God. This was horrid. Women *liked* this?

And what the heck was that noise? Like splintering wood?

"Settle down, ladies, we're getting to the good part. Go, Amy Jo."

Amidst shouts of *Amy Jo, Amy Jo, Amy Jo*, AJ inhaled a deep breath when the stripper turned around. She slid the twenty beneath the G-string above his right hipbone. She'd almost made the corner of the fabric to tuck the money into the pouch, when the outer door to the bar burst open.

Curious men poured in, including Cord McKay.

Their eyes locked. And her mouth was dangerously close to a stripper's...pole.

Rage flared in his dark blue eyes.

For the first time in her life AJ felt the urge to be contrary. Cord was already pissed, how much madder could he get? So amidst the confusion, keeping her gaze firmly on Cord's, she dropped the cash in the man's banana hammock and used her teeth to snap the stripper's G-string like a rubber band.

Cord was infuriated.

The stripper yelled, "Ouch!" When he caught sight of the deputy's arrival, the stripper snatched his duffel bag and slunk out the back door half-naked.

Glenda shouted, "Amy Jo wins!"

AJ hopped up and snagged her prize off the podium and hefted it in the air like she'd won the gold buckle at the rodeo.

A few women noticed and clapped.

Carolyn McKay floated her a thumbs up before she and her sister snuck out.

The deputy and male bar patrons stared in horror at the decorations and the leftover food. And Bebe and Toots were having a sword fight with two monstrously long and anatomically correct penis-shaped swords.

Which wasn't nearly as much of an eyeful as the three women bouncing on a six-foot inflatable penis like it was a buckin' bull. And two other women slow dancing with their life-size phallic partners.

Oh yeah. Keely would be absolutely pea green with envy.

Liza kept a silly grin on her face as Noah climbed up on the stage and helped her to her feet. "My Prince Charming."

"My drunken bride."

She giggled. "It was a grr-reat partay."

"I see that. Ready to return to the castle, princess?"

"Yep." Liza grinned at AJ as Noah scooped her into his arms and carried her out. "They'll be talkin' about this one for years."

"That they will." When she turned back around she saw Cord, standing in the same place, staring at her coolly. Like he didn't know every inch of her body. Like it hadn't bothered him a bit to see her on stage with a male stripper.

Like he didn't care about her at all.

Say something. Come up here and chew me out. Drag me out. Don't stand there and pretend you don't know me.

Of course, Cord didn't do anything.

Disappointed, AJ spun around to regain control of her emotions. Stupid rum punch and bridal games always made her weepy. She stacked the chairs on the stage and carried them to the wall.

When she looked back Cord was gone.

Chapter Twenty-five

But he hadn't gone far.

Cord fumed in the shadows of the parking lot as he leaned against his truck outside the bar.

AJ had had her lips on another man.

His woman had her mouth near some half-naked punk's groin.

In public.

And she'd been enjoying it.

Had she been drunk?

Didn't matter.

Women stumbled out of the bar for the next half hour under the watchful eye of the Crook County deputy. Husbands, boyfriends, in a couple of cases fathers, picked up the bachelorette party attendees. A couple of women walked arm in arm down the sidewalk singing, "Save A Horse (Ride A Cowboy)" but they'd changed the words to, "Save A Horse, Ride An Inflatable Penis" which wasn't particularly funny, yet it sent them into gales of laughter.

Finally AJ came out. Alone. She nodded to Deputy Shortbull and headed for her Jeep.

Cord sauntered out of the shadows.

She jumped back. Then tried to start his goatee on fire with her glare. "Did you give your mom and aunt a ride home?"

"Nope."

"Then why are you here?"

"You know."

"No, actually I don't, Mr. McKay."

He scowled. "What's with the *Mr. McKay* shit?"

AJ shot a look over her shoulder. "Are you sure you should be talking to me? Since we're not supposed to know each and all? Someone might see. Spread rumors that you're secretly diddling me and God knows we couldn't have that."

"Jesus. Are you drunk?"

"What does it matter if I am? Are you taking a poll?"

This was not going well.

"Wrong answer."

"Do I get another prize for giving you the right response?"

"Knock it off, AJ." He glanced at the box in her hand. "What's that?"

"The prize I won."

"What is it?"

She opened her mouth to snap off something smart, but changed her mind and smiled cagily. "A vibrator."

"No fuckin' way. What the hell do you need one of those—"

"—for? Comparison? That might be interesting."

He stared at her steadily, wondering if the steam blowing out of his nostrils was the same color as the steam blowing out of his ears.

"Fun as this conversation has been, Mr. McKay, I need to be getting home. Might need to stop and pick up some double A batteries first."

"Like hell. You ain't goin' no place until you tell me why you haven't been around for the last three days."

"Been busy."

"Busy havin' your mouth next to another guy's dick?"

She looked at her watch. "Wow. It's half-past I don't give a shit what you think, Cord McKay."

He growled.

"You don't have the right to talk to me like that."

"Yes, I do."

"Why?"

Because you're mine.

Where the hell had that come from?

"Because...Christ. It's hard to have a serious conversation with you when you're wearin' lighted cocks on your head."

AJ defiantly thrust out her chin and the penises bobbled. "We aren't having a conversation. You're giving me tough-guy attitude. If you won't acknowledge me in public, you don't have the right to chastise me for anything I do in public or in private. And now you lost the right to *do* anything to me in private either, bucko."

"Quit bein' so goddamn childish."

Her eyes narrowed to silver slits. "Quit bein' such a goddamn dickhead."

"You're the one with dicks on your head, baby doll."

"Yeah? I can take mine off any old time I please, but you wear your dickhead status like a second skin. Or should I say as a second foreskin?"

"You tryin' to piss me off?"

"No, I'm trying to go home. So step aside."

"Tough shit. You ain't in no condition to drive."

"I'm fine."

"Says who?"

"Says Deputy Shortbull. He forced me and everyone else to take a Breathalyzer. I passed. So hah!"

Don't let her go like this. Stall.

"If you walk away from me, AJ, I swear to God your penalty will double. Triple maybe. You already owed me for the last two nights. Don't make it worse on yourself."

"Bring it, cowboy. In fact, you'd better bring a rope and hogtie me because that's the only way you'll ever get me back in your bed. But we both know you won't do it."

"Wrong."

"We're done with the hot horny divorced cowboy and the virginal babysitter fantasy. And no, I won't cause a hysterical crying scene that'll embarrass poor proper rancher Cord McKay. This will end like it began—as our dirty little secret. But it sure has been fun."

AJ pivoted on her stiletto, her hips swinging, the penises on top of her head swaying with every step of her long, sexy legs as she promenaded away from him.

Oh yeah. Little Miss Baby Doll just earned herself one helluva punishment.

Chapter Twenty-six

The next morning Cord woke up an hour earlier than usual. He finished his chores, cleaned up and was at AJ's house by eight a.m.

He called her cell phone. "I'm comin' up the driveway to get you. Easy or hard, your choice. But you will be leavin' with me, AJ. I suggest you be dressed and ready. Don't make me hogtie you because contrary to your smart little remark, you know I *will* do it. In public. In front of your family. With complete and utter joy." He hung up.

He parked. Waited a minute. Hopped out and passed her Jeep. On the passenger's seat was the flashing penis headband, a button proclaiming, "I sucked balls at Liza's bachelorette party" and...the vibrator she'd won. Still in the box.

Heh. A little comparison might be interesting, huh? He'd see about that. He snagged it and put it in his truck under the seat. To be ornery, he draped a rope over his shoulder, just so Little Miss Smartypants knew he wasn't kidding.

Cord knocked on the front door.

Jenn answered. "Cord McKay? What on earth are you doing here on a Saturday morning? Is everything all right?"

"Fine. I'm lookin' for Amy Jo. Last week she offered her help and I'm here to take her up on it."

"What kind of help?"

"Dealin' with my horses. Since we've been cross breedin' for a couple of years with your stock, I'd sure like her opinion on which ones I oughta sell when she sells yours."

"Come on in and have a cuppa coffee. She's a regular Dale Evans when it comes to horses. I'm sure she'd love to help."

First thing Cord noticed were the boxes stacked everywhere. Second thing he noticed was AJ glaring at him.

"Mornin', *Amy Jo*. I was just tellin' Jenn about you helpin' me out today with my horses. Doin' a little ridin'."

"But I can't possibly help today. As you can see"—she gestured to the stack of flattened cartons—"my hands are full."

Was she really challenging him? He mouthed, "That's one."

Her back snapped straight.

"Oh pooh, you don't need to stick around here, Amy Jo. Take a break. Spend time outside. You deserve it. The kids and I have gotten really good at packing in the last week." Her eyes zeroed in on his shoulder. "What's the rope for?"

Cord kept his gaze on AJ's. "I figured I might have to drag her out. She can be stubborn."

A bit of unease flashed in AJ's stormy gray eyes.

Jenn laughed. "Now that I'd like to see."

He grinned, knew it looked predatory and didn't care. "Comin' along peacefully, Amy Jo? Or do I have to prove to you and your sister just how good I am with ropes?"

"I'm coming." She stood and snatched her purse off the counter. "I'll follow you in my car."

Like hell. "I can bring you back, no problem." He bestowed his best aw-shucks-I'm-a-good-ol'-boy grin on Jenn. "She'll be gone all day. And to show that I ain't a total ingrate, I'll probably take her out for supper."

A kid screamed, another one yelled, "Mom!" Jenn sighed and disappeared upstairs.

Cord gave AJ's jeans and T-shirt a once over. "Get your boots on."

"Cord—"

"Now."

"They're in the entryway."

He held the door open for her. "After you."

AJ reached for the red ropers lined against the wall with the others. He noticed the silver spiked-heeled boots and pointed at them. "Bring those too."

"I can't ride in those."

"You can for the kind of ridin' I got planned."

"Fine." She slipped on the boots and grabbed the other pair.

"Get in the truck."

"Bossy much?"

"Oh, you ain't seen bossy, baby doll. Not by half."

She swallowed hard and climbed in.

Cord purposely didn't speak to her at all during the ride to his place. He didn't crank the radio either. His silence would keep her on edge, right where he wanted her.

He parked in front of his house and stared straight ahead as he spoke. "You've pushed me to the limits of my control, AJ. Today ain't so much about discipline, but playin' catch up for the nights you've missed. Today I'm gonna give you a taste of me not holdin' back. I'm warnin' you; I will be relentless in takin' what I want. You won't deny me anything."

AJ didn't say a word.

"Go on in the house. You have five minutes to strip to nothin' and do whatever you need to prepare yourself for me before I'll expect you in the living room. Five minutes. Not a second more."

He watched her hustle in the front door. After two minutes passed, he reached for the box under the seat and headed in after her. A quick trip upstairs to drop off his goodies and her time was up.

She positioned herself in front of the windows, naked, with her arms folded over her chest.

"C'mere."

Her footsteps were silent on the wood floor. When she was close enough, he curled his hands around her face and rested his forehead to hers. She melted against him, returning his affection without hesitation. Then Cord kissed her for a good long time, mostly to please himself as he walked her backward past the couch. He nudged her onto the coffee table.

"Sit. Lean back on your elbows and spread your legs."

She didn't argue.

He scooted her forward until her butt hung off the edge. "Just like that. Don't move." Cord licked her from her throat straight down to her pussy.

AJ moaned.

Lord. She did like a little kink—was already wet and he'd barely touched her. He dropped to his knees and stared at the feminine bounty before him. Soft. Pink. Glistening with want. He burrowed his tongue into her channel, inhaling her sweetness as he began to work her over with his mouth. Long sweeps of his tongue from her clit to her tiny puckered hole. He suckled her pussy lips, used his teeth on her clit while circling his wet thumb across that tight rosette.

When she began to bounce her hips and that kittenish whimper echoed in his ears, he latched on to her sweet spot and sucked. As she started to come, he plunged two fingers into her ass and his thumb pressed just inside the entrance to her juicy pussy.

"Oh-man-oh-man-oh-man. Cord!"

He scissored the fingers in her ass, his thumb stroking the sensitive spot of her wet sex, his mouth suctioned to the swollen bud, every action in tune with the blood pulsating in her body.

She screamed.

Cord didn't back off until AJ exploded again. His attention to her pleasure triggered a sweet, thick female ejaculate and she literally came all over his face.

It was unbelievably fucking hot.

As she was floating down from the last orgasm, he kissed her, checking to see if she'd be uncomfortable with the taste of herself on his tongue. But she lapped at him like a hungry kitten, digging her fingernails into the back of his neck.

His dick was so hard it threatened to drive a hole through his jeans to get out.

Cord helped her up. "On your knees on the rug, baby doll. Hands behind your back." He grabbed the rope.

"What are you doing?"

"Makin' sure you can't use your hands." He bound her

crossed wrists. "Too tight?"

"No."

"Good." He watched her watching him as he unbuckled his belt and unzipped his jeans. Lowered them to his shins. He shoved the boxers down and his cock bounced like it was spring loaded. "Come closer."

AJ wet her lips and walked three steps on her knees.

"That's right. Get your mouth nice and wet for me. First I want you to suck my balls."

He widened his stance and placed his hands on the top of her head. "Might have to crane your neck."

She nuzzled his groin and kissed down the length of his shaft until her hot breath reached where his sac hung. AJ licked around his left nut before bringing it into her warm mouth.

"Ah. Both of them now. Like that." When Cord glanced down and saw her face buried in his crotch, her eyes closed in enjoyment, his dick jerked against his belly. "Suck nice and slow. Get 'em really wet. Roll 'em over your tongue...oh hell yeah." After his balls had drawn up, he stroked her cheek and said, "Enough."

AJ released them. "I love the way you smell. All musky, manly, salty goodness."

"You're gonna love the way I taste too." He tipped her head up and he circled the weeping tip of his cock over her lips. "Open wide, 'cause I'm goin' deep."

He fed his cock into her mouth an inch at a time. Jesus. He loved that supremely wet heat and how the soft tissues of her mouth molded to his hardness.

"We're gonna work past your gag reflex until you feel me in the back of your throat." Cord placed his hands on her head to guide her. "You're doin' fine. That feels so goddamn good. You can take it all." The cockhead crested her soft palate and her lips were pressed against his abdomen at the root. "Breathe through your nose."

AJ tried to speak and the vibration of her voice box traveled up his shaft and electrified his balls.

"Do that again."

A humming noise this time.

"Christ. Now I know why it's called a hummer. Suck me hard as I'm pullin' out."

Her lips stayed tight around him until the head popped free. "Do I—"

"No questions, baby doll. My show." Cord pushed the length back into her mouth, building a rhythm that brought her bottom teeth into contact with the sweet spot underneath his cockhead on every withdrawal. His legs started to shake with anticipation. Everything primitive and male inside him roared satisfaction at seeing his dick coated with her saliva and her chin shiny wet.

The silky glide and the way AJ alternately sucked and licked jerked his balls up tight. His thrusts became faster, shorter. He gently held her head between his palms and her baby soft hair spilled through his fingers.

"Oh yeah, flick that wicked tongue, right there. Work just the tip. Make it drippin' wet. Like that. Open wider." He pumped four more times. The last one kept his cock deep. Cord arched as the spasms sent his seed jetting down the back of her throat.

She swallowed with gusto.

White noise detonated in his brain. When not a single twitch of his cock remained, he eased out of her mouth.

AJ's big gray eyes were on his as he yanked up his boxers and jeans and refastened his belt.

Cord dropped to his haunches and wiped her chin. "You get any better at that and you'll send me into a coma." He kissed her in a long, slow, seductive tangling of tongues, which left them both breathing hard.

"Go upstairs and wait on the bed for me." He stood and helped her to her feet, watching shamelessly as her breasts bounced, her ass shook and her shiny blonde hair swayed across the middle of her back when she climbed the stairs buck-ass nekkid.

Chapter Twenty-seven

It was difficult to stretch out on the bed with her wrists tied behind her back, but AJ managed.

Why wasn't she seeing red at his high-handed behavior?

Because maybe high-handed means he cares about you.

Right. It meant he cared that she was a sexual plaything willing to flesh out his darkest fantasies.

She could work with that.

AJ closed her eyes and ran her tongue around the inside of her smooth lips. He hadn't been kidding about showing her his dominant side. Not that she minded. Having him lose control, mindless for the release only she could give him, hearing tough guy Cord McKay whimper. That was powerful, knowing how thoroughly she'd pleased him.

The creak of the door startled her, but she wasn't in any position to panic.

Cord perched on the edge of the bed close to her. Completely dressed. He smiled.

She smiled back. "Are you still mad at me for last night?"

"A little."

"What for?"

"Mostly because you were right." He skimmed his fingertips over her face. "You're beautiful and vibrant and young and sweet. Everything I'm not. You don't embarrass me, AJ. Me not wantin' anyone to know about what we were doin' wasn't to protect me; it was to protect you. Some folks think it's funny, the reputation the McKays have. It's not. You saw how Colt's been behavin'. I'd never let you get caught up in it. You deserve better."

"Cord—"

He cut off her protest with a kiss. Seemed he always did that. Seemed she always let him. But there were worse ways to elicit a subject change, in her opinion.

"Two questions, baby doll. You ever seen the movie *9½ Weeks*?"

She shook her head.

"You scared of water?"

"Like you throwing me in the stock tank with my hands tied like this? Yes."

"No. I mean like takin' a shower."

Cord had showed up so unexpectedly she hadn't had time to shower. Did she smell bad?

"I know that look. No, you don't stink. I just wanna play some water games with you."

She flashed back to the hot tub incident the night he'd meted out her penalties. After blowing him while he'd floated on the surface of the water, he'd fucked her tits again. Slower, longer, taking more time to arouse her by playing with her nipples and letting her suckle just the tip of his cock. Then he'd bent her over the edge, perfectly aligning her clit with a water jet and mounted her from behind like a stallion and fucked her until she screamed her release.

"AJ," he warned.

"And if I say no?"

"I'll say tough shit, we're doin' it anyway."

"Sorta thought you might say that."

"Roll over. I need to untie your hands."

He made quick work of the rope. Before she sat up, he trailed his lips down the curve of her right butt cheek, and back up the left. She tried to get up but he pushed his hand in the middle of her back and held her down.

"Ah-ah-ah. Not so fast. For this next lesson, you're gonna be blindfolded too."

Something cool slipped over her eyes. "Wait a minute...you

said *too.*"

Cord slithered the rope across her spine and chuckled.

"You're tying me up again?"

"Yep."

"I'm starting to get worried about your penchant for bondage, McKay."

His breath was hot in her ear. "Only with you. Only *for* you. Come on." He tugged her upright and led her into the bathroom. "Small step up. Hands above your head. Back up. Perfect. Hold still."

He tied her arms to the metal showerhead. "What in the world—"

"No talkin'. Don't make me gag you, because I will."

She stuck out her tongue.

He caught it between his teeth and gently bit down, then sucked it like he'd sucked her clit. "Last warnin'. Be right back."

Her heart beat harder. She listened to bottles chinking against the tile and the sink being turned on and off. She heard him unbuckle and unzip his Wranglers, the whooshing thud as they hit the floor. Strange how tuned in she was to the sound of him stripping.

Cord stepped inside and said, "Cold?"

She sensed him drooling over her hard nipples. "Is it obvious?"

"Uh-huh. Let me see if I can't warm you up."

AJ expected him to turn on the shower, not fasten his mouth to her nipple. By the time he finished worshipping her breasts, he'd heated her up past warm to the boiling point.

Cord pressed his hot, naked body against hers. He nuzzled her throat. "Got something I want you to taste."

"Didn't I just do that?"

"Mmm. Funny. Open up."

She shrank back. "It's not soap, is it?"

"No. Open up and stick out your tongue."

"Fine." She did. A heavy, sticky dollop landed dead center. She closed her mouth and swallowed.

He murmured, "What is it?"

"Honey?"

"Good answer." Droplets of that same sticky substance landed on her breasts. Her belly. The tops of her thighs.

"What are you doing?"

"Makin' you my personal lollipop. I'm gonna lick it all off. Every. Single. Drop."

Everything inside her went red-hot with want.

"Open up and stick out your tongue."

She did. Something warm ran off the sides and down her chin. She licked her lips. "Chocolate syrup."

"Very good." Cord drizzled warm syrup down her neck. He squirted so much on her breasts she felt it dripping from her nipples. He coated the inside of her thighs. Then he licked her chin and her lips before he blew her mind with another soul kiss. "Tasty. Open your mouth and stick out your tongue."

"How many flavors am I gonna be?"

"Anxious to feel my tongue on you? Licking off every bit of sweetness?"

Her sex clenched hard. "Cord. You're making me crazy."

"I know, baby doll, that's the point." He used his teeth to tug her earlobe, sending goosebumps through her from her scalp to her curled toes. "Now be a good girl and stick out your tongue or I'll turn on the shower and let it clean you off instead of me."

"No! I—I'll be good. I promise." AJ stuck out her tongue. A solid blob this time. She closed her mouth and chewed. "Peach jam. Specifically your mom's peach jam."

"I'm impressed."

"We have half a dozen jars at our apartment. It's the one food thing Keely refuses to be without. She's making me bring a couple more pints home to Denver when I go back."

A beat of silence, then, "I'm not smearin' jam on you. So, open your mouth for the next one."

AJ wondered what'd thrown him. A reference to the fact she'd be returning to that apartment? Or the idea Denver would be her only home?

"AJ," he warned.

She opened her mouth. More sticky liquid dribbled down her chin. "Chokecherry syrup."

"You have highly developed taste buds, let's see how *mine* feel against your skin."

Cord began his onslaught at her neck and licked his way down. Sometimes fast. Sometimes slow. Sometimes scraping his teeth on her flesh. Sometimes using suckling kisses.

But every sweep of his tongue, every hot breath, every groan and sigh only pushed her further to the edge. Her heart, her arms, her belly, her legs—all trembled. Her pussy in particular quivered for the feel of that brilliant tongue.

Finally he said, "Spread your legs."

Her blood seemed to pound right out of her veins as she slid her bare feet across the cool tile.

"Do you remember the prize you won last night?"

"Uh. Yeah. Why?"

A buzzing noise sounded beside her right ear.

"No. Is that the...?"

"Yep. Picked up off the front seat of your car. Didn't want your sister or your nieces and nephew to find it first. Plus I thought we might need it today. You know, for a little comparison."

"Cord—"

"Oh, no need to thank me, baby doll. Watchin' this plastic cock disappear into your pussy will be thanks enough." The buzzing stopped. "I lubed it with K-Y, but hold still while I put it in."

The vibrator slid in easily. Whoa. Talk about bizarre, having a plastic cock inside her; no warmth, no life, no heat, no pliancy. What was the appeal?

Then Cord turned it on and she knew.

"Oh-man-oh-man-oh-man." The part inside her pussy vibrated differently than the one on her clit. The interior wand seemed to be spinning. Slow. Fast. Slow. Fast.

"Does it hurt?"

"No. It feels...weird. But in a good way. In a really good way all of sudden." She felt him smile against her breast.

"I ain't gonna turn it to warp speed. While it's doin' it's thing, I'm gonna do mine. God, I love your tits. Especially without the condiments."

She arched when Cord sucked her nipple, which pressed the outside apparatus more firmly against her clit. Her whole body shook. The darkness, the sweet scents in the enclosed damp space, the hunger of Cord's mouth, the feel of his hard body, and the loss of the use of her hands—all overpowering sensations. The unrelenting vibrations inside her pussy and on her clit were setting her on a path to the fastest orgasm of her life.

"It's too much, it's—" She gasped as the climax struck fierce as chain lightning, in intense bursts, flash after flash of light behind her eyelids and then it was gone.

The buzzing stopped. Cord removed the vibrator and his mouth was on hers. He untied her hands.

She sagged against him. He turned the shower on, letting the cold water hit his back until it heated. Droplets of water sprayed her face and scented steam filled her nostrils.

Cord washed her off as he kissed her; his rough hands seemed bigger when they were wet. He said, "I want you like this. Turn around."

He braced her hands on the wall, bending her forward until she was nearly at a right angle. He kicked her feet apart, tilted her hips and slid into her to the hilt. And stopped.

"Cord?"

His chest pressed into her spine. "I want to fuck you like an animal—"

"Then do it. Take what you want. You have the reins."

He groaned and sank his teeth into the back of her neck, sending a fresh batch of tremors through her body before he stood up and slammed home.

Over and over. Harder than he'd ever done before.

Cord didn't speak beyond grunts. He just systematically fucked her into oblivion.

Good thing she'd braced herself. It was almost like he was trying to fuck her through the wall. When he came, snarling, pounding his flesh into hers, she swore even his semen burned hotter.

She sensed a shift in him. His breathing leveled, resembling a wave of shame as he retreated from her body with exquisite care. AJ walked her hands up the wall. She spun around blindly, reaching for him.

God, she loved this man. She loved his gruff, sweet, thoughtful sides. And his edgy side. She wasn't in love with the perfect Cord McKay she'd been fantasizing over forever, but the real flesh and blood man. The real man. Flaws and all.

And she knew without a doubt he'd break her heart. His stubborn pride would stand in the way of them being together. She had too much pride to do all the work of making him see how good they could be together for the long haul if he'd just be patient. She'd been doing all the work in all aspects of her life and she deserved a man who would meet her halfway. She deserved a man she didn't have to beg to love her.

AJ coiled her arms around his waist and kissed his chest, above his heart, making a wish. *Please love me. Please see what we could have together. Please figure it out on your own.*

"You okay?"

"Tired. Your water games wore me out."

"Hang tight." He removed the blindfold, returned with a fluffy towel, dried her off thoroughly and guided her back into the bedroom to tuck her between his sheets. "Rest, baby doll."

"What time is it?"

"Not even noon."

"So we still have all day?"

"Yep. And all night if you want it."

AJ smiled and sank into the pillows. "Good. I'll just take a little catnap."

"You do that." He kissed her forehead.

She expected him to leave. But Cord swept her hair from her face and dragged his rough-skinned knuckles up and down her cheek.

As AJ drifted away, she heard him murmur, "What the hell am I supposed to do now?"

She tried to fight her way back to consciousness to give

him a couple of realistic options, but a veil of darkness covered her and she was out.

Chapter Twenty-eight

Rather than pace while AJ napped, Cord made lunch. Rather than dwell on the fact that in two short weeks he wouldn't be able to drive to her place and kidnap her for a full day of wicked sex games, he thought about how they'd spend the rest of the afternoon.

Naked, obviously. But what else?

What else do you need? Wasn't this deal supposed to be a way to prove that sex was separate from love and companionship?

Not love. Logically his need for companionship made the most sense on why he was so insanely crazy about her. He was missing his son and spending time with AJ was a substitute. The minute Ky arrived, things would be back to the way they'd been.

Wouldn't they? Wouldn't he be happy then?

Cord knew he shouldn't be such a damn ostrich about this stuff, but he wondered if the "out of sight; out of mind" adage would hold true once AJ was gone.

He piled food on a tray and carried it upstairs. AJ was lying on her side, breathing evenly. "AJ? I made lunch."

"What?" She scrambled upright. "Where am I?"

"You fell asleep in my bed."

"Oh. Wow. How long ago?"

"Little more than an hour. You hungry?"

AJ stretched. "Always. What's on the menu?"

"Cold cuts. Cheese. Fruit. Nothin' fancy."

"Sounds good. Do you have a robe I can borrow?"

"A robe? What the devil do you need a robe for?"

"I don't want to sit in the kitchen naked."

He grinned. "Who said anything about eatin' in the kitchen? I brought you lunch in bed."

"Aren't you worried about crumbs?"

"No. We'll do a number on the sheets anyway." Cord scooted closer and plucked up a grape from the tray. "Open."

Her gaze narrowed thoughtfully on the piece of fruit. "Are you gonna smear condiments all over me again?"

"Would that be so bad?"

"No. I just wish I could've taken a turn." She scrutinized the tray. "Where are the cookies?"

"What cookies?"

"Exactly. Lunch isn't lunch without cookies."

"You sound just like Ky," he said dryly.

"Ky is a boy after my own heart."

A tiny stupid flare of jealousy appeared: Cord wanted to be the man after her heart.

You could be. Just take the chance. Admit this is long past a simple roll in the hay.

"Your son and I even have the same favorite cookie."

"Peanut butter kisses?"

"Yep."

Cord leaned closer. "I don't have any peanut butter kisses. How about a real one instead?" He granted her a quick peck and dangled a fat green grape above her lips. "Open up."

AJ sucked the grape from his fingers with deliberate sensuality, which made his dick stir. "This makes me feel like a lady of leisure. Laying in this soft bed. Having a hot guy hand feed me. You have palm fronds hidden somewhere too?"

"Hot guy. Right. You mean *old* guy."

"So you have a few years on me. Hasn't kept you from keeping up with me." She purposely looked at his groin.

"True."

"It's never mattered to me." Her serious gray eyes searched

his. "Do you remember the time I fell off my horse? When I was five? And you picked me up, wiped my tears and calmed me down?"

Cord frowned. Didn't ring a bell. "You gonna be upset if I say no?"

She shook her head. "I'd be surprised if you *did* remember. But I've never forgotten it. Never. You were a Western knight in a white cowboy hat. You've been my fantasy man since that day all those years ago."

"AJ, that's not me. Then or now—"

"It is. Don't spoil the memory for me by denying it. Don't spoil this moment either. Be Cord my sexy fantasy man, not Cord the responsible rancher who thinks too much."

A section of her hair was stuck to her cheek from where she'd slept on it. Cord peeled it away and rubbed the damp, white-blonde strand between his fingers. So soft. Such a contrast against his rough, callused hand. "You are sweet."

AJ blushed. She picked up a chunk of salami and held it to his mouth. "I want to feed you too."

By the time the food was gone, they'd teased each other to the point Cord was crazed to have her again. He sat in the middle of the bed and wrapped her legs around his lower back as she shifted down slowly, encasing his cock in her tight, wet heat.

"I like it this way."

"Me too, baby doll. Me too." Cord clutched her ass cheeks in his hands as they maintained a slow, sensual pace. Her soft skin brushed his everywhere. He consumed her mouth, her neck, her nipples, never completely leaving the heaven of her pliant pussy. She climaxed and brought him along with her, in a deliciously sweet throbbing that seemed to last an eternity.

With their bodies and mouths still connected in the aftermath of lazy, but passionate loving, he realized he'd never clicked with anyone on this level—heart, body and soul. He also realized he didn't know what the hell to do about it.

AJ licked his Adam's apple. "Mmm. Sweaty, yummy sexy man."

"I can get some more food if you're still hungry."

"I'll just nibble on you, if that's okay."

"Fine by me." He arched his neck when her teeth scraped up to his ear and released a shudder. "God. I love that."

"Then I'll keep doing it."

His hands were on her butt and his thumbs idly stroked the crack of her ass to the puckered rosette. On the next slow stroke up, his thumb lingered on that tiny opening.

Immediately she tensed up.

"You don't like that?"

"No. I do, but I don't think I'm ready for umm...more than that."

"We can go slow."

She said nothing—which alarmed him because she always spoke her mind.

"AJ? Look at me." She lifted her head. Cord didn't like the fear in her eyes. He especially didn't like the fact he'd put it there. She'd given her body over to him without hesitation, with eagerness, with utter trust, with joy. He'd be a fool—and a bully—if he let his sexual desires overrule her panic. "I'd never make you do anything you didn't want to, baby doll. If you're not ready, no big deal, okay?"

"But you said—"

"Forget what I said. I'm a controllin' dickhead sometimes. I'm used to bein' obeyed. Period." He kissed her with reassurance. "No hurry. I can wait until you're ready. In the mean time"—he flipped her on her back—"I want you again."

AJ murmured, "I'm so glad *Cosmo* was wrong about the male recovery time thingy."

He chuckled against her throat and wondered how he'd ever let her go.

After spending nearly all day in bed, AJ needed a break. She unfolded from Cord's embrace and reached for her clothes that he'd brought up from downstairs.

"Where's the fire?"

"Nowhere. Don't you have to check cattle?"

"Yeah. Why?"

"Can I come along?"

Cord raised both eyebrows. "Really?"

"Sure. Can we take the horses instead of the truck?"

"Takes longer."

"I don't care. I like being outside."

He rolled over and mumbled something as he reached for his clothes.

"What? If you don't want me to come along, just say so."

"It's not that. Just shocks the hell out of me that you want to."

"It shouldn't. As much as I bitched about it when I had no choice but to tend to everything, I'm a ranch girl through and through. I think you forget that sometimes."

"I'm tryin' to."

Not touching that comment, cowboy. I can't wrestle your demons anymore than I can make you change your mind or see the truth.

Downstairs, as AJ slipped on her ropers, Cord waggled the silver boots at her. "You still haven't worn these. Now you'll have me thinkin' of all sorts of scenarios in which you're wearin' nothin' but these *fuck me* boots when we get back."

She snatched them and threw them in the coat closet. "Wrong. Out of sight; out of mind."

Cord froze.

"What?"

"Do you think that'll really work? Pretendin' somethin's not there when it obviously is right in front of you?"

AJ had the strangest feeling they weren't talking about a pair of boots. "No. Come on. Let's saddle up."

Within ten minutes they were riding the fenceline. The late afternoon sun was hot, not unbearably so, but warm enough that AJ wished she'd grabbed a hat. Cord wore his, a finely woven cream-colored straw, not the frat party variety, but the type ranchers needed in the summertime to reflect heat. She couldn't help but think the white hat just reinforced the white knight image she'd held of him her entire life.

After they'd checked the herd, they continued clopping

along. The serenity of the scenery negated the need for idle chatter. Cord led; she followed.

"See that stock tank? Race—"

The second she heard the word *race* she was gone. He didn't come close to catching her. "Maybe you should ride this horse next time, McKay. I've beaten you both times."

"I won once."

"Want to go best three out of five?"

"No. You have a daredevil streak, Ms. Foster. How come I never knew about it?"

"Because being a wild child was Keely's reputation, not mine. I was too busy working in my dad's stead to be wild." After she realized what she'd confessed, she kicked her heels into Nickel's sides and they were off.

Cord reined up beside her. "You gonna explain that, or are you gonna make me guess?"

She said, "Guess," deciding he wouldn't figure out what no one else had during those years.

"Let's see. I moved back here seven years ago after bein' in Seattle for two years, so you would've been fifteen. I don't remember you chummin' around with Keely until you were at least eighteen, after Ky was born and Marla took off. So durin' those missin' years you were—"

"Wow. Look. A red-tailed hawk." AJ pointed to the bird circling in the vibrant blue sky off to the west.

"Baby doll, I could be sarcastic and list a buncha things you might've been doin', but I'm askin' you to be honest and tell me the truth."

"And if I don't want to?"

"Do it anyway."

AJ met his hard gaze. "I was working the ranch. Daddy had a debilitating heart attack when I was thirteen. Mama and Daddy didn't want anyone to know about his health problems, so all the doctor's visits were done in Cheyenne."

"So you're sayin'? What? You did everything? Ran the ranch by...yourself?"

"I couldn't do the haying. But I knew what else needed to be done, so I did it. End of story."

Colt looked like she'd punched him in the gut. "You ran the ranch? From the time you were thirteen? Why didn't anyone in the community notice? For Christsake, why didn't anyone in *my* family notice?" He demanded, "Did Keely know this?"

"Not until a few years ago. She always teased me about being such a goody-goody. But the truth was, I was too damn tired to care about being the belle of the county." After she'd told Keely the truth, Keely had been suitably appalled by her own clueless behavior. She'd also been embarrassed by the McKay family's tendency to take care of their own to the exclusion of all others. AJ had sworn Keely to secrecy and they'd become friends on a much deeper level than she'd ever imagined possible.

"You took care of the cattle? And the horses? And fixin' fence and mowin' ditches? And breedin' and brandin'?"

"After the first calving season Daddy started selling off cow/calf pairs. By the time I was fifteen all the cattle were gone. Dad told everyone he wanted early retirement and we leased most of the grazing land. Then I just had to deal with the other ranch stuff you're always talking about."

"You didn't ask my dad, my brothers, my cousins, or any of the McKays? You have to know that someone in my family would've helped you out—"

"Which family, Cord? Colby was rodeoin'. Cam joined the service. Carter was at college. You were living in Seattle, which left Colt. Your McKay cousins, Kane, Kade, Quinn and Bennett had to do all the rest of the work—except for Chase who was still in high school—and they had to hire out, remember? The McKay ranch is fifty times the size of ours. So your family couldn't have helped us even if my dad hadn't had too much pride to ask."

"AJ—"

"I'm warning you, Cord, drop it."

"Like hell."

AJ reined Nickel the opposite direction, snapped the reins and raced back to the barn like the hounds of hell nipped at her heels.

Cord was right on her horse's tail. But all thoughts of continuing the discussion were lost when she noticed Colby's pickup screaming up the driveway as she reached the fence beside the barn. She jerked Nickel to a stop, causing Cord to do the same with Jester.

He snapped, "What now?"

"Do you want me to hide in the barn until Colby leaves?"

"Fuck that. I'm sick of this hidin' shit. I think it's time we told everyone the truth about us—"

"Cord!"

They turned to see Colby running toward them.

A sick feeling churned in AJ's stomach. Colby. Running.

"You gotta come. Dag had an accident."

"Dag? What the hell happened?"

"We ain't sure."

"He okay?"

Colby shook his head. "He's dead."

Shock hung in the air.

AJ said, "Go on, Cord. Be with your family. I'll take care of the horses."

Neither he nor Colby said another word as they climbed into Colby's truck and roared off.

Chapter Twenty-nine

Four days later…

Cord sat next to his brother Carter in the church basement after Dag's funeral service. Everyone was somber, still in a state of shock over Dag's death.

Sometimes a tragedy will pull a family apart. But it had the opposite effect with the Wests and McKays, by putting an end to the rift between them. Carson and Cal and Charlie McKay and all of Dag's male McKay cousins—less Cam who was in Iraq—were pallbearers right alongside the eight West cousins.

The church had been packed with family, members of the community and lots of young rodeo cowboys. They'd all been holding up fairly well until Dag's buddy Trevor Glanzer brought the traditional riderless horse to the funeral procession of cars headed to the graveyard.

In the last four days, Dag's father, Harland, aged twenty years. He refused to let his daughter, Chassie, out of his sight. Cord's mother shooed Chassie away to give her a much needed break from her father's overwhelming grief, and Carolyn stayed beside her grieving brother. The only other time Cord had seen his mother so distraught was two years ago when Colby nearly died from a rodeo injury.

Cord's gaze swept the table. Carter and Macie. Colby and Channing. Keely. Kane and Kade. Chase McKay and his older brothers Quinn and Bennett. Cash Big Crow. Trevor. But Trevor went to comfort Chassie and they disappeared outside. Cord imagined it wouldn't be much longer before he'd be hearing another set of wedding bells. Better that than the somber tones of a funeral dirge.

Colt was conspicuously absent. He'd been at the service and the burial, but no one knew where he'd gone afterward. No one said it, but everyone knew his brother was drinking someplace. And of all the stupid fucking things to do...drinking was what'd gotten Dag killed.

Dag had still been half-drunk from a hard night of partying when he'd started chores Saturday morning. The assumption was Dag passed out on the tractor, drifted into the ditch where the tractor flipped on top of him and crushed him. Luckily Trevor discovered Dag that afternoon, not Harland. God knows that would've killed his uncle and they'd be having a double funeral.

Ranching was a dangerous life. Fatal accidents happened all the time. Not in their family in recent years. And not because of a bad decision that could've easily been avoided.

A fucking senseless waste of a life.

Jesus. He couldn't believe Dag was dead. None of them could.

Voices murmured. Cord loosened his tie and Keely caught him looking at his watch.

"What time do you have to leave?"

"In about an hour."

"You sure you want to go alone? I could drive you."

"Thanks, sis, but I'll be fine. It's gonna be a quick trip."

"Did you talk to him today?"

"Yeah. He don't understand and I've done a poor job explainin' it to him." By the time Cord decided to tell Ky what'd happened to Dag, his son had plain gone into hysterics and demanded to come home. Oddly enough, Marla agreed Ky should be with him. They'd changed the plane reservations and Cord was scheduled to leave on the last flight out of Cheyenne to Denver, en route to Seattle. As happy as he'd be to see his boy for the first time in a month, a layer of sadness dimmed his enthusiasm. Death changed everything.

Carter shoved his empty cup across the table. "Sorry I'm gonna miss seein' the little squirt, but we can't stick around."

"My fault," Cash said. "I doan wanna leave Gem alone with the twins overnight. She says she can handle them but she shouldn't have to. We brought two horse trailers and we still need to load up the horses I bought from AJ before we take off."

Cord's stomach clenched at the mention of AJ's name.

"That means you guys are leavin' me to deal with Colt once I track him down?" Colby asked.

Shit. Cord hadn't thought of that. "Can it wait until I get back?"

"What am I, Colby, chopped liver? I didn't get to knock some sense into Carter the last time we had a McKay fall out of line, so I'm entitled to let loose on another one of my stupidly clueless brothers." Keely gave Cord a pointed look.

"What?"

"You know *what.*"

Kane said, "Don't sweat it. Kade and I'll be around."

Quinn scratched his head beneath his hat. "Count me and Bennett in, if you give us enough warning so we can make the drive. Chase has gotta get back on the road too."

"Where you competin' next?" Cash asked.

"Wichita. Big purse. Lotsa points."

"That's a long way. You drivin' straight through?"

Chase nodded.

"Good luck and be careful." When Cash stood to leave, everyone at the table followed suit.

After Cord was on the road, he heard his cell phone beeping and he saw he'd missed a call from AJ. Damn. They'd been playing phone tag for a couple of days. The day after Dag died she'd gone to Billings with Jenn to get her mother moved into the assisted living facility. She wouldn't be back until after he and Ky returned.

Yeah, he knew it was over. He knew he shouldn't call her back. He should just let it go. He should just let *her* go. But the idea of not seeing her again? Not talking to her? Not laughing with her? Not touching her? That was just another reason why his reunion with Ky would be so bittersweet.

He hit redial anyway and left her another message. Cell service through Wyoming was spotty at best so he knew chances were slim they'd actually connect. Why did everything in life have to be so goddamn hard?

Why don't you just buck up and tell her how you feel?

Right. So she could walk away from him?

Maybe she'd stay.

Nah. The die was cast. The ball was in play. There was no way to go back and he really couldn't see how he and AJ could go forward when they'd literally be miles apart from Sundance to Denver.

It was a damn long, lonely, depressing drive to Cheyenne.

Chapter Thirty

Two days later...

While Kade and Skylar waited for the check after a crappy meal at Ziggy's sports bar, which neither of them tasted, he saw Colt.

Happy as Kade was to know his cousin wasn't dead, because no one had seen him since Dag's funeral, he was less than happy when Colt stumbled to their booth drunk as a skunk, high as a kite with a vulgar look in his bleary eyes.

"Hey, cuz. Who's the purty lady?"

"Skylar. Skylar this is my very drunk cousin, Colt McKay."

"Colt. Nice to meet you."

"So how come you haven't brought her by the Boars Nest? 'Cause she ain't the adventurous type?"

"No. Because I don't live there anymore." Kade had a moment of panic. What if Colt was here with Kane? Why in the hell after half a dozen dates hadn't he come clean about his real identity? Because it'd gone too far and he was a total fucking dumbass.

"Excuse us, we were just leavin'."

"Hold on, hold on. I'll let ya go get lucky," he winked lewdly at Skylar, "soon as you tell me what the hell Kane did with my extra set of truck keys. Can't find 'em anywhere."

"Is my brother here?"

"No, your brother ain't here. That's what I'm sayin'. The bartender took my keys. I keep an extra set in my glove box and they're missin'. Kane didn't give 'em back last time he borrowed my truck."

"You shouldn't be drivin' anyway."

"When did you turn into such a fuckin' pussy, Kade? Jesus."

"Shut up, Colt, and go someplace else. For Christsake go sleep it off in your truck."

"Think you got the right to tell me what to do like everyone else in my goddamn life? Fuck that. I'll knock you into next week, you smarmy cocksucker."

Skylar said, "Take it easy, Colt. You're confused. Maybe Kane and I should take you home."

Colt frowned and looked around wildly. "Kane? He's here?"

"He's right there." Skylar pointed at Kade.

No no no. Kade knew everything was about to go horribly wrong.

"Darlin', I may be drunk as shit, but you're the one who's confused. That ain't Kane. That's Kade."

Skylar stared at Kade as if she expected him to dispute it. While she waited, two more shadows fell across the table and they both looked up to see Colby and...Kane.

Fucking great.

Skylar gasped. Her gaze zipped back and forth between the twins. "There are *two* of you?"

"Skylar? What the hell are you doin' here with my brother?"

Her eyes were black with rage when they connected with his again. "*Kade*, I presume?"

"Look. I can explain. When I found out what a dick Kane was to you on your date that night—"

"You took it upon yourself to pretend to be him that lunch date in Moorcroft? And then all the times after that?"

"Yes. I mean, no. Shit. I wanted to show you I'm not him. Just because we're identical twins doesn't mean we have identical behavior."

"Unless you want them to, purty lady. These guys fulfilled quite a few women's fantasies of bein'—what'd Jazz call you that night she fucked both of you at the same time?—a twin beefcake manwich."

"Colt, shut your fuckin' mouth," Colby snapped.

"I'll bet you're having a big goddamn laugh about this, *Kade.*"

"I ain't laughin', Sky, 'cause it ain't a joke. I planned to tell you—"

"Right after you screwed me in the parking lot of a honky tonk not an hour ago?" she hissed. "Was it all a lie? A trick? See if I'd notice the difference between you two?"

"No!"

"Aw, sweet darlin', there's plenty of us McKay men around if you wanna give me a shot. I'm up for anything." Colt ran his fingers down Skylar's arm.

Kade jumped up and clocked Colt in the jaw. Colt stumbled but remained upright. "Don't you ever fuckin' touch her. Don't you even look at her, you drunken piece of shit."

"At least I don't have to pretend to be someone I'm not in order to get some pussy."

Kade lunged for him again and Colby held him back as Colt hit the ground.

He noticed everything and everyone in the bar came to a dead stop.

"Come on." Colby and Kane each had one of Colt's arms as they dragged him outside.

Somehow, Kade found the balls to face Skylar's justifiable fury. He boxed her in so she couldn't escape until he'd said his piece. "No matter what you think, I was *me* when we were together. Me. Kade McKay. Everything I did, everything I said, every damn time. None of it was a lie. The way I feel about you ain't a lie either."

She whispered, "Just go away and leave me alone."

"I'm takin' you home."

"No. Just go."

"But—"

"Don't humiliate me any more than you already have. Go."

Miserable, he walked out.

Colt had passed out in the parking lot. The three of them threw him in the back of Kane's truck with more force than necessary.

"How'd you track him down?" Kade asked.

"The bartender called me. We've put the word out to all of Colt's regular waterin' holes that we're lookin' for him."

Colby was pissed and as close to losing it as Kade had ever seen him. "What the fuck am I supposed to do with him? I can't take him home. Ma is already a mess over Dag's death and she's worried sick the same thing is gonna happen to Colt.

"If I leave him by himself to sleep it off, he'll disappear again, or I'll find him dead from chokin' on his own vomit. You guys can't stay up all night and babysit him because we've all gotta work tomorrow. We're short-handed since Cord's been gone and Colt ain't been around to pick up the slack."

"Colt ain't done shit for months, Colby. None of us are happy about that."

Colby paced. "My pregnant wife is fuckin' hysterical because she's afraid my stupid brother will do somethin' to get me killed. Now she refuses to let me work anywhere around him. How am I supposed to tell my folks that? When Colt and Cord can't work together anymore either."

Softly, Kane said, "She's right."

"Well, what the hell am I supposed to do? We've got a goddamn ranch to run! None of us can spend our time worryin' about soap opera family shit like this."

They remained quiet, lost in their own thoughts.

"I'll stay up with him at the Boars Nest tonight," Kade said. "I'm too wound up to sleep anyway and Ma will know somethin' is wrong with me if I go home."

"Guess that gets you outta mornin' chores," Kane said.

"Talk to Uncle C about this. I'll talk to my dad. We'll come up with somethin' because far as I'm concerned, tonight was the last straw for Colt's employment anyplace on the ranch."

Kane retrieved the keys from the bartender and drove Colt's truck home, then helped Kade get Colt into the house.

After they'd dropped Colt fully clothed in his bed, Kane said, "About what happened with Skylar—"

"Not talkin' about it with you now, or ever, Kane. Let it alone."

He nodded and Kade heard the door to his brother's room close.

It was a long night.

ꟹ

Colt stirred around eight o'clock when Kade dumped a bucket of cold water on him. "Get up, asshole."

Colt rubbed his jaw and wiped water from his face. "What happened last night?"

"I hit you."

"Why?"

"Because you're a drunk and an asshole and an embarrassment to this family."

Colt leaned over and threw up in the bucket on the other side of the bed. When he got to the dry heave stage and finally sat back up, Kade tossed him a bottle of water.

"I don't remember nothin'."

"You'd be the only one. It's sure to be all over Crook and Weston Counties today."

"Shit." He closed his eyes. "Am I really that far gone?"

"Afraid so." Kade paused. "You remember Dag is dead?"

He nodded. "What else has happened?"

"Channing doesn't want Colby to work with you because she's afraid you'll get him killed."

"Great. My sweet sister-in-law fuckin' hates me."

"Not hate, she's scared, Colt. We all are. Then there's the situation between you and Cord."

Colt's eyes opened. "What situation?"

"You got into a fistfight with him at the Golden Boot." When Colt continued to have that same blank stare, Kade filled him in on everything else up through last night.

His head drooped to his chest in absolute shame. "I'm sorry. I'm so fuckin' sorry." His deep baritone was scarcely above a whisper. "What the hell has happened to me? I don't remember nothin'," he repeated.

Kade didn't answer. He just let Colt soak it all in.

After a while Colt stood and shuffled to the bathroom.

Half an hour later Colt propped himself against the doorway to the kitchen. He cleared his throat. "I need help."

Kade didn't offer anything.

"I need help in a bad way. No more drinkin'. No more druggin'. No more whorin'."

When Colt met his gaze, Kade wasn't the least bit surprised to see Colt's tears.

"I know I don't got no right to ask you, but will you help me? Will you take me some place to dry out?"

"You want me to call your brothers?"

"No. They have enough shit to deal with. Call Keely. Have her and our cousin Nick find a place in Denver. Someplace away from here."

"You sure?"

"Yeah."

"Okay. But I'll hafta tell the family why I ain't gonna be able to help out the next coupla days. The truth about you goin' in for treatment oughta come from you, cuz, not me."

Colt nodded and took Kade's cell phone and disappeared into the kitchen.

Kade McKay to the rescue again. While he waited for Colt, he took stock of his own situation.

His life was a screwed up mess. Living with his parents. He'd try like hell to get Skylar to forgive him and give him another chance, but he figured with his luck, he'd already lost her. Not that he blamed her. He'd done a stupid thing by not telling her the truth and now he was paying for it. Just like Colt was.

Losing a woman like that seemed a damn steep price to pay. He hoped Cord was smart enough to not make the same mistakes he had. One of them deserved a shot at happiness that didn't have a goddamn thing to do with the fucking ranch.

Ten minutes later Colt shouldered an overnight bag and trudged past Kade to his truck without another word.

They'd have plenty of time to talk on the road, if Colt

wanted to. But Kade wouldn't be surprised if the trip to Denver toward sobriety was completely silent.

Chapter Thirty-one

Three days later...

"Daddy, how come Gran-gran is so sad?"

"Because Uncle Colt made some bad decisions and he had to go away. Gran-gran misses him like I missed you."

"Did he go away like Dag went away?"

Cord looked up from buttering toast. "Not the same, Ky. Dag ain't comin' back. Colt will be back next month."

"Okay. Is that how come you're sad too?"

"Yeah." But Cord couldn't help feeling relieved that his brother finally acknowledged a problem and had taken control of his life. They'd deal with the changes when Colt returned.

"I know what'd make ya happy."

AJ. Seeing AJ would make him very happy. "What?"

"Playin' Go Fish."

"You know, that'd probably do it. We'll play a game first thing when I get home later this afternoon."

"How come I gotta go to Gran-gran's? Why can't I help you?"

Cord counted to ten. "As I've already explained three times, I can't be worryin' about you today while I'm changin' out the pump. And Gran-gran missed you bad. Don't you wanna cheer her up?"

"No." The spoon in the cereal bowl clattered. "I wanna stay with you. Why are you sendin' me away? I wanna stay in my own house and play with my own tools and be with my own daddy—"

Ky launched himself off the barstool, coiled himself around Cord's legs and blubbered. He'd been clingy too—another thing Cord hadn't dealt with before. He hoisted his son up and tried to calm him.

When Ky quit sobbing, Cord finally understood what Ky had been saying over and over—*I don't wancha to die too.*

No way could he leave the kid today. No way.

He called his folks' house. "Ma. No, we're not runnin' late. He's not comin' over today. Because he needs another day with me, and I could use another one with him. Yeah, I know we're short-handed. So? The pump will keep another day. I'll call you later."

Ky finally stopped shuddering and peeked out from where he'd hidden his teary face in Cord's neck. "Is she mad?"

"Nah. Disappointed, but not mad."

Cord gazed down into Ky's somber blue eyes. The kid looked so much like him it was like looking back in time.

"You mad at me now, Daddy?"

"For being a kid? Not on your life." He kissed the top of his head. "But I will be ticked if you beat me at cards, boy."

Ky giggled and wiggled to be let down.

Cord felt like one piece of his life clicked back in place. Oddly enough, he still felt like another piece was missing.

cs

AJ's cell phone rang at nine o'clock and she knew it was Cord before she saw the caller ID. "Hey. What's up?"

"Ky's in bed. And I haven't seen you in over a week."

No small talk. Not a surprise. "You wanted this 'deal' to end when your son returned."

"I know."

Silence.

"So? Why'd you call me?"

"To see if you'd come over."

Why? Because you missed me? Or missed the sex?

Did it really matter? She was leaving in a couple of days. Hadn't she wished for a chance to be with him again?

"AJ?"

"Yeah. Give me half an hour."

A sense of displacement and sadness rolled over her as she looked at the empty walls. Nothing remained of the years the Foster family spent here besides memories and the boxes stacked in the kitchen. Where would Macie and Carter start making changes? Plenty of repairs and updates dogged this old ranch house—repairs the Fosters hadn't the skill or the money to implement. She doubted Macie would see the charm in leaky faucets, drafty windows, doors that stuck, a cellar with an uneven floor and an unreliable heating system.

Speaking of...she wiped her sweaty brow. Why was it so damn hot in here? She'd shut off the window air conditioner because it kept shorting out, and she'd closed the windows because of the bugs. But it shouldn't feel like the damn furnace was running. Stupid coal heater in the cellar was acting up again.

Nothing she could do about it now and it wouldn't be her problem much longer anyway. Day after tomorrow the movers would load up everything and take it to the storage facility in Billings. Then she'd make a final walk through with the McKays and the banker and be on her way to Denver to finish school.

It was weird to think she wouldn't see her mother until Christmas. Not as weird as imagining Christmas wouldn't be here, at home, in this house, ever again.

Pull up your bootstraps, girl. Life goes on.

That it did. AJ had cried at Liza and Noah's wedding ceremony as they'd begun their life together. As she'd cried for Dag West, his life cut short too soon. It'd served as a reminder that things could be much worse in her life than moving away from home and unrequited love.

She grabbed her purse and drove to Cord's. He waited for her on the front porch swing. After a prolonged kiss, without saying a word, he took her hand, led her upstairs straight to his bedroom and locked the door. He stripped her bare. The need on his face ripped straight into her soul.

His clever hands and hungry mouth were everywhere and

attempted to set her skin on fire. He perched her on the edge of the bed and fell to his knees, nudged her thighs wide and bent to taste her. A few teasing swirls and he latched on to her clit and sucked.

The intense concentration on that bit of flesh and nowhere else launched her into orgasm like a rocket booster.

While she attempted to return to sanity, Cord kissed his way up the center of her torso, tickling her nipples with his lips. "Roll over onto your stomach."

Cord's rough fingers caressed her arms, the sensitive backs of her thighs and calves as he placed her exactly how he wanted her—butt in the air, arms stretched above her head. He lapped her spine from tailbone to the nape of her neck, sending another wave of shivers across her body.

He maneuvered his cock inside her on a slow smooth glide. "Every bit as good as I remembered. So goddamn good." When he layered his muscled chest over her back to drag kisses over her shoulder, she arched, craving the contact of his warm male skin on hers. While he drove into her, he straightened up and curled his hands around her hips.

AJ looked over her shoulder at him and her heart nearly stopped. Her fantasies paled in reality to this man, so ruggedly beautiful lost in passion. Eyes squeezed shut, jaw clenched. Lips full and soft from kissing her. Sweat gleamed on his torso. The veins in his arms bulged.

Cord sensed her staring at him and opened his eyes.

AJ didn't say a thing. His restraint snapped. He slammed into her over and over. She half expected to feel the bite of his teeth on her throat like stallions did during mating.

A guttural groan burst forth from Cord as she felt the end of his cock twitching, and her interior muscles contracted around the rigid shaft and sent her flying into an orgasm that stole her wits.

AJ collapsed face first on the bed. Firm lips feathered up her calves. He used his tongue on the back of her knees. More lingering kisses up her thigh. Then the other leg. On her butt. Cord spent a lot of time kissing, licking and nuzzling her lower back. Equal treatment to her arms and shoulders and by the time he flipped her over, she was shaking.

Cord kissed her until she was dizzy. Until she was sopping wet with need.

He whispered, "Again," and picked her up, carrying her to the rocking chair in the corner. He straddled her legs across the arms of the chair and sank inside her. "Always so ready for me, baby doll."

"You know how to touch me to make me that way."

"You're so damn sexy I never know where I wanna touch you first." He lifted her breasts to his mouth level. "How about I suck these while you're ridin' me, cowgirl? I wanna feel your nipples throbbin' on my tongue when you come."

This go round was slower, a solid, steady rocking of the chair and a longer climb to pleasure. In the aftermath, Cord kissed her like he couldn't bear to have their lips be apart.

They didn't talk. They returned to bed and touched and kissed and made love until they were exhausted.

Sleepy, AJ shivered beneath the covers.

"You're always cold." Cord rummaged in the dresser alongside the bed. "Here's a T-shirt."

She slipped it on. Pathetic, but she had every intention of stealing it so she'd have something to remember him by.

"I've gotta check on Ky. I'll be right back."

When he returned, AJ noticed he'd left the door cracked open. Cord spooned against her and breathed in her hair. "Stay. Just a little while. I'll wake you up before dawn."

"Mmm. Okay." She knew he'd keep his word because he wouldn't want Ky to find them in bed together. She allowed herself to drift away.

Two sharp pokes on her arm startled her awake. Her gaze flew to the alarm clock. Five thirty.

Dammit. It had happened again.

Two more insistent pokes and AJ moved her head to see mini-Cord, aka Ky—wearing Superman pajamas, peering at her suspiciously. "Amy Jo? Hey, how come you're havin' a sleepover in my daddy's bed?"

Crap. She elbowed Cord in the ribs.

"You coulda had a sleepover in my room."

By Ky's petulant expression he was upset because he considered her *his* friend, not his father's friend. Her fingers automatically reached out to smooth Ky's dark sleep-tousled hair. "No way, Jose. You snore."

Ky smiled. "Daddy snores louder."

"No kidding."

"So did you move back for good? I shore missed you." Ky hopped up on the bed, right next to her. "Are you gonna babysit me today? We could bake some of them cookies. And ride horses. Hey, wanna see the pitchers of the ocean—"

"Hang on, sport," Cord said in a husky morning voice. "Let's have breakfast before you go makin' any plans."

"Are you stayin' for breakfast, Amy Jo?"

"I-I don't know—"

"Please?" Two enthusiastic bounces. "Pleeeeaaase?"

She was such a sucker for this kid. "Okie-dokie, artichokie, but you'd better have a coffee cup out for me by the time I get down there."

His face bloomed with a devilish grin that was pure bad-boy McKay. "I knew you would. You can even sit by me." The look Ky sent his dad dared him to argue about seating arrangements.

"Why don't you get dressed and we'll meetcha downstairs?" Cord said.

"Okay." Ky stood on the mattress and bounced twice before he hurled himself off the bed like a long jumper.

AJ gasped.

Cord sighed.

"Better'n last time, huh, Dad?" Ky's little chest puffed up. "Pretty soon I'll be able to make it all the way to the door." He scampered out.

Before AJ could comment, Cord's mouth was on hers for a deep kiss. He broke away and smiled. "Good mornin'. And before you worry about my son catchin' us in bed, let me say it ain't the end of the world." He nuzzled her neck. "Makes me think maybe we oughta go public with this. Maybe we oughta get...married."

A whack upside the head couldn't have stunned her more

than a marriage proposal. From Cord McKay. First thing in the morning.

"What say we get hitched? We're compatible—in bed and out. You know what it takes to be a rancher's wife. You like my kid and he adores you. You'd be a great mother to him and any other kids we have."

"And I have all my teeth and I can cook, too," AJ snapped and jumped out of bed to scramble for her clothes.

"What?"

"I am not a goddamn broodmare, McKay."

"Fine. Maybe the reasons don't sound romantic, but why ain't it a good idea? You love it here. This could be your new home. You already know the land and my family. You could stay right here and you wouldn't have to go back to Denver."

"*Have* to go? I *want* to go to Denver. I want to finish school because it is the single thing in my life I'm doing for myself and no one else." She yanked on her jeans. In the last few weeks Cord hadn't listened to a damn thing she'd said. He wanted her simply because...she suited him.

At one time that might've been enough for her, but not now. Marriage should start with a declaration of I-love-you-and-can't-live-without-you. Period. It didn't make her childish to expect love, not compatibility, as a reason to spend her life with him; it just made his reasons emotionless and selfish.

"AJ, listen—"

She whirled around. "Do you love me, Cord? Is that why you're hinting you'd like my boots under your bed every night?"

Cord averted his eyes. "There are more important things in a relationship than love."

Not for me there isn't.

The front door slammed and voices echoed in the foyer. Before either of them knew what the ruckus was about, footsteps pounded up the stairs. The bedroom door was flung open and Carolyn McKay raced in, Carson and Ky on her heels.

Carolyn threw her arms around AJ. "Thank God. Oh, thank God you're okay, Amy Jo. We thought..."

AJ couldn't breathe, Carolyn was squeezing her so tight.

Ky announced, "Amy Jo had an overnight with Daddy,

Gran-gran."

Cord groaned. Carson cleared his throat. AJ felt her cheeks flame.

"That's good. Real good that she was here and not there."

"There? What is going on?"

Carolyn eased back and tucked a strand of hair behind AJ's ear. "Sweetheart, I don't know how to tell you this."

All the blood drained from her face. "Did something happen to my mother?"

"No, but your house caught fire and burned to the ground."

AJ stared, in utter shock. "What? When?"

"About two hours ago, near as they can figure."

"You're sure?"

"Yes."

"But...how?"

"No one knows. It went so fast the volunteer firefighters didn't get there in time to save anything. And we thought you were inside..."

"Until I realized your Jeep wasn't there," Carson said. "We called Keely when we couldn't get you on your cell and she told us to check here."

"The house burned?"

"Yeah, honey, I'm sorry."

"Is there anything left?"

"Didn't appear to be. Didn't spread to the barn or any of the outbuildings so they're assumin' it was just somethin' in the house that somehow ignited."

AJ nodded numbly. "I know Ma told you we'd been having problems with both the propane and the old coal furnace. Some of the wiring was kinda iffy too. I can't believe it. If I would've been there, maybe—"

"Don't say it, don't even think it, AJ," Cord snapped.

"Not your fault. Sweetheart, we're just so glad you weren't there."

"But everything else was. All our family pictures and furniture and the movers were supposed to come and get it all tomorrow..." Tears broke free like a dam breach.

Carolyn wrapped an arm around her shoulder and led her from the room. She offered to make coffee; all AJ wanted was to see the wreckage that used to be her home. Alone. But Carolyn insisted on coming along.

Pumper-trucks and pickups filled the yard. When AJ caught the glimpse of the smoking pile of rubble, she covered her face and sobbed. The only thing that remained was the foundation and the cement walkway.

Poof. Everything gone. Carolyn held her while she cried. She stayed close when AJ called her mother and her sister, and the insurance agent. Luckily they'd kept the house insured until the final step of the deed transfer, which wouldn't be for another couple days.

Hours passed before the firefighters declared the last embers out. It was late afternoon and she was alone with her scattered thoughts, lost in the smell of smoke, guilt and tears. Carolyn had saddled up Lucy and rode her to the McKay homestead, promising to take care of her horse until AJ was settled. Wherever and whenever that might be.

AJ wondered if she'd ever feel settled again. Not only had she lost her home, she'd lost decades worth of family history. She literally had nothing but the clothes on her back.

She knew things could be replaced. She knew she was lucky to be alive. She knew it, yet, she mourned. And dammit, she figured she had a right to it.

Cord's big truck rumbled up the driveway. With all that'd happened she'd completely forgotten their early morning conversation. AJ hoped Ky was with him because he wouldn't speak so freely about future plans with his son around.

But Cord was alone and he didn't get out of his truck for the longest time, he just stared at the debris pile. When he climbed out, he ambled straight to her and enclosed her in his big strong arms.

Why did *he* feel like home?

Wishful thinking.

She allowed his comfort and managed not to cry. Finally she untangled herself from him. "It's probably better it burned now, rather than after Carter and Macie moved in with their sweet little baby, none of them suspecting what horrors were awaiting them in this old crappy house. I couldn't live with myself if it would've happened to them." AJ walked away to try a sense of balance.

Cord chased her down. "You're damn lucky it didn't happen to you and you weren't here last night."

"Maybe if I had been I could've saved something. Picture albums. Letters. My great grandmother's tatting. Anything."

"Goddammit, AJ. Look at me." He grabbed her arm. "None of that shit is more important than your life."

She jerked back. "Easy for you to say. You have everything in your life that I just lost."

"Have you forgotten what I said this morning? I offered you everything I have."

Everything except love.

"This—" he gestured to the rubble behind them, "—is gone. It sucks. I'm sorry. But now you can move on." His jaw tightened. "Now you can move in with me."

"Move on? Just like that? Forget about everything in my life going up in flames and move in with you?"

"I want to take care of you, baby doll. What don't you understand about that?"

AJ looked him dead in the eye. "I don't want you to take care of me, Cord McKay, because I've been taking care of myself my whole life. All I ever wanted was for you to love me. Just love me. What don't you understand about that?"

He didn't respond—he actually looked a little sick to his stomach. At the prospect of loving her?

Enough. She'd had enough heartache to last a lifetime. "Goodbye Cord."

She climbed in her car and didn't look back. There was nothing here for her anymore.

Chapter Thirty-two

Don't let her go. Jump in your truck and chase her down.

AJ left him. Just like Marla had.

She would've stayed if you'd had the balls to tell her the truth.

What truth? That he nearly went out of his freakin' mind because she could've died last night? When he wanted to hold her up she preferred his mother's comfort and company to his? That she handled everything by herself again, when he'd offered to fix it for her, and added insult to injury by tossing his offer back in his face?

What did you offer her?

What she needs.

No. You offered her what you *need. You don't even know what she needs.*

Me. She needs me. Why won't she admit it?

Dammit. He hadn't planned to handle it this way. He'd imagined approaching her about them getting hitched over a nice romantic dinner. Between Ky's questions, ranch business—including Kade volunteering to head the cattle experiment up in the northeast section over the next few months—and his mother's constant cell phone updates about Colt, he hadn't had a chance to consider an approach about how he'd convince AJ to accept his proposal for her own good.

Now it didn't matter because she was gone for good.

ଓ

Two weeks later...

Cord was on edge, snappy with Ky, his dad, his mom, Colby and his cousins. Seemed everyone was avoiding him and leaving him to his own devices.

Alone in his own damn house again. He paced to the kitchen for a beer to ease his frustration when he noticed the sinkful of dirty dishes. Dammit. Why did crusted eggs remind him of AJ? Why did everything remind him of her? Fuck it. He headed to the porch and his dad's truck parked in the driveway.

Ky hopped out of the cab, followed by Cord's mother and Keely.

What was Keely doing here?

His son bounded up the steps and Cord caught him in a one-handed hug. "Hey, where you goin', slick?"

"Thought if I ran by you really fast you wouldn't have no time to yell at me."

Cord froze. "What? Why would I yell at you?"

"You been kinda grouchy lately. Aunt Keely says it's 'cause you got your head up your—"

"Kyler! You weren't supposed to repeat that."

Ky grinned and ran in the house.

"I didn't know you were gonna be around to corrupt my son, Aunt Keely."

"I'm on break and have a couple of things to take care of before I go back."

He wondered if AJ was on break too. He sipped his beer.

Keely sighed. "See, Ma? I told you. He's the most stubborn of all of them."

"Yep. Just like his father."

"What'd I do? Why you gangin' up on me?"

His little sister teetered on the tips of her boots and stuck her nose right in his business. "Why don't you ask the damn question I see in your eyes, Cord?"

"Fine. Why ain't she returnin' my calls?"

"Because you're a clueless asshole who doesn't deserve her."

"Keely West McKay," Carolyn said sharply, "that isn't helping."

"I don't care. She's mooned around you for years—years! Why? She's shouldered more responsibilities than anyone should, which is probably why she was so drawn to you in the first place, Mr. Large and In Charge—"

"Whoa, back up. Whatya mean mooned around me for years? She's twenty-two."

"She has some crazy notion she's been in love with you since she was five."

"No," he breathed, but the truth pummeled him from every direction as the things AJ said came rushing back.

Because I'm definitely smitten with you.

I've had a crush on you for so long.

You've been my fantasy man since that day all those years ago.

Keely's eyes burned with anger and tears. "You think it's a coincidence she was untouched? No. AJ saved her virginity for *you.*"

I'm so glad I waited. Waited for you to be ready for me.

"I thought it was stupid, I still do. I tried to talk her out of waiting because I didn't think you could love her like she's dreamed of her whole life."

Just like this. Love me like this, slow and easy and for a long time. Make it last forever.

"She's the closest thing I have to a sister and I hate that my brother is just like every other man—taking what's offered and giving nothing in return."

"Cord West McKay. Is that true?" his mother demanded.

Cord's cheeks grew hot. Partially because his mother was listening to the conversation; partially because he felt the need to defend himself. Keely was dead wrong. "She came to me. So don't you go blamin' me for nothin'. I offered to marry her."

"Like you were doing her a favor," Keely snapped. "Like she was just one of the fringe benefits of taking over the Foster ranch."

"That's not true. I care about her."

"Care? Jesus, Cord. You care about horses, and cattle, and the ranch. If you care about a person, you tell them you love them. Hell, you shout it from the rooftops."

All I wanted was for you to love me. Just love me.

"Why haven't you done that?"

"I don't know!"

"That's bullshit," Keely said. "AJ deserves better than you. Why should *she* have to be the one to convince you she's worthy of *you*? You oughta be on your knees proving that you're worthy of *her*. Instead, you're here glaring at me, acting as pigheaded as every other man in this testosterone-laden family." Keely opened her cell phone and whirled away.

He snagged Keely's elbow. "What do you want me to say? I nearly lost my fuckin' mind when I realized no one in my entire family knew what she'd been through all those years to keep that goddamn ranch when she was merely a girl? That I nearly wept with fear when I considered I could've lost her forever if she hadn't been in my bed the night her house caught fire?

"Should I tell her that I can't sleep, I can't eat and I miss talkin' to her? Or just sittin' with her? That I miss the secret way she smiles at me? That I constantly think about the way she smells, the taste of her mouth, the feel of her skin, and the sound of her laughter?

"That she's the only woman I've ever met who gets everything about me? My moods, my needs, my ties to the land? She sees the beauty in a patch of weeds out in the middle of nowhere Wyoming? That I love she can saddle and ride a horse faster than me? That she ain't as shy as she pretends? That she doesn't mind muckin' out stalls? And checkin' cattle?

"She loves sunsets and bakin' cookies and holdin' babies and two-steppin' and all that corny country shit? She loves my son, and how was I supposed to tell her how much I love her, when I was scared to death she'd leave me—and then that's exactly what she did anyway?"

He was breathing hard and damn near tears. "You tell me how I'm supposed to deal with that, Keely, 'cause I sure as hell don't know."

The sudden silence was like more salt in his wound.

"You stupid jerk. You really do love her." Keely all but

tackled him in a bear hug. “She didn’t leave you.”

“Well, she ain’t here.”

“But she will be if you give her a reason to come back.” She tipped her head back and stared into his eyes. “You do realize how important it is for AJ to finish school? For herself? There’s so little she’s done for herself: like you, everything she’s done has been for her family.”

“Guess I didn’t understand. Guess maybe I thought school was a whim—”

“—like marrying a Wyoming rancher and hightailing it back to the big city when it didn’t work out? AJ is not Marla. But you will lose her if *you* don’t take the first step this time. She gave you her trust, it’s time for you to give her yours and toss in your heart to up the ante.”

“How am I supposed to do that?”

Carolyn snorted.

Cord’s and Keely’s eyes swiveled her direction.

“Why don’t you ask your father? He’s had to grovel a time or two hundred. He’s got lots of pointers.” Her smile faded. “But if you really want to show Amy Jo she matters to you? Prove you listened to her thoughts and opinions, hopes and dreams over pillow talk or during dinner or while you were cleaning the barn. She gave you the map to her heart, son, you just gotta learn to read it.”

A gust of wind rattled the chimes on the porch, breaking the lingering silence.

Cord smiled and let the sage-scented breeze soothe his troubled mind. He could do this. He *had* to do this. “A map, huh? I can work with that.”

Chapter Thirty-three

Four weeks later...

AJ was dragging butt after a long day of classes. She waited for the elevator, clenching and unclenching her fists. Her hands hurt. Had she given everyone in the free world a massage this week?

The apartment she shared with Keely was dead quiet. AJ let out a sigh of relief. As much as she loved her roommate, she needed some down time. Keely was a whirlwind of activity. When she wasn't studying or working she had to be out doing things and she demanded AJ come along for the ride.

It hadn't taken long for AJ to get back into the swing of school. Between the three extra classes and finishing an extra work-study course in four days, she was still on track to graduate right before Christmas.

Not that she had a clue what she'd do once she received the diploma. As much as she loved her mom and sister, she'd rather live in Denver than Billings. She'd filled out the paperwork for the Wyoming economic development's no-interest loan, an initiative for opening her own studio in Sundance, but she wouldn't have the final word on whether she'd received it until after the first of the year.

Every week different businesses would come to the college to recruit students. AJ could probably pick and choose where she wanted to work—but none of the health care companies were in Wyoming. Where her heart was.

Her weary head fell into the couch cushions. For the first two weeks after her house burned down and she'd returned to Denver, Cord called her every day. Sometimes twice a day. She never picked up. The messages weren't sweet and loving, but terse. Typical. Then he'd stopped calling altogether.

AJ knew things were crazy at the McKay ranch. Colt had returned home after a month-long stint in rehab. Channing's pregnancy wasn't going smoothly and the doc put her on partial bed rest, which worried Colby. Carter postponed his art show to help out on the ranch since Kade was gone for the whole winter. Quinn and Bennett pitched in. Macie ran into major remodeling snags with the diner, which required her constant on-site supervision.

And Cord...well, evidently Cord was the glue that held it all together.

So who held him together?

No one. She had no doubt Cord worked all day, came home and cared for his son, and fell into bed exhausted and alone every night.

Which made her heart hurt. AJ hadn't stopped loving him, she was pretty sure if Cord could love any woman, it would be her. She wondered fifteen times every day if she'd done the right thing in walking away from him, when he'd offered her exactly what she'd wanted from him.

Wrong. You wanted his love. You didn't get that.

Two loud raps on the metal door startled her. She stood and looked out the peephole. A deliveryman. With flowers.

The safety chain clicked. "Yes?"

"Flower delivery."

Great. More flowers for Keely from one of her many admirers. Still she knew to ask before she opened the door. "Who're the flowers for?"

"AJ Foster."

"Really?" she squealed and flung open the door. She'd never gotten flowers before. Ever. She took the bouquet to the table to rip open the card:

AJ—Close as I could get to Wyoming wildflowers. Hope it reminds you of home. I miss you. Cord

Her mouth hung open. Cord had sent her flowers? She

peered at the small purple daisies and the big yellow mums and the thick greenish-yellow stem which sort of resembled goldenrod. And the tiny white baby's breath, which reminded her of cow parsnip. She sniffed. Yep. He'd even had the florist use sage as the greenery. She grinned. Probably cost him an arm and a leg for that extra touch. Still, his sweetness touched her.

The next week Cord sent her two tickets to the Big and Rich concert at the Pepsi Center. Shocked her he'd remembered they were her favorite band. She dragged Keely along and bought a "Save A Horse (Ride A Cowboy)" concert T-shirt and wore it to bed instead of his T-shirt she'd ended up with after the fire.

The following week a plain brown box arrived with *FRAGILE* stamped all over the outside. AJ opened it to find dozens of peanut butter kisses cookies. The note read:

Ky helped make these. Not as good as your sweet kisses, baby doll. Think of me while you're eating these and studying...Love—CWM.

Oh man. The man was trying. Really trying.

Less than a week later, she received a box with the silver boots she'd forgotten in his front closet—along with a new ballcap that read:

You Gonna Cowgirl Up and Ride? Or Lay There and Bleed?

No note. She wondered if the hat was a challenge.

Only two days passed before his next gift arrived via her cell phone. A streaming video of her horse running alongside Nickel and Jester and Ky's pony, Plug, in the frost-covered field behind Cord's barn. Then a close up of Lucy from the star on her nose to the tip of her long chestnut tail, the gorgeous autumn sunset as the backdrop, with Cord's husky voice in the background. "She looks happy here, huh? Ky and I are takin' good care of her until you come back. I think Jester's got a thing for that stubborn mare. I know the feelin'. Quit bein' stubborn and call me, baby doll. I miss you somethin' fierce."

The screen went blank.

AJ could scarcely see it through her tears. She hit redial and held her breath when Cord answered on the first ring.

"AJ? Is that really you?"

She sniffled and nodded.

"You okay?"

I am now. "Ah. Yeah. Thanks for the video."

"You're welcome."

"And the tickets. The concert was awesome even if Keely got a little out of hand."

He chuckled. "Don't need the details on that one."

"Thanks for the flowers, too. They were so..." She started to cry.

"Hey, now. No tears. I've been waitin' to hear from you for two and a half damn months and it'll bust my heart even more if you're sobbin' on the line the whole time. I can't take it."

"Okay."

Pause. He sighed. "Please, tell me everything you've been doin'. Don't leave nothin' out."

So AJ talked, half-afraid the conversation would be hopelessly one-sided, but Cord seemed eager to chat. An hour passed. Reluctantly, AJ said, "I have homework to finish."

"Can I call you again? Same time tomorrow?"

"I'd like that."

He cleared his throat. "I have somethin' to say. I wish I could say it to your sweet face, but I ain't about to let the opportunity pass me by again. When you asked me if I loved you, I should've manned up. I didn't. I was a chickenshit, plain and simple. The truth is, I do love you, AJ. More'n you can possibly imagine."

"Cord—"

"Let me finish while I still got the guts to do so. The last time I told a woman I loved her? She left me. So in my screwed up way of thinkin', I thought if I didn't tell you, you wouldn't leave me."

AJ was glad she was sitting down because she was light-headed and weak-kneed.

"You left anyway. I understand now that even if I woulda told you how I felt, you still woulda left—and your leavin' had nothin' to do with me."

"You do?"

"Yep. Our partin' coulda been a lot sweeter, though."

"I think you telling me how you feel is pretty sweet."

"Oh, you ain't seen sweet, baby doll. Not by half."

She smiled even when her belly did a little flip.

"Talk atcha tomorrow. Think of me."

"Always."

Cord hung up.

AJ snapped the phone shut after she watched the video again.

They'd take this one day at a time. Might not be the fairy-tale ending she'd envisioned, but it was a start.

☙

For the next two months Cord wooed AJ over the phone.

Once a week he sent her a package. Sometimes the items were funny, like a miniature windup dancing horse he'd picked up at the farm supply store. Or sweet, like a silvery camisole that he claimed matched her eyes. Or thoughtful, like a pair of flannel pajamas because he knew she was always cold. Or raunchy, like the fur-lined adult novelty handcuffs.

No matter what he sent, he included a hand-written note with the words *I LOVE YOU* written in all caps and underlined. Heavily underlined. Ky frequently contributed a drawing to the weekly mailing, in addition to demanding to talk to her at every opportunity.

If she thought she'd loved Cord before, it was nothing compared to the way she felt about him now.

AJ looked at the clock and smoothed the wrinkles from her denim skirt. Cord would be here any minute. Lord. They hadn't seen each other in over four months. Longest four months of her life. And yet, getting to know Cord on a non-physical level gave her a whole bunch more to appreciate about him.

She'd taken her last test and was officially a certified massage therapist. Seemed weird not to have a graduation ceremony. Seemed even weirder not to have a plan firmly in place about her future. She just hoped Cord was in it.

Three knocks sent her scurrying to the door. She flung herself into Cord's arms the second he stepped inside.

"Oh God. You're here. You're really here."

Cord kicked the door shut and just held her. He tipped her face back to look into her eyes. "Before I kiss you, before I touch you, let me say this: I love you. Sweet baby Jesus. I love you so damn much." He kissed her with a mix of tenderness and passion that had tears springing to her eyes.

When she broke away, she whispered, "I love you too."

"Then marry me, AJ. Not because we're compatible, or because you are a born ranch woman, or because you'd make a good mother. Marry me for me. Marry me because I'm a selfish bastard and I want you to be mine forever. Marry me because I don't know if I'll survive the rest of my life without havin' you by my side every damn day. Please say yes, baby doll. Make your home with me. With us. Make me the luckiest man in the world."

"Yes."

Cord kissed her again.

All the need and hunger that'd been dormant inside her ignited like a brush fire. She tugged him toward her bedroom.

He gently dug his bootheels into the carpet. "Nuh-uh. No hanky-panky until you're wearin' my ring and you're my wife."

"But—"

He lifted an eyebrow. "That's one."

"Can I have the swat now? I'll even take my skirt off. Shirt too." Her hands went to the buttons on her blouse.

"Amy Jo. You ornery cuss. Keep them clothes on."

"I missed you. I want you. I don't wanna wait." She nipped his chin and scraped her teeth down his throat. "Bet I can getcha to change your mind."

"Probably. But we ain't got much time, so there's two things we hafta talk about first." He reached inside his suit coat pocket and removed an envelope. "Your mama gave me this to give to you."

"What is it?"

"I have no idea."

AJ opened the letter and her heart caught at the familiar formal handwriting:

Sweetheart-

I'm glad Cord finally knows the truth about what you did to keep our ranch going. I'm thrilled he's asked for permission to marry you and I know you'll be happy to be home in Sundance where you belong and with a man who loves you like crazy.

You've no idea the guilt your father and I felt about how you worked so hard and got nothing in return but more work. In hindsight, we knew what we did was wrong. There's no way to make up for the lost time now, except to offer you this check as "back wages" and hope it eases the way for you to start your own business. You earned it. I'm so proud of you for finishing school. I miss you. Bring your new hubby and son up for a visit after you get settled. Congratulations!

Love you, baby girl,

Mama

She glanced down, in utter disbelief, at the check for thirty-five thousand dollars. "I don't understand. Where did she get the money?"

"Our buyout was very generous, AJ. But I had nothin' to do with this." He pointed to the check. "I ain't gonna argue that you earned it. You shouldn't argue either."

AJ's mind was already whirling. She could rent that storefront space in Sundance she'd been eyeing. Heck, she had money to renovate even if the loan from the state didn't come through. She looked up at Cord. "Do you know if that space in the Sandstone Building next to Macie's restaurant is still up for grabs?"

He shook his head. "Afraid not. It's spoken for."

"Shoot."

Cord put a finger under her chin. "By you. I leased it in your name, AJ, last month."

"Why? Did you know Mama was gonna give me this money?"

"No. I know you. I have faith in you. I know how good you are at givin' massages and so will everyone else in the county. Even if you wouldn't have gotten this unexpected windfall, I figure the state of Wyoming ain't dumb enough not to fund your business. I didn't want you to miss out on the space you'd set your heart on."

"Really? You did it for me?"

"There ain't nothin' I wouldn't do for you." Just as he bent down to kiss her, the door opened and Keely and Colt burst in.

"Did she say yes?"

"Of course she said yes. The woman's been in love with me since she was five." He whispered, "I've got a lot of catchin' up to do."

Keely squealed and AJ smacked Cord in the arm before Keely squeezed her tight. "We're really gonna be sisters now. This is so cool! So, you guys ready?"

"Ready for what?"

Cord cursed.

"You haven't told her?" Colt grinned. "Typical."

He sauntered over and hugged AJ. "Welcome to the family. I'm gonna enjoy teasin' my bro about bein' a cradle robber for a long time to come."

AJ looked at Colt. He looked fit and healthy, even when a sense of wariness surrounded him that hadn't been there before. She whirled back around and faced her intended. "Tell me what?"

"That we're goin' to Vegas. Tonight. To get married. Thought I'd surprise you. Colt and Keely are standin' up for us."

She stared at him, stunned.

Which caused him to babble. "Come on, baby doll. I love you. You love me. I don't wanna wait. You told me when we talked about gettin' married on the phone the past coupla weeks that you didn't want a big weddin' ceremony. Colt and I got three days before we're needed at home. Keely said she'd kill me if she didn't get to see us tie the knot. Ky's stayin' with my folks, though it's makin' him mighty antsy waitin' for us to come home. I thought we could get hitched, and spend the night in the honeymoon suite of a swanky hotel. Then we'd come back here, pack your stuff and you could come home with me for good."

She continued to stare at him.

"Ah, hell. Are you mad?"

"No. Just trying to wrap my head around the word *home* and *you* in the same sentence."

Cord's eyes softened. "Same thing, in my opinion."

She melted. The feeling of rightness, of inevitability, flowed over as sweetly as it had when she'd been a young girl. But unlike then, she now knew real, true love earned through trial and error was better than any one-sided fairy tale love from afar.

"You guys gonna stand here makin' goo-goo eyes at each other? Or are we goin' to Vegas?" Keely demanded.

"Whatcha say, cowgirl mine?" Cord asked.

She grinned at the man she'd love for the rest of her life. "I say it's about damn time."

About the Author

To learn more about Lorelei James, please visit www.loreleijames.com. Send an email to lorelei@loreleijames.com or join her Yahoo! group to join in the fun with other readers as well as Lorelei. http://groups.yahoo.com/group/loreleijamesgang.com

One tempting heiress. Two sexy cowboys. Three means fun beyond her wildest dreams—until her Cord starts to unravel.

Take Me

© 2007 Mackenzie McKade

Thoroughbred rancher's daughter Caitlyn Culver has always wanted playboy Cord Daily, even after her daddy threatened to bankrupt him. But winning a racehorse in a poker game means Cord is no longer just a cattle rancher. He's come back wealthier and more wicked than ever.

Snaring this cowboy won't be easy for Cait, and keeping him will be even harder. Still, his sexual antics and taste for ménages won't scare her off. She knows the best way to snag a man like Cord is to pretend indifference. So when he comes onto her in the barn, she plays along—only to leave him tied to a ladder, aroused and unfulfilled.

It's payback time.

Cord seeks out Cait and brings along his playboy cousin, Dolan Crane. The two cowboys are enough to set her body afire. She's bound and determined to resist their sexual allure, but ends up experiencing a night beyond her wildest fantasies. Now Dolan wants Cait for himself. Cait's father wants Cord's racehorse. And Cord wants Caitlyn to choose—her father's money or her cowboy's love.

Warning, this title contains the following: explicit sex, graphic language, ménage a trois, and BDSM.

Dirty Deeds...when good, clean fun isn't an option.

Dirty Deeds

© 2006 Lorelei James

Just once, good girl Tate Cross wants to experience a red-hot, no-strings-attached affair. She's temporarily left her graphic artist position in Denver to settle her aunt's estate in Spearfish, South Dakota. However, Tate receives a city mandate: she must comply with new landscaping regulations before she can resell the property. Given Tate's precarious finances, she asks her friend, Val, for advice. Val swears her brother—owner of a local construction company, and a man well-versed in purely physical relationships—might consider trading dirt work for art lessons. When Tate meets the mysterious Casanova, can she convince him to toss in a few sex lessons as well?

Nathan LeBeau believes few women look at the Native American man beneath the filthy work clothes and hard hat. He's kept past liaisons casual—a fact his sister shared, hence Tate's sexy proposition of wanting a hands on demonstration of his sexpertise. But in truth, he's tired of relationships based solely on sex. His goal of proving he's not completely hopeless in matters of the heart is second only to his dream of expanding his business.

What happens when Tate desires no-holds-barred sex and Nathan favors a good old-fashioned romance?

A battle of wills ensues.

And Tate is willing to get down and dirty to get what she wants.

Available now in ebook and print from Samhain Publishing.